Liv
A JEN

The world of TV news

Just ask Jenny McKay... She's a TV reporter in search of a break, a boyfriend, and a reason to feel good about turning forty. The high sleaze and low ratings of New York's WTBK aren't exactly what she aspired to—but hey, it's a living. And when broadcasting turns to crime-solving, she uncovers the city's deadliest secrets.

It's a dirty job—but someone's gotta do it.

PRAISE FOR
BROADCAST CLUES
A Jenny McKay Mystery...

"NOT ONLY IS THIS BOOK TOUGH TO PUT DOWN,
YOU END UP HOPING BELSKY IS WORKING
ON A SEQUEL."
—*Associated Press*

"SEX, MAYHEM, GOSSIP, HEADLINES,
EXCLUSIVES, TV DIRT, AND SOCIETY JUICE...
A FLAVORFUL READ!"
—*New York Post*

"ENGAGING!"
—*Kirkus Reviews*

"AN EXCELLENT STORY... A FINE STORYTELLER."
—*Cedar Rapids Gazette*

"VIVIDLY RE-CREATES THE GRITTY, DOG-EAT-DOG
WORLD OF TV NEWS... A RIVETING
THRILLER PENNED BY A NEWS PRO."
—*Star Magazine*

"A LIVELY TALE... FIRST-RATE!"
—Cleveland *Plain Dealer*

"WONDERFULLY FUNNY... A TERRIFIC BOOK.
PLEASE LET US HAVE MORE OF JENNY McKAY!"
—*KMB Newsletter*

MORE MYSTERIES FROM THE
BERKLEY PUBLISHING GROUP...

THE INSPECTOR AND MRS. JEFFRIES: He's with Scotland Yard. She's his housekeeper. Sometimes, her job can be murder...

by Emily Brightwell
THE INSPECTOR AND MRS. JEFFRIES   THE GHOST AND MRS. JEFFRIES
MRS. JEFFRIES DUSTS FOR CLUES

JENNY McKAY MYSTERIES: This TV reporter finds out where, when, why...*and* whodunit. "A more streetwise version of television's 'Murphy Brown.'"   *—Booklist*

by Dick Belsky
BROADCAST CLUES   LIVE FROM NEW YORK

CAT CALIBAN MYSTERIES: She was married for 38 years. Raised three kids. Compared to that, tracking down killers is easy...

by D. B. Borton
ONE FOR THE MONEY   TWO POINTS FOR MURDER

KATE JASPER MYSTERIES: Even in sunny California, there are cold-blooded killers... "This series is a treasure!"   *—Carolyn G. Hart*

by Jaqueline Girdner
ADJUSTED TO DEATH   MURDER MOST MELLOW
THE LAST RESORT   FAT-FREE AND FATAL

RENAISSANCE MYSTERIES: Sigismondo the sleuth courts danger—and sheds light on the darkest of deeds... "Most entertaining!"   *—Chicago Tribune*

by Elizabeth Eyre
DEATH OF A DUCHESS

PENNYFOOT HOTEL MYSTERIES: In Edwardian England, death takes a seaside holiday...

by Kate Kingsbury
ROOM WITH A CLUE

CHARLOTTE GRAHAM MYSTERIES: She's an actress with a flair for dramatics—and an eye for detection. "You'll get hooked on Charlotte Graham!"   *—Rave Reviews*

by Stefanie Matteson
MURDER AT THE SPA   MURDER ON THE SILK ROAD
MURDER AT TEATIME   MURDER AT THE FALLS
MURDER ON THE CLIFF

DICK BELSKY

J

JOVE BOOKS, NEW YORK

LIVE FROM NEW YORK

A Jove Book / published by arrangement with
the author

PRINTING HISTORY
Jove edition / December 1993

ISBN: 0-515-11265-8

A JOVE BOOK®
Jove Books are published by The Berkley Publishing Group,
200 Madison Avenue, New York, New York 10016.
JOVE and the "J" design are trademarks
belonging to Jove Publications, Inc.

PRINTED IN THE UNITED STATES OF AMERICA

10 9 8 7 6 5 4 3 2 1

This is for Laura.

Opening Credits

A woman political reporter was called into the office of the TV producer and told she had a new assignment. He wanted her to cover cooking stories. Not fluff, explained the producer, not girl stuff, but "hard news" cooking stories—food as news. The woman reporter thought for a moment.

"Oh. Now I understand," she said. "If a 707 crashes this afternoon, you want me to take my camera crew to the pilot's house, and when his wife comes to the door, you want me to ask her what she would have cooked him for dinner if he were coming home. Is that right?"

—Linda Ellerbee
And So It Goes

The media consultant showed me a tape of anchorwomen from all over the country, one after another. It was uncanny how they all looked the same, talked the same and wore variations of the same clothes and makeup. Chicago looked just like Cleveland, just like Miami, just like Denver. Finally a woman with some spunk popped up. She seemed different, intelligent, street-wise and spunky. "Oh no," the consultant said, "I don't want you to see her . . . she's much too assertive."

—Christine Craft
Too Old, Too Ugly,
and Not Deferential to Men

Prologue

My name is Jenny McKay, and I'm a TV reporter for WTBK News in New York.

TV. The boob tube. The vast wasteland. The idiot box. From the same folks who gave you "My Mother the Car" and "The Dukes of Hazzard" and Phyllis George and Maria Shriver reading the news.

Me, I don't look a lot like Phyllis George or Maria Shriver. I'm forty-one years old, single, no kids, and with no one exactly breaking down my door to change that status. Sometimes men tell me I'm pretty, but it's generally during moments of bedroom passion, which really doesn't count. I'm also kind of strong-willed. This seems to make a lot of men—particularly the men who run TV stations—very uncomfortable. Like Christine Craft, maybe I'm "too old, too ugly, and not deferential enough to men" for this business.

A long time ago I was a real journalist. I worked for a New York City newspaper—which no longer exists—and I did a number of things I was really proud of. Once I got a deputy mayor indicted for embezzling city funds. Another

time I was nominated for a Pulitzer prize for a series I wrote
on urban renewal. I saved all these articles and keep them in
a big yellow scrapbook at home. Sometimes, late at night,
I'll page through it and wonder if the person who did all that
was really me.

Now I do celebrity news and cooking tips and quick
"sound bites" from media press conferences, and I try to
squeeze it all into minute and a half segments so that people won't get bored and switch the channel to reruns of
"Gilligan's Island" or "The Facts of Life."

Hey, it's a living; it pays well, and it's not illegal.

But every once in a while something happens that . . .

Well, did you ever see a movie called *Farewell, My Lovely*? It's set in the summer of 1941, and at the end Robert
Mitchum muses about how the great Joe DiMaggio's record
fifty-six–game hitting streak finally ended.

Bagley and Smith, a couple of run-of-the-mill pitchers,
stopped DiMaggio.

I guess maybe they had something extra that night.

I like to think that sometimes I still have a little extra,
too.

This is a story about one of those times.

1

She's Joan Lunden, and I'm Not

Rikki Stiles walked into my life one wet afternoon in early November.

It was pouring outside—a cold, driving rain that pelted loudly against the window next to my desk in the WTBK newsroom, an unmistakable reminder that winter was only a few weeks away. Some people love the fall. They go to football games, carve out pumpkins, and drive to the country to watch the leaves change. Not me. To me, fall just means winter is on the way. Cold, lifeless, and barren. Sort of like death. Or my love life.

I needed something to cheer myself up, something new and exciting.

There was an ad in the *Times* for cut-rate Caribbean vacations. "We'll Tailor Your Vacation to Your Budget!" the ad proclaimed in big type. Next to it was a list of potential vacation spots—places like St. Thomas and Martinique—along with the prices for each. And a picture of a white beach in Martinique with a smiling man and woman walking hand in hand along the water. The picture was appealing, but the prices weren't. In fact, after studying the price list closely, I determined that the only way I could tailor a Caribbean vacation to my budget was by not eating until February. If I opted for eating, then the furthest south I could afford to go was Roanoke, Virginia.

On the next page there was an ad for a snappy leather skirt and top ensemble. The model wearing it looked a little like Madonna. Maybe if I wore it, I'd look like Madonna too. On the other hand, the model had a waist of about twenty-seven inches and weighed twenty pounds less than I did. On me, it might be your basic Roseanne Arnold look.

"What are you doing, Jenny?"

I looked around. It was Bob Carstairs, the WTBK news director.

"Trying to get my life together," I told him.

"Oh, nothing important then."

I sighed. Sometimes Carstairs and I got along okay, sometimes we didn't. Right now we were going through one of the times we didn't. I knew why too.

My station, Channel Six, was into this big promotion at the moment called "Live From New York"—which meant we covered the news with a lot of live remotes from all over the city. Live coverage like this has a lot of advantages over videotape. It also has some disadvantages. One of them happened a few days ago when my microphone went dead on the street and I cursed out loud, thinking we were off the air. Only we weren't off the air.

Since then my relationship with Carstairs had been . . . well, strained. Mostly, he wouldn't give me anything to do.

Funny, when I first got into TV, I thought I'd have a news director like Lou Grant on "The Mary Tyler Moore Show." You know, he'd call me "Jen" and I'd call him Mr. Grant, and I'd talk over my personal problems with him and sometimes have him over my house for dinner. Only it hasn't worked out like that. Carstairs and I are not Mary Richards and Lou Grant. Actually, we're more like Gomer Pyle and Sergeant Carter.

"So how long is this going to go on?" I asked him now.

"What do you mean?"

"This punishment bit. Me not getting any decent stories to do. I'm a good reporter and—"

"Good reporters don't say the F word on TV."

"The F word? You actually call it the F word? What are you, six years old? Bob, I said, 'fuck.' "

"Jesus . . ."

"Actually I said it twice."

"Huh?"

"The exact quote, if I remember it correctly, was, 'Holy fuck, now we're really fucked.' "

"Jenny, I don't think you realize the seriousness of this. . . ."

"What seriousness? Hey, I didn't kill anybody. I didn't advocate the overthrow of the government. I just said a bad word. So wash my mouth out with soap and put me back on the air."

Carstairs shook his head. "A million people heard you say that, Jenny. Some of them are young impressionable children who may be traumatized permanently by—"

"Oh, c'mon, Bob," I groaned. "I really think most of these kids are going to hear that word someplace else."

"Nevertheless, FCC regulations specifically state . . ."

"Give me something to do. I'm going nuts."

Carstairs nodded. "See that woman over there?"

He pointed to a woman standing on the other side of the newsroom. She was a stunning-looking thing who appeared to be in her mid-twenties. She was wearing a pair of formfitting designer jeans, a silver chain-link belt, and a low-cut pale blue sweater that left little to the imagination. Her hair was blond and cascaded down over her shoulders, falling loosely over a pair of jade earrings. Everything about her face was striking—piercing blue eyes, unblemished skin, and the kind of high cheekbones you see on fashion models. She was probably at least five foot ten in her stocking feet, and now she was wearing a pair of spike-heeled boots that put her well over the six foot mark. She was a real looker, no question about it.

"Her name is Rikki Stiles," Carstairs said. "She just walked in off the street. Says she's got a story for us. I want you to talk to her."

He motioned to her to come over.

I made a face. "Oh, Christ, thanks a lot," I said sarcastically.

People were always walking into newsrooms with what they thought were great stories. Mostly they turned out to be a waste of time.

"You wanted something to do," he growled.

"I wanted a story."

"This will keep you busy."

"You want to keep me busy? Why not just have me clean out the goddamned ladies' room too while you're at it?"

Rikki Stiles was standing next to us now.

"Miss Stiles, this is Jenny McKay, one of our best people." Carstairs smiled. "She'd very much like to listen to everything you have to say."

I shot him a dirty look, and he disappeared in a hurry. Then I shrugged and pointed to a chair in front of my desk. "You might as well make yourself comfortable," I said. She sat down, and I did too.

"So," I began, "exactly what can I do for you?"

Rikki Stiles took out a cigarette, put it in her mouth, and lit it with a gold cigarette lighter from her purse. Her fingers were long and elegant, with nails polished a brilliant shade of red. Everything about her seemed flawless, as a matter of fact. Except for one thing. Up close I noticed a dark discoloration on one of her cheekbones, a bruise of some sort that even the makeup she was wearing couldn't hide. There was something else too. Her hand was trembling as she held the cigarette. She seemed nervous, worried about something.

"I know who pulled the Lancaster Hotel job," she said.

I stared at her. The Lancaster Hotel was one of the poshest in the city. Elizabeth Taylor stayed there when she was in town, so did Princess Caroline and Nancy Reagan. A few months ago, six masked gunmen had broken into the hotel's safety deposit boxes and made off with six million dollars in jewelry and other valuables. The list of victims read like the pages of the Society Register, and the story was at the top of the news for days.

"Who?" I asked her.

Me and Barbara Walters, we like to ask the tough questions.

"Johnny Camancho."

I stared blankly at her. "Who?" I said again. Boy, Barbara would be proud of me.

"Johnny Camancho. Look, I know you probably never heard of him. He and his brother Nicky live in Brooklyn. Bath Beach. They're involved in all sorts of rackets and things, and he did the heist."

I nodded. "How exactly did you come into possession of this information?" I was rolling now.

"Well, in my line of work, I meet a lot of people. Hear a lot of things. This was one of them."

"And exactly what is your line of work?"

"I guess you could say I'm sort of a social therapist," she said.

"Huh?"

"I work with people—men, actually—and try to ease some of their tensions.

"Could you be a little more specific?"

She shrugged. "I'm a hooker."

"That's pretty specific," I said.

"Look, I've slept with this guy Johnny Camancho a few times. He tells me things. Everyone does. It's part of the whole mystique, I guess. You know, the hooker with the heart of gold who understands them when no one else does. It happens all the time. It's just that no one's ever told me anything like this before. Frankly, I'm nervous. Can you help me, Miss McKay?"

I looked out the window. The rain was coming down in sheets now, turning the intersection in front of the WTBK building into a huge lake. My umbrella was at home in my closet. If I went out now, I'd be drenched. I turned back to Rikki Stiles.

"Have you talked to the police about this?" I asked her.

"Yes, I went to see them first."

"And what happened?"

"Nothing. I guess they didn't believe me."

"Why not?"

"How do I know? Listen, Johnny Camancho was one of the guys who did the Lancaster job. I know that for a fact. Are you going to do anything about it or not?"

"Okay, let's say you do know who did it," I said. "Why tell me or even the cops? What's in it for you? You don't exactly strike me as somebody who's looking for a good citizen's medal."

She smiled. "There's a reward for the capture of the holdup gang and the return of the money. A big reward. Fifty thousand dollars. I figure if you crack the case with information from me, then I'm entitled to it. And I need that money."

"Who doesn't?" I laughed.

"No, I mean I really need the money." Her face got that same tense look she'd had when she was lighting the cigarette. She was nervous about something, all right. And I wasn't sure it was just about Johnny Camancho and the Lancaster heist.

She saw me looking at her. "You don't really believe me, do you?" she said. "You think I'm just making this all up, don't you?"

"No, I believe you." I smiled.

But the truth was I didn't believe her, any more than the police probably did when she went to them with the story. I didn't really think this guy Johnny Camancho had anything to do with the Lancaster job or that she even knew anything about it. I didn't even know if Johnny Camancho existed. I mean the cops didn't take her seriously, and they're professionals. So why should I?

I looked up at the assignment board in the center of the newsroom. There were some good stories around. Manhattan District Attorney Elliott Carson had just announced a new series of racketeering indictments against mob figures. There'd been a derailment at Grand Central Station. The President was in town for a press conference. And a woman in Brooklyn won twelve million dollars in the lottery by using digits from her dead husband's Social Security number. I wished I was working on one of those stories. Instead, I was sitting here wasting my time listening to a hooker who was probably just out to make a fast buck.

Except . . .

Except she seemed to be in trouble. There was something about her that got to me somehow. She seemed—well, she seemed scared.

"Look, I'm not asking you to do all that much," she was saying. "Just make some checks. You'll see what I'm telling you is the truth. Like I told you, this is important to me. I really need that money."

"Why's that?" I asked. "The prostitution business not paying too well these days?"

"I'm looking to get out of it," she said. "I want to quit being a hooker. Try to do something different. Maybe go back to art school. I can draw pretty well, that's one of the reasons I came to New York in the first place. I'd like to give it another shot."

"Sort of like a mid-life career change, huh?"

"Something like that. Will you help me?"

I didn't say anything for a few seconds. She sat there waiting. There was nothing but the sound of the rain on the window.

"Okay," I said wearily, "I'll talk to a few people about it."

"You will?" Her face brightened. "Hey, that's great. I was hoping you would, but I wasn't sure. . . . Listen, you're really swell."

"Yeah," I said, "swell."

But I didn't feel swell at all.

Mostly I just felt stupid.

After she left, I sat there for a while watching a TV monitor on the wall above me. It was tuned to Channel Seven, the ABC affiliate, and they were doing a promo for a Joan Lunden interview with Robert Redford on "Good Morning America" later in the week. Great. She gets to interview Robert Redford and all I get is the Unhappy Hooker. Plus she gets paid at least a million a year.

I guess blondes do have more fun.

I ran my fingers through my hair which ranges—depending on when I last washed it—from auburn to dirty brown. Maybe I should become a blonde. I tried to picture myself as a blonde. Then I took some of my hair and pushed it to the side and up in the back the way Joan Lunden sometimes used to do.

"Got a headache?"

I looked around. It was Alan Sanders, a camera guy I do a lot of work with. I was still holding my hair up.

"Imagine me as a blonde and with this hairstyle," I said. "Who does it remind you of?"

"Phyllis Diller?"

"I'm trying for the Joan Lunden look," I told him. "Does it work at all?"

He studied me carefully. "Definitely Phyllis Diller."

"Oh," I said.

Funny, I never knew Joan Lunden looked like Phyllis Diller.

2

Sweeps, Sex, and Other TV Phenomena

People who watch a lot of TV news think they know everything about it.

They know Dan Rather likes to wear sweaters and topcoats and which words Tom Brokaw has trouble pronouncing and how much Diane Sawyer made by jumping from "60 Minutes" to ABC and even what Maury Povich and Connie Chung like to eat for breakfast.

On the local side, they can tell you what stations are into a happy news format, which ones are trying for the tabloid or authoritative feel, and the names of every newscaster, sports reporter, and weather reporter on the air, even the weekend fill-ins.

They talk about all of them on a first name basis, as if they're all friends, which I guess is a big part of the mystique.

Let me tell you something, these people know nothing about TV.

Hey, I've been doing it for a couple of years now and I'm not sure I understand it either. But if I had to sum it up,

I guess I'd do it like this—TV news is to journalism what Barry Manilow is to music. Or what Jim Bakker is to the ministry. Or what Brooke Shields is to acting. It's really bad, really phony, and it makes really big money.

We were in the middle of something called Sweeps Week.

Sweeps arrive regularly, like locusts, every November, February, and May. During these weeks, ratings are especially important because they are used to set the rates TV stations charge sponsors. Each tenth of a rating point can be worth hundreds of thousands of dollars during a Sweeps Week. So if TV people would kill for ratings during the regular part of the year, you can imagine what happens during a Sweeps Week.

On network TV, this is when you get all your miniseries and TV movies with Vanna White and sitcom moms giving birth to new babies. One November during Sweeps Week, Bill Cosby imagined he was having a baby, Roseanne fantasized about being waited on by beefcake studs right out of Chippendales and then killing her own family, and Carla's ex-husband died on "Cheers" when he was run over by an ice-making machine. And this was only November. You can imagine what February and May were like.

Local news saves up its really big guns too for Sweeps Week. Stuff like "Does Your Husband Have a Mistress?" or "New Yorkers' Ten Favorite Sexual Fantasies" or "Date Rape: Could It Happen to You?" Do you sense a pattern here? Besides sex, there's also hard-hitting exposés on things like "How to Get a Good Night's Sleep," "Diets: They Can Change Your Life," and "Forty Doesn't Have to Be Fatal."

The other day I suggested to Carstairs that we do one called "How Living Out Your Sexual Fantasies With a Secret Lover While Dieting and Getting Plenty of Sleep Can Help You Live to Two Hundred."

He said no.

I think he thought about it though.

Maybe I'm jaded because I'm one of the few TV reporters these days to come from print journalism. It used to be that was how TV got its reporters. They'd find people from newspapers or magazines who knew how to report a story and then they'd teach them about TV. Now it doesn't work that way. Now they hire beauty pageant winners and models and actresses and just put them on the air to do the news. As Linda Ellerbee once pointed out: "It's interesting to note that in recent years about half the contestants and several winners of the Miss America pageant, when asked what they wanted to be when they grew up, answered 'a television anchorwoman.' It's also interesting to note the great number who have gotten their wish."

We've got one of them at WTBK.

Her name is Liz St. John, and she's blond and beautiful and bland. If you've never seen her, that's okay—she's just like the ones over at Channels Two or Five or Seven or in Fort Worth or Des Moines or Atlanta. I think that she was Miss Artichoke or something and then she did a little modeling for *Vogue* and wound up selling orange juice and panty hose on TV. Terrific résumé, huh?

The other day she actually broke an exclusive. An announcement that a local congressman was going to run for the Senate. She had it first. Afterward, I asked her how she did it. Hard work? Diligence? Poring over campaign filings?

"Well," she said slowly, "actually I just rolled over in bed and Bill said, 'He's going to do it.' "

I stared at her. "Bill? As in Bill Lewin, the congressman's press secretary?"

"Yeah. You know him?"

"You slept with Bill Lewin?"

"Yes."

"You slept with a news source!" I said incredulously.

"Uh-huh."

"That's wrong."

"Wrong?" She looked at me blankly. "No, we didn't do anything wrong. I mean there was nothing kinky or anything. We just had sex."

Maybe that's how she won Miss Artichoke too.

I probably ought to say something here to emphasize how strongly I feel about the matter of whether or not to sleep with a source to get a story.

This is not an issue in which there is any grey area. Either you do or you don't. You don't say "I'll only do it for a really great story." Once you do that, it's like a guy I know who was asked at a party if he'd have sex with a dog if someone paid him fifty dollars. He said no way. How about for five thousand dollars? He thought for a minute and then asked: "What breed?" Once you ask "what breed" in the news business, it's too late.

My position on sleeping with sources is very firm and clear.

I don't do it. Ever.

Well, almost never.

I mean, if I would normally have slept with a man anyway and I'm not doing it to get the story and I just happen to get a story in the process—well, you get the idea.

That's okay.

I think.

The detective handling the Lancaster Hotel investigation was a lieutenant named Rick Gallagher, who worked out of the 17th Precinct on East 51st Street. I got Gallagher on the phone and said I needed to talk to him. I said I had a hot tip on the Lancaster robbery. He suggested I come up to the station house.

WTBK is way down on South Street, near Chinatown and the seaport, which means it's about a twenty-minute cab ride uptown to 51st Street under optimal conditions. A torrential downpour is not an optimal condition. First it took me a long time just to find a cab. Then, because the East River Drive was flooded, the cab driver went up First Avenue which turned out to be like a giant parking lot. After crawling block by block into the forties, I finally gave up in frustration and walked the last ten blocks or so. By the time I reached the 17th Precinct, I was tired, drenched, and contemplating several exquisite types of torture for Bob Carstairs. I plopped down in a chair in front of Lt. Rick Gallagher's desk in the second floor squad room. The chair made a squishing sound when I moved.

"I think I know who pulled the Lancaster Hotel job," I announced.

Gallagher grunted, stood up, and walked over to a small counter in the corner of the room with a coffeepot on it. He asked me if I wanted any. I said I did. He poured some into two foam cups and brought them back to the desk. He pushed one of them toward me.

"Give me a name," he said.

"Johnny Camancho."

Gallagher snorted in disgust, then started laughing.

"Johnny Camancho. That's great, McKay. That's really great."

I took a sip of the coffee. It tasted awful. "You don't think he held up the Lancaster?"

"Johnny Camancho couldn't hold up his pants without a pair of suspenders. He's a loser. A small-time nobody. You know anything about him?"

"A little," I said defensively. This was not going well. "He lives in Brooklyn. And he's got a brother named Nicky."

"The Camancho brothers run a small auto repair shop in the Bath Beach section," Gallagher said. "They do a little business repairing cars, I guess, but mostly they're into things like fencing stolen property, dealing drugs to neighborhood kids, doing a little extortion on local shop owners . . . well, you get the idea."

"They're not exactly members of the neighborhood improvement association," I said.

"Right. Now every once in a while the local precinct busts one or both of them on something. Then they go off and do a few months in jail upstate or—most likely—their lawyer gets them off on some kind of technicality or probation. In any case, pretty soon they're right back out there in Bath

Beach doing what they always do."

"So what does all this have to do with the Lancaster Hotel job?" I asked, taking another sip of coffee. "Why couldn't they have pulled that?"

Gallagher shook his head. "You're not listening to what I'm saying. Two-bit extortion scams, drugs to local kids . . . these are small-time operators. And dumb. Johnny Camancho couldn't even find the Lancaster Hotel, much less hold it up. And his brother, Nicky . . . well, he makes Johnny look like a genius. These guys are nothing. Just some flotsam in the bowels of Brooklyn."

He opened up a desk drawer, took out a large manila folder, and flipped it over to me. The label on it said: "Lancaster Hotel Robbery." It was thick, maybe more than an inch high, filled with typewritten pages and computer printouts.

"Read a little bit of it," he said. "Not all of it, just the first page or so. There's a summary there. Get a feel of the flow of it."

I read for a few minutes, then put it down and looked back at Gallagher.

"So what's it say?" he asked.

"That the Lancaster robbery was a highly professional, sophisticated heist carried out by a team of at least six burglars. Their timing was impeccable. Probably weeks of research involved. They went in at the one time of the weekend when there was no one around, managed to short-circuit an expensive alarm system, and got away with six million dollars in jewels and cash from the safety deposit boxes in less than thirty minutes. A real precision job."

"Does that sound anything like the description of Johnny Camancho I just gave you?"

I shook my head. "I guess my source was wrong."

"That's for sure. Anyway, we already know who was behind the Lancaster job. Jerry Rossiello."

"The mob boss?"

"Yeah, the only problem is we can't prove it. Rossiello's just too slick to pin anything on. He's got more lawyers than he's got hired guns. And he's got a lot of hired guns, believe me. I don't know how to get him on it."

There was a copy of the *Daily News* on Gallagher's desk. The front page headline said: "DA CARSON INDICTS ROSSIELLO ON RACKETEERING CHARGES." I remembered something about that from the WTBK assignment board too.

"Well, he was just indicted for something else." I shrugged, pointing down at the *Daily News*. "So it looks like he's going to be out of commission for a long time."

"Maybe," Gallagher said.

"You don't sound very optimistic. You don't think the DA's got enough on him?"

"I don't know. I don't work for the Manhattan DA's office. It's just that I have a feeling Elliott Carson—our esteemed District Attorney—is the kind of person who really likes to see his picture in the paper. He's trying to make a big splash. People that ambitious tend to get sloppy. Make mistakes. Jerry Rossiello doesn't make mistakes. He's methodical, precise, and very careful. You're not going to nail him easy. But what the hell, that's Carson's worry, not mine."

I stood up to leave.

"Anyway, you're convinced he was behind the Lancaster heist," I said, "and that this tip on Camancho is a bum steer?"

"Absolutely. Listen, I'm sorry."

I shrugged and started for the door. "It happens."

"Hey, McKay. You want to talk about it more over coffee sometime?"

I turned around.

"Talk about what, Lieutenant? Johnny Camancho?"

"Whatever?"

"Are we discussing a date here?"

"If that's the label you want to give it." He smiled.

I looked him over. He was a little older than me, maybe mid-forties, with light brown hair that hung long in the back and over his ears. An affectation of youth. Not bad though; I've done worse. A lot worse. I looked down at his left hand. There was a ring on it.

"Are you married?" I asked.

"No." He saw me staring at the ring. "I mean, yes."

"Pick one."

"Well, I mean I was married, but I'm not now."

"Uh-huh."

"Honest."

"You divorced?"

"Yes."

"And you just wear the ring to remind you of that."

"Well, I mean I'm getting divorced. . . ."

"Separated?"

"Well, we're in the process of . . ."

"Good-bye, Lieutenant."

I walked outside and down the front steps of the precinct. It had stopped raining, but it was already dark out. I hate it when it gets dark early. I heard someone coming down the steps behind me and turned around. It was Gallagher.

"Look," I said, "don't take it personal. I just don't go out with married men, okay?"

He shrugged. "Okay."

I started down the street.

"How about when I break up with my wife?" he yelled after me.

"Doubtful," I said.

I went over to the Lancaster Hotel on Fifth Avenue and spent an hour talking to employees there. Security people, managers, and bellhops. No one had anything to add. No one believed my source. No one could understand why I was wasting my time.

So that was that. It all seemed to be a nonstory. I headed for home that night convinced I knew everything I needed to know about Johnny Camancho, Jerry Rossiello, and Rikki Stiles.

But the truth was I didn't know anything.

3
Death and Taxes

I was living downtown on Mulberry Street, in a third floor apartment above an Italian restaurant called Enrico's.

New Yorkers know Enrico's for two things—it's indescribably delicious veal parmigiana and its bloody mob rubouts. Both are ordered with great regularity. The most famous mob killing there was the shooting of Sal (the Barber) Columbo in 1985. Columbo was trying to choose between the fried Buffalo mozzarella and the shrimp Fiorentine for an appetizer one night when three men with machine guns burst in and rendered the decision academic. Legend has it that a party of twelve at the next table never even paused in wolfing down their veal during the entire time the bullets flew.

The owner of Enrico's is an underworld kingpin named Anthony (Big Tony) Mosconi. I was living upstairs from Enrico's because I'd once done a favor for Big Tony. Sort of. You see, a seven-year-old girl was missing, and I broadcast a picture of her and an appeal for her return. Someone found her wandering on the subway and she got home safely. It turned out she was Mosconi's granddaughter. He came to meet me afterward and said he was in my debt if I ever needed anything.

Me, I needed an apartment. I'd gotten into this big fight with my landlord in the Village. The lease was in an ex-boyfriend's name so I offered the landlord some money under the table to transfer it to me. He asked how much money. I said $500. He said $5000. I went to $750. He repeated the $5000 figure. When I demurred, he pointed out that it was his lease and he could do whatever he wanted with it. I suggested that he stick it in a bodily orifice in a manner that may have been a physical impossibility. The conversation went downhill from there.

Anyway, that's when Mosconi told me about the vacant apartment over his restaurant. The apartment suddenly had become vacant when the previous tenant, one of Mosconi's people who Big Tony found out was secretly a spy for a rival gang, had gone to Enrico's and someone delivered the house special to his table. And I don't mean the veal.

Did I go through an ethical dilemma before I moved in? Well, sure. I mean my new landlord was a killer, a crook, and probably a dope pusher and an extortionist too. On the other hand, so are a lot of other New York City landlords. Besides, these are desperate times in the apartment-hunting market. Desperate times require desperate measures. I took the place.

It was a little after eight when I got home. I opened the door, let myself in, and was immediately attacked by something black and furry. It was my dachshund, Hobo. I'd found him a year or so earlier wandering the streets and took him in. Some people say it's cruel to keep a dog cooped up in an apartment all day, but I don't think Hobo seems to mind. He's got his couch and his bones and his three walks a day and me. My guess is he's pretty happy.

The first thing I do when I get home is tell him a joke. It doesn't matter what it is. Animal experts say that the act of telling the joke projects happy emotions that make the dog feel safe and at peace with the world. Makes sense to me. The one I told him went like this:

A guy goes to a doctor's office, gets a physical, and the doctor tells him he's got good news and bad news.

"What's the bad news?" he asks.

"You've only got six months to live," the doctor tells him.

"Jesus," the guy says, then remembers the rest of it. "What's the good news?"

The doctor smiles. "I had sex with my nurse this morning."

I laughed loudly, and Hobo licked my face.

Afterward I walked him, fed him, and then tried to decide what to have for my own supper. There was some lettuce in the refrigerator. A nice healthy salad would be good for my figure. And I'd been putting on a few pounds recently. Or I could go downstairs to Enrico's and pick up a take-out order of angel hair pasta, with some cheesecake for dessert. I opted for Enrico's. Maybe I'd start a diet tomorrow.

On the way out I noticed the light flashing on my telephone answering machine. There was one message waiting. I clicked it on.

"Miss McKay, this is Agent Michael Stoner of the Internal Revenue Service Investigative Unit. I need to talk to you at the earliest possible moment. Could you give me a call at 827-5301? Thank you."

Uh-oh.

The IRS had notified me two weeks ago that I was being audited for the past two years. Something about my cash flow not being commensurate to my tax liability. Or maybe it was the other way around. I don't know. I'm really bad with money.

I looked at the time. Eight-thirty. Probably this guy Stoner was long gone by now. I dialed the number anyway. At least I could say I tried.

"Mike Stoner," a voice at the other end said.

"Boy, justice never sleeps, huh?"

"Pardon me?"

"My name's McKay. Jenny McKay. You called me."

"Oh, right. I've been assigned to do an on-site inspection of the home office you've claimed as a business deduction on your returns. This means I'll have to make a visit to your apartment sometime at your convenience."

"You're kidding me."

"I'm afraid not. You see we need to verify that you're using this area of your home exclusively for business. That means no TVs, video games, stereos, or anything like that there. And it has to be stocked with the proper amount of equipment and supplies."

"I bought a new box of paper clips the other day," I told him. "Does that help?"

He laughed. "A little. I'd like to get this done as soon as possible. Would next week be all right?"

I liked his laugh. His voice too. It sounded young and pleasant. Maybe this would be interesting. Probably not though. Probably Mike Stoner was about sixty years old with a face like Broderick Crawford and bad breath.

"Sure," I said, "why not?" We made an appointment for the following Thursday night at nine. "Hey, you guys over there ever listen to the *Revolver* album by the Beatles?"

"Excuse me?"

"You know, the first cut on the first side by George Harrison." I started to sing the lyrics from "Taxman."

Stoner cleared his throat. "I realize we're not always the most popular people, Miss McKay. Nevertheless a proper income tax system is necessary to keep our country functioning. The money you pay into it allows Washington to provide you the services essential for—"

"Boy, that's a bunch of bull," I said. "Most of the money goes to bail out places like Lockheed and so that the Army can build more missiles that don't work and blow up on the launching pad. Why don't you just forget about my money and blow up one less missile this year? Who's going to know the difference?"

"An interesting thought. I'll pass it on to the Defense Department next time they call. In the meantime, I'll see you next week."

"Yeah, sure." I paused. "Listen, do you guys bring your own rubber hose and cattle prod to work me over, or do I have to pay for that too?"

"You have to pay for it," he said. "But don't worry, you can deduct it on next year's return."

"Funny," I told him. "Really funny."

I ate my pasta and cheesecake in front of the TV while watching a rerun of "L.A. Law." Harry Hamlin was defending a woman accused of shooting her husband. Maybe I could get him to defend me in my case with the IRS. Maybe then we'd fall in love and . . . maybe I was fantasizing too much. It was eleven o'clock now. I pushed aside the pasta, let Hobo lick the plate, and switched on a videotape of the Channel Six News from earlier in the night.

Conroy Jackson's face appeared on the screen. He's the co-anchor who's been on the air for nearly twenty years and the station bills him as "the most authoritative anchorman in New York." The truth of the matter is he's—how can I say this—well, dumb. Big-time dumb. Dullardsville. Single-digit IQ country. Running a couple of quarts low.

Right now he was describing a ship that had sprung a huge oil leak in the East River just off of Houston Street and the FDR. The pronunciation of the street is "house-ton." Only Jackson kept saying it like the city in Texas. The gist of the piece was that the oil spill was being cleaned up, but officials were worried about the environmental impact on birds and sea life in the area.

Liz St. John came on next. I thought maybe she might correct Jackson's pronunciation of Houston, but she didn't. Probably didn't even know it was wrong. Instead she smiled at him and said:

"Well, you know what they say, Conroy—the oily bird always gets the worm."

They both laughed loudly.

Terrific, I thought. They're on the air, and I'm not. Life sucks.

I looked over at Hobo, who had curled himself into a ball on the couch and was snoring loudly.

"Hey, Hobo!" I said. He opened one eye slowly. I pointed toward the TV screen. "What do you think of Conroy and Liz as an anchor team?"

He closed both eyes again and resumed snoring.

"Me too," I said.

I got a good night's sleep, woke up bright and early, and made it to the office thirty minutes before Carstairs did. Then I planted myself outside his door and waited for him. When he showed up, I ambushed him before he even got his coat off.

"Remember that woman—Rikki Stiles—you had me talk to yesterday?"

He nodded.

"She's a hooker."

"No kidding?"

I told him about her story.

"And?"

"The cops say there's nothing to it. So do the investigators the hotel has on the case. And I checked around on this guy Camancho, who seems to be exactly what the police say he is. A two-bit hoodlum. Certainly not the type to pull off something like the Lancaster job."

"So." Carstairs shrugged. "Just forget it."

"Okay. Then what about me?"

"What do you mean?"

"I was a good girl. I checked out her story like you told me. So put me back on the air."

Carstairs sighed. "We'll see."

"That's no answer. Am I on or not?"

"Probably."

"Probably?"

"We'll talk about it this afternoon. Okay?"

"Okay." I stood up and started for the door, then turned around. "Oh, one more thing. The Stiles woman was pretty desperate for money. I think she's trying to get out of the hooker business. Can you spring loose a few bucks for her?"

"Why? We're not the Salvation Army here."

"I know, but maybe we could give her a little something for coming to us, just to help her out. Nothing big. Say maybe one hundred, two hundred dollars. We pay for story tips all the time."

"Yeah," Carstairs said, "for story tips. She didn't have a story. You said so yourself."

"I know, but it could have been true. Who's going to miss a couple hundred dollars? You can write it off on your expenses easy. Pretend it's just another long lunch at Lutèce or something."

Carstairs arched an eyebrow. "Just for the record, McKay, my lunch yesterday was a peanut butter sandwich and an apple from the diner downstairs and—"

"Bob, I really think she needs help," I said.

He reached into his desk drawer and took out a cash withdrawal slip, made it out for $150, and handed it to me.

"Thanks," I told him. "I really appreciate this."

"Just tell Rikki Stiles to do a little more checking next time before she comes to us with a story," he grunted.

I could have put the money into an envelope and mailed it to her, I guess. But I wanted to talk to her face-to-face one more time. Maybe I wanted to confront her on why she sent me off on a wild-goose chase with the hokey story. She'd given me an apartment address before she left, so I got the cash and headed over there.

The apartment turned out to be on Sutton Place. That surprised me. Sutton Place is superposh. Not exactly the kind of place you'd expect a woman to live who said she needed money. Rikki Stiles's building was a swanky-looking high rise, where the apartments probably started at about two thousand dollars a month. I thought again about her story of needing money and felt a little foolish making such a big deal over the $150.

There was a doorman in the lobby—a young guy, maybe mid-twenties, probably Hispanic. Behind him a TV camera made a sweep from left to right, taking in all of the lobby and the sidewalk out front. A set of TV screens was on the wall so he could monitor anyone's movements at all times. Next to the TV screens was a big sign which said: "Absolutely no one allowed in without doorman ringing first."

I wondered if the doorman was going to give me a hard time, like they sometimes do in fancy buildings, but I needn't have worried. He was engaged in deep conversation with a girl in a tight blue blouse, bright red leather miniskirt, and platform heels. They were talking in Spanish, which I barely speak. But I made out enough to understand that he was suggesting they get together after he got off work. Some things come across in all languages.

Rikki Stiles lived in Apartment 18B. I walked past the doorman, past the security camera, and got onto the elevator and pressed the button for eighteen. Crack security system, all right. Probably cost the landlord a minimum of one hundred thousand dollars. It pays to buy the best.

On the ride up, I thought again about why I was doing this. I didn't have to give her the money. I didn't owe her anything. Anyway, she seemed to have more money than she needed from the looks of this place. She'd given me a tip, it didn't check out—end of story. Except . . . except there was something more, something she wasn't telling me that was going on here. I wanted to know what it was. Maybe if I talked to her again.

The elevator doors opened, and I walked out into a plush carpeted hallway. Apartment 18B was the second door on the right. I rang the bell. There was no answer. I banged on it for a while, then rang the bell again. Still nothing.

"Rikki, are you in there?" I yelled. "It's Jenny McKay. From Channel Six."

Not a sound from inside.

I should have left right then, I guess. Just got on the elevator, went down to the street, and gone back to the office. But I didn't. For some reason, I pushed on the door. It opened. That startled me. Nobody in New York City leaves their door open, not even in a building like this. I went inside.

The apartment was big. The living room had a picture window with a view looking south toward the Chrysler and Empire State buildings. There was a door on the other side leading out onto a terrace overlooking the East River. In the center of the room was a velvet couch with a long mahogany coffee table in front of it. There were two empty glasses on the table and a bottle of champagne. Of course. With a setup like this, Rikki Stiles probably charged a pretty hefty fee. The customer wanted his money's worth. You couldn't expect a girl to just serve him Miller Lite before the ol' roll in the hay.

"Rikki, are you here?" I said.

More silence.

I started to edge my way down a long hall toward two rooms, apparently bedrooms, on the other side of the apartment. This is crazy, I thought to myself. I'm probably going to walk in on her in bed with a customer.

The first bedroom was empty. The bed was made, the drapes drawn. Everything very much in order.

I found her in the second room.

She was wearing the same clothes she'd had on when she came to see me. The designer jeans with the chain-link belt, the fancy boots, and the low-cut blue sweater. The front of the sweater was splotched with blood. So was the bed she was lying on. Her eyes stared upward at nothing, but her face seemed peaceful. Almost serene.

"Oh, Jesus," I said out loud.

Rikki Stiles had been looking for a way out, all right, but now it looked like someone had beaten her to it.

4

Live From New York!

PRODUCER: Jenny, are you standing by?

McKAY: I'm here.

The producer's name was Barry Kaiser. He was back in the WTBK studio on South Street. I was standing on Sutton Place, in front of Rikki Stiles's building, listening through an earpiece and talking into a microphone.

KAISER: Good. We're going to go to you about ten minutes after the hour. First Liz will lead with the Mayor being pelted with eggs today in Bensonhurst, then Conroy will do a follow on Rossiello, the mobster being indicted by the DA, and then they do a short intro and switch over to you: "Here's Jenny McKay, live at the scene of a late breaking murder on Sutton Place . . . blah, blah, blah." Got that?

McKAY: Right.

KAISER: Is that enough time for you to get ready?

McKAY: Plenty of time.

KAISER: You got everything you need?

McKAY: No problem.

KAISER: [pause] You feel okay, right? I mean you don't need a drink of water? You don't have to go to the bathroom or anything?

I sighed. One day when I was doing a remote I needed to go to the bathroom a few minutes before going on the air. I thought I had time. But the ladies' room turned out to be down two flights of stairs and on the other side of the building. I barely made it back just as they were switching to me, and I was panting and gasping for breath during the whole segment. Several viewers called in and thought I was having a heart attack.

McKAY: I'm fine, Barry.

KAISER: Okay, stay close.

I was with Alan Sanders, my cameraman, and Artie Jacobson, who handled the sound. I'd called both of them as well as the police from inside the apartment after I found the body.

"You know, you ought to be more careful how you talk to the bosses," Sanders observed now. "I mean there's only about one hundred dazzling beauties lined up across the country who'd love to stick their fingernails into you to get this job."

"Are you saying you think they might fire me?"

"It has been known to happen in this business."

"Let 'em. The IRS is about ready to garnish my salary anyway. I'd make more on unemployment."

"The IRS? You still having trouble with them?"

"Yeah." I told him about the phone call from Mike Stoner.

"We brothers don't have tax problems," said Sanders, who is black. "That's because we don't have money."

I groaned. "Is this going to be the story about how you grew up in a two-room tenement with twelve other people and no food and a cockroach for a pet?"

Sanders's father is a corporate lawyer and his mother trades stocks and bonds on Wall Street, and I happen to know he grew up in a three-story mansion in the suburbs.

"Well, maybe not me," he said defensively, "but my people. My brothers. . . ."

"We're all brothers and sisters in the universe, Alan. Listen, what am I going to do about this tax thing?"

"You need some professional help."

"I had professional help when I filled out the forms."

"Jenny, a guy you met in a singles bar named Murray who told you he was an accountant is not professional help. Why'd you listen to him anyway?"

"Well, he had nice eyes."

"Oh, the IRS is going to love that. Where is he now?"

"He sorta disappeared."

Sanders shrugged. "I'll ask my father. Maybe he can recommend someone. Hey, Artie, how about you—you know a good tax lawyer?"

Artie Jacobson looked up from the crossword puzzle he was doing. Artie was always doing crosswords. He started out with the *Times*, then did the *Post*, *News*, and *Newsday*. After that it was the Jumble words in the *News* and Scrabble in the *Post*. Sometimes—if he finished all that—he even did the kiddie "connect-the-dots" stuff. I asked him once why he liked doing puzzles so much. He thought for a minute and then said: "Kills time."

Artie was not a particularly articulate man.

"My brother-in-law is a tax lawyer," he said now.

"No kidding?" Sanders said. "He any good?"

"Good enough to get me a sixty-five-hundred-dollar refund last year."

"Can you call him for me?" I asked.

"I suppose I could. But it wouldn't do you much good."

"Why not?"

"Because," he said, "he's doing five to ten in Lewisburg for tax fraud."

I stared at him. "You're kidding, right?"

"Yeah, I'm kidding."

"I thought so."

"Actually he copped a plea bargain and only got disbarred."

My earpiece crackled to life. "Okay, here we go," Kaiser was saying from the studio, "get ready. Are you watching a monitor?" I said I was. On the screen in front of me now was a Hyundai commercial. Then it switched to a Channel Six logo, a quick cut to the newsroom, and then the theme music began.

ANNOUNCER: And now, direct from New York's liveliest newsroom, it's the News at Six on Six. With the WTBK team of newsbreakers: Conroy Jackson and Liz St. John at the anchor desk; Bill Hanrahan on sports; Stormy Phillips with the weather; and live reports from all over New York. Now here's Conroy and Liz:

ST. JOHN: Good evening, ladies and gentlemen. Here's what's happening. The Mayor went to Bensonhurst today to try to mend some political fences and inject some good humor into his feud with the area's residents over a controversial housing project. But it turned out the "yolk" was on him as demonstrators pelted him with eggs . . .

I watched the way she talked. Her mouth looking as if it was stuffed with cotton, emphasizing key words, staring at the teleprompter for every thought, a silly smile plastered on her face—and the latest viewer surveys showed the people out there loved her. That was scary. It meant more people on TV would start talking like her. Maybe even impressionable teenage girls watching would start too. Then little girls just growing up. Pretty soon the world would be made up of Liz St. John clones. Sort of like *Invasion of the Body Snatchers*.

I heard Kaiser's voice again in my earpiece. "Okay, Jenny . . . stand by . . . stand by . . . stand by . . . he-e-e-re we go. . . ." On the monitor, Liz was saying:

ST. JOHN: And now we check in with our reporter, Jenny McKay, who's standing by live on Sutton Place in Manhattan, where police are investigating a very gruesome murder. Jenny?

The scene switched to a picture of me. I was standing there in front of Rikki Stiles's building, trench coat on, notebook in hand, holding a microphone in front of me, my hair blowing slightly in the wind. I looked good. Ms. Newswoman. Ready for action. I hoped somebody from a network was watching.

McKAY: A young woman was found murdered this afternoon inside her posh apartment in this building on Sutton Place.

The picture shifted to film clips shot earlier inside the building—Rikki Stiles's front door and then a view of the interior of the apartment, including the bedroom.

McKAY: I discovered the body myself in this front bedroom overlooking the East River shortly after 1 p.m. The victim's name was Rikki Stiles. She had been shot to death.
The picture was back to me.

McKAY: Although Rikki Stiles told people in this building she made her living as a free-lance artist, WTBK has learned that she was really a prostitute—a high-priced call girl. In the living room of her apartment were two empty glasses and a bottle of champagne. I have with me Police Lt. Nicholas Ruggerio. Lieutenant, do you think that she may have been killed by one of her customers?

Cut to a picture of the lieutenant talking with me.

RUGGERIO: Well, that would be a likely scenario. It does look like she was getting ready to entertain someone before she died.

McKAY: Was there evidence of a sexual attack?

RUGGERIO: Nothing apparent. But we won't know for sure until the autopsy.

McKAY: Did you find anything in her apartment?

RUGGERIO: Not really. A lot of expensive clothes in the closet. Some cash—some jewelry hidden underneath a drawer. A cabinet of art supplies—sketch pads and colored pencils and stuff. But nothing personal. No diaries. No photographs.

I realized as he was talking that I had noticed the same thing when I was in the apartment. There was a bareness about it, an emptiness, despite all the expensive furnishings. It was as if Rikki Stiles had lived there, but she didn't really live there. Like a Holiday Inn you spend a few nights at, then move on down the road.

McKAY: Thank you, Lieutenant, for taking time to talk to us.

I turned back to the camera.

McKAY: And that's the situation right now on Sutton Place. A dead call girl in a posh apartment, but no clues and no motive. This is Jenny McKay, live in New York, reporting for the News at Six on Six.

ST. JOHN: Thanks, Jenny. Jenny, you said you discovered the body yourself. Why were you there?

A good question. Someone must have fed it to her. She usually asked dopey questions when she tried to do this sort of repartee on the air.

McKAY: Rikki Stiles came to see me yesterday with some information I promised to look into for her.

ST. JOHN: Can you tell us more about that information?

McKAY: Well, it turned out not to be true, so there's really no point. . . .

ST. JOHN: I see. One more thing, Jenny. When you found Rikki Stiles's body, what did she look like?

I looked straight ahead at the camera and tried to keep my composure. This was a typical Liz St. John question.

McKAY: Well, she looked dead, Liz.

ST. JOHN: Oh, I see. [She seemed somewhat flustered.] Well, we'll certainly be keeping tabs on this story. Thanks for that report.

She turned back to the camera in the studio.

ST. JOHN: Ladies, do you suspect your husband may be cheating on you? Well, now you can find out by taking a ten-point quiz called "How to Know If the Man In Your Life Has a Mistress." We'll be talking to the author of that after this message. . . .

We were packing up our equipment to go when I saw a face I knew coming out of the building with some other cops. It was Lt. Rick Gallagher, the guy I'd talked to about Rikki Stiles's tip on the Lancaster robbery. He saw me too and walked over.

"Hello again, Jenny McKay."

"What are you doing here?" I asked.

"Oh, I just wanted to check it out. I had some dealings with the dead woman in the past."

"What kind of dealings?"

He shook his head. "It's confidential. I can't have it being broadcast on the air."

"Off the record?"

He thought for a minute. "Okay, off the record. Rikki Stiles did some work for us a while back. She was a police snitch. A paid informer."

"Jesus!" I said.

"What?"

"Remember when I came to you yesterday with the tip about the Lancaster Hotel heist? I told you I had a source that said she knew who did it?"

"Sure."

"Well, Rikki Stiles was my source."

Gallagher laughed. "No wonder that Lancaster Hotel story sounded familiar."

"You mean she came to you with it first?"

"She must have. It didn't make any more sense then than it did coming from you. Anyway, we weren't listening to her anymore by that point anyway."

"Why not?"

"Look, she worked for the cops for a few months or so. She came to us and volunteered. People who move in the circles she did hear a lot of things, you know. This Stiles chick used to tell us some of it from time to time, we'd slip her a little money for the information and then follow it up. She was okay too. For a while."

"What went wrong?"

"Too much bad information. It was like she was desperate for money somehow and was feeding us anything. Who knows why? Maybe she had a drug habit or something."

"A snitch," I muttered. "Rikki Stiles was a snitch for the Police Department. How much did you guys pay her?"

"I don't know. A lot. Some of her stuff was pretty helpful. Until she went bad."

"Just for telling you things?"

"Don't act so surprised. This sort of thing happens all the time. Of course, being a snitch can be dangerous too. The wrong person finds out she's doing it, and she's in trouble."

I thought about the bruise on the side of her face. Maybe the wrong person had found out.

"So what do you think?" I asked. "Somebody found out she was talking to the cops and knocked her off?"

"Maybe."

"You don't think so?"

"I can hear the wheels clicking in your head, McKay. It makes a neat little package that way, doesn't it? She tells us something somebody doesn't like so they shut her up. A good story too. Except it doesn't have to be that way. Hookers get killed all the time. It could have been just a dissatisfied customer. No connection whatsoever to anything else."

"What about the Lancaster Hotel tip? Maybe this guy Camancho . . ."

Gallagher shook his head. "But it's not true. We've already agreed on that. I mean we'll pick up this guy Camancho for questioning, but I don't think it'll do much good. If he didn't do the Lancaster robbery, what's his motive for killing her?"

"Yeah," I said, "I see what you mean."

"It was a violent world she lived in, McKay. There doesn't have to be a reason. The world is filled with weirdos."

A couple of guys from the Medical Examiner's office came out of the building now carrying a stretcher with Rikki Stiles's body on it. It was inside a green plastic bag with a zipper up the front. They had trouble getting it through the front door at first. Finally, after the doorman opened it up wider, the two ME guys made their way down the steps and loaded it into an ambulance waiting on the street. Must be a helluva way to make a living, I thought to myself.

"One thing I don't understand," I said. "You say she was desperate for money, giving you phony information and all. And she certainly seemed like it with me too. But yet she had this great setup. Fancy East Side apartment, nice clothes. I don't get it."

Gallagher smiled. "She worked for Victor Galena. Ever hear of him?"

I shook my head.

"Who's he?" I asked. "Her pimp?"

"Well, you could say that, but it's not exactly like you think. This guy Galena deals only in high-class goods. He works out of a penthouse on the Upper East Side. Has maybe fifteen, twenty girls. They all have their own apartments too, mostly in swanky neighborhoods like this. We're not talking about twenty-five bucks a pop in the backseat of a car, we're talking about high rollers—execs and the like willing to plop down two grand or so for a night of loving company."

I made a whistling sound. "Whew! Two thousand dollars. That's a lot of bread. An operator like Galena must take in a fortune."

"Sure. Remember the case of the Mayflower Madam a while back? The blue blood chick who was running the posh call girl ring? She had this black book with a lot of fancy clients in it and all. Well, that's the same sort of operation Galena runs."

"Okay," I said, "so Galena takes his cut and makes a lot of money. That still should leave a lot of money left over for someone like Rikki Stiles."

"It doesn't work out like that. A guy like Galena takes everything, the whole ball of wax. He sets up some chicks like Rikki Stiles in fancy apartments, buys them expensive clothes, nice jewelry—the works. But that's it. Nothing's really hers. That way he's always got a hold on her. She's living in the lap of luxury. But she can never leave because she's got nothing but the clothes on her back, and even those belong to Galena. It's a real trap."

Sanders and Jacobson were waiting for me in the mobile van. Sanders stuck his head out the window now. "Carstairs wants to talk to you," he said. I nodded.

"I gotta go," I told Gallagher. "Thanks for the information. Maybe I'll talk to you later."

He smiled. "I certainly hope so."

When I got to the WTBK van, Sanders handed me the mobile phone. Carstairs was on the other end.

"A very nice job, Jenny."

"Really?"

"Really. Of course, I could have done without the dumb answer to Liz at the end. . . ."

"Dumb question, dumb answer," I said.

"Yeah, well. . . ."

"So am I reinstated? Is all forgiven?"

"All is forgiven."

"Great!"

"But Jenny, be careful what you say when you're on the air from now on. Okay?"

"Okay."

I hung up the phone. Sanders and Jacobson were staring at me, waiting to find out what Carstairs had said. I gave them a big smile.

"Well, boys and girls," I said, "we're back on the air."

5

A Talk With the DA

By Monday, everything was pretty much back to normal.

I was assigned by Carstairs to do a feature on a soap opera actress named Carlotta Gayle who moonlighted in her off-hours as a New York City taxicab driver.

"Why?" I asked.

"Why what?"

"Why does she moonlight as a taxi driver?"

"I don't know. Who cares?"

"I do. You should too. We're journalists, remember? Every story should have the five W's—who, what, where, when, and why. This is why."

"To make ends meet, I guess." He shrugged.

I snorted. "Doesn't this sound just a little like a publicity stunt?"

"So?" Carstairs asked.

"So don't you have any good stories for me to do?"

"Jenny, Jenny." He sighed. "Every story can be a good story if you make it good."

"Whew, that's inspirational," I said. "Maybe you could

embroider that on a pot holder or something and I could hang it on my kitchen wall."

"Have a nice day, Jenny," he said and walked away.

I hadn't forgotten about Rikki Stiles, but I really didn't know what to do about her. The cops said Johnny Camancho and his brother couldn't be found; Victor Galena, her pimp, hadn't been of much help; and the investigation was pretty much at a dead end. Just another dead hooker in New York City.

It was a little after eleven when my telephone rang. The person on the other end was someone named Carrie Macklin in the Manhattan District Attorney's office. I didn't know a Carrie Macklin. I didn't know anyone in the DA's office. I told her that.

"I understand," Carrie Macklin said, "but would it be possible for you to drop by sometime today to meet with Mr. Carson?"

"Elliott Carson?" I asked. "The District Attorney?"

"That's right."

"Do you mind if I ask why?"

"Well, I'd prefer to let Mr. Carson discuss that with you."

"But I don't even know Elliott Carson. . . ."

"You have heard of him, haven't you?"

"Of course. The way he gets his name in the newspapers, I'd have to be from the planet Venus not to have heard of him."

She laughed, but it seemed forced.

"Mr. Carson would very much like to talk to you," she said. "He has an opening at twelve-fifteen. Could you stop by then?"

My interview with the soap opera actress wasn't until two. Plenty of time to see what the ol' DA had on his mind.

"Sure, that's fine."

"Good. We'll see you then."

I had an hour to kill before the meeting. It was going to be a busy afternoon, so I decided to grab an early lunch at a McDonald's near City Hall. I got there at eleven-fifteen, which is bad timing at a McDonald's. The breakfast was over, and a lot of the hamburgers weren't ready yet for lunch. I had a choice—I could eat Chicken McNuggets or wait fifteen minutes for a Big Mac. I finally decided to order the Big Mac and then ordered Chicken McNuggets to eat while I waited for it. Tough problems require tough solutions.

I'm a connoisseur of fast-food places in the way some people are connoisseurs of fine wines or elegant restaurants. I mean I can tell you all about the sour cream baked potatoes at Wendy's or the salad bar at Roy Rogers or how many White Castle hamburgers with onions a normal human being can consume before becoming significantly nauseous. (The answer is ten, although on occasion I've made it to twelve.) Once, back when I worked for a newspaper, I suggested writing a regular column on all this in the same way that papers run wine or restaurant columns. I even came up with a name for it: "The Garbage Gourmet." The editor thanked me profusely for my suggestion, but respectfully declined. It's like Paul Newman says in *Butch Cassidy and the Sundance Kid*—"I've got vision, and the rest of the world wears bifocals."

The Manhattan DA's office is located at 1 Hogan Plaza, which is a few blocks away from City Hall and about ten minutes from the WTBK studios. The front part of the building on Centre Street is the Criminal Courts section. It's run-down and dismal. If you go in the building that way, you run into an army of drug pushers, prostitutes, pimps, and other assorted lowlifes waiting for their court appearances. The Hogan Plaza entrance in the back is a bit more civilized. It's used mainly by the DA's people, law enforcement officials, and the like. I went in the back.

A receptionist directed me down a hall to an office which said ELLIOTT CARSON, MANHATTAN DISTRICT ATTORNEY, on the door. Inside I was taken to a neatly furnished office where a woman sat working behind a desk.

"Jenny McKay, I'm so glad you could come," the woman

said, standing up. "I'm Carrie Macklin."

Carrie Macklin was about thirty-five or so, but she had the look of someone almost fifteen years older. Her hair was a dull brown, and she had it pulled back behind her head in a severe bun. She wore only the barest makeup and no jewelry. A pair of eyeglasses dangled from a chain around her neck. Her clothes were as plain and conservative as you could get. There was a grey skirt and top that looked as if it had last been in style sometime during the Eisenhower Administration, flat-heeled black shoes, and dull grey stockings. She was not exactly what you'd call that "*Cosmopolitan* Girl."

"Hi," I said. "Listen, I'm still not really sure why I'm here, Miss Macklin."

"Carrie, call me Carrie. We want to be friends here."

I nodded. "Sure, Carrie."

"Anyway, why don't I let the District Attorney talk to you about that, Jenny. I think it would be better that way. He'll be with you in just a few minutes. In the meantime, have a seat and relax."

She pointed to a couch near her desk, and I sat down.

Carrie Macklin's office matched the way she was dressed. It was very austere, businesslike. No paintings on the walls. No pictures of children or dogs. Just a few shelves filled with law books. Her desk was the same way. Several stacks of papers placed in neat little piles—everything organized, everything in its place.

I took out a cigarette to kill time, started to light it, and then realized I couldn't find an ashtray.

"Jenny, I'd appreciate it if you wouldn't do that," Carrie Macklin said.

She pointed to a little sign near the corner of her desk which said: THANK YOU FOR NOT SMOKING.

"Sorry, Miss Macklin," I said. I put the cigarette away.

"Carrie," she reminded me with a smile.

"Right, Carrie."

"I don't mean to be rude," she said, "but I really can't stand cigarette smoke. It's so dirty. You know, the smell

clings to your clothes and hair for days if someone lights
up in the same room with you. It's very unpleasant."

I reached back in my purse and found a stick of chewing
gum. I looked around the office again. There didn't seem to
be any signs against that, so I stuck it in my mouth.

She leaned over and pressed a button on the intercom on
her desk. A few seconds later a secretary appeared from
another room.

"This schedule you typed up for the District Attorney is
wrong," Carrie Macklin told her.

The secretary got a tight look around her mouth. "Wrong?
But I don't understand. I checked it. . . ."

"It's wrong. Do it over."

She pointed to a spot about two thirds of the way down
the paper.

"It says there that he's scheduled to arrive for the fund-
raiser in the Hilton at eight o'clock. The correct time should
be 8:05. He's not scheduled to be there until 8:05."

"But I thought it was all right to make the time an estimate. . . ."

"We never estimate or guess at anything in this office,"
Carrie Macklin told her evenly. "We check the facts and are
exact. Now please do it over."

The secretary took the paper back, still with that tight look
around her mouth, and stalked out of the office.

"She's a nice girl," Carrie said to me after she was gone,
"but sloppy. Always trying to take the easy way out. I don't
like sloppiness. Sloppiness is the Devil's handiwork, I think
sometimes. What do you think, Jenny?"

"You may be right, Carrie," I said.

Carrie was starting to get on my nerves.

"Too many people in this world are sloppy," she said. She
paused for a second. "And negative thinkers too. They're
always worried about what they can't do, not what they can
do. I'm a positive thinker."

She leaned back in her chair and looked around the office.
"Let me give you an example of positive thinking. Every

other government office in this city starts work at nine o'clock. And most of the people don't show up until near ten. Well, I make everyone here show up at eight o'clock sharp every morning. Do you know why?"

I'll bite, I thought. "Why?"

"Because it gives us a positive outlook, a positive start on the day. We're in charge of making sure the law is carried out in this town, so it's important we're one step ahead of the lawbreakers all the time. Being here at eight o'clock gives us an hour's head start on the rest of the world."

I nodded thoughtfully. "There's only one problem with that," I said.

"What's that?"

"What if all the criminals get up at seven?"

Carrie Macklin didn't smile. Just sat there and stared at me strangely. Probably writing me off as a negative thinker.

The intercom buzzed and she stood up.

"The District Attorney is ready to see you now, Jenny. This way please."

We went through a set of connecting doors and into another office. Elliott Carson was sitting behind a big walnut desk with a window facing out over Chinatown. He was in his mid-forties, with thick, dark, curly hair and a ruddy complexion. He was wearing a dark blue suit, white pin-striped shirt, and blue and gold Ivy League tie. Pretty good-looking as politicians go, and he looked like the type who knew it.

"Jenny McKay, I'm really glad to get a chance to meet you," he boomed. "Sit down. Sit down."

I sat down in front of the desk. There were several plaques on it from various organizations honoring him as their Man of the Year for his achievements. On one corner was a picture of his family—a smiling, rather plain-looking woman and three dark-haired children. Next to it was a picture of Elliott Carson riding a white horse. He sat tall in the saddle and his hair billowed behind him in the wind. I remembered reading somewhere that Carson was very big on horses—owned a slew of them upstate.

"Now remember you have a two o'clock appearance at the Plaza with the Bar Association," Carrie Macklin was saying to him. "Here's your speech. I have it all prepared for you. It's exactly twenty-three minutes long. That'll give you enough time for cocktails and allow you to get to your meeting with the Mayor on time. All right?"

Carson nodded. "I'm sure it will work out fine."

Carrie Macklin turned, gave me a small smile, and left the room.

"She takes good care of me," Carson said admiringly after she'd gone. "That's one hell of a little lady."

"Yeah, she's great," I said. "I think I once had a school-teacher just like her."

Carson laughed. "Okay, I know what you mean. She is a bit overbearing at times. But she's worth her weight in gold to me."

I didn't say anything.

"Listen, I'm glad to get this chance to meet you," Carson told me. "I mean I know most of the media people around town—Chuck Scarborough over at Channel Four, Bill Beutel at Seven, Conroy Jackson at your station. . . . Some of the network people too. Tom Brokaw, Dan Rather. Do you know Rather?"

"Nope," I said. "Never met him."

"Helluva nice guy. Not stuffy or stiff or anything like that. Nothing like you see on camera. Of course, none of them could hold a candle to some of the real old pros like Walter Cronkite. Or Edward R. Murrow. Now Murrow, he practically wrote the book on TV journalism, didn't he?"

"Murrow was great," I agreed.

"Yeah, he sure was. . . ."

His voice trailed off.

"Well, Miss McKay, I imagine you're wondering why I asked you to come here today."

"Jeez, no," I said. "I just figured you wanted to impress me with how many media names you could drop into a conversation."

Carson stared at me for a second and then laughed. Loudly.

"Very funny. Very sharp. I like sharp people. In fact, I like you and . . ."

The door opened and Carrie Macklin came in. She told Carson he had signed some papers in the wrong place and waited while he did them over. She wasn't exactly disapproving about it, more like a mother explaining something patiently to a child. Carrie Macklin was a pip, all right.

When she left, Carson turned back to me.

"Now where were we?" he asked.

"You were telling me how much you liked me."

"Right. Look, Miss McKay, I happened to catch you on TV the other day. You were doing a piece about some prostitute who died. A woman named . . . ah . . ."

"Rikki Stiles," I said.

"Right. Rikki Stiles. Anyway, it was impressive. Damn impressive. I mean you actually met the girl the day before she was killed?"

"Yeah," I told him, "it was really strange. She came to see me, just like I said on the air, because she thought she had something that might be a story for us."

"Really?"

"Uh-huh. She thought she knew who pulled off a robbery."

"What kind of robbery?"

"The big one at the Lancaster Hotel."

He looked surprised.

"Yeah, I know. Everybody tells me it's crazy. Anyway, the tip didn't pan out and now she's dead. But the cops don't think the two are related. They figure it was just a call-girl murder. It can be a pretty dangerous occupation, even when you work at the luxury level like she did."

Carson nodded. "I can imagine. Anyway, I'm watching you do this report on TV and I say to myself—this is a woman with a bright future. Me, I think I've got a bright future too. Maybe we should get to know each other."

"That's very flattering."

"How about a get-acquainted lunch? Maybe in a few days?"

"I never turn down a free lunch."

"I've got a story or two you might be interested in. Stuff I'd like to make public, but in a private way. You know what I mean?"

"Off the record? As a source?"

"Yes. It could work well for both of us." He smiled at me. "I like to have friends in the media."

"I never turn down a story either."

He leaned back in his chair. "So tell me a little about yourself, Miss McKay."

I went through a recap of my career.

"My, my—newspapers, magazines, TV. That's quite a checkered career for someone so young. What are you— thirty-two, thirty-three?"

"I'm forty-one," I said.

Carson let out a low whistle. "No kidding. Hey, you look real good."

"I think that's a sexist remark, but thanks anyway."

"You ever do anything besides journalism?"

"Well, I worked for a big public relations firm for six months or so in between two of the newspaper jobs."

"How'd that go?"

"Not well. I got fired."

"Why?"

"They said I didn't fit their corporate image."

"What did you do?"

"I called the president of the company a dickhead."

He laughed again. "Well, let's make that lunch date. . . . Now where is my calendar?" He began shuffling through papers on his desk without any success.

"Why don't I just call your office and set it up?" I suggested.

"Good idea."

The intercom buzzed. It was Carrie Macklin again. "You need to leave soon," she said.

"I've got to be going myself," I said.

I stood up. Carson did too and started to walk me to the door.

"I'm glad we talked," he said. "Who knows, maybe we never would have met if I hadn't happened to see you doing that report on . . . what was her name again?"

"Rikki Stiles."

It didn't seem like that hard a name to remember, especially for a DA, but then what do I know?

"Right." He shook his head. "She comes to you with a tip, and then she's dead. And that's all she told you? This phony tip about the Lancaster Hotel robbery?"

"That's all."

"Life's funny sometimes."

I walked out through the waiting area. As I left Carson's office, I heard him back at his desk muttering something about not being able to find his speech for the Bar Association. Carrie Macklin was talking again to the woman with the tight look on her face.

"I think he needs you, Carrie," I told her.

The soap opera star, Carlotta Gayle, turned out to be as big a publicity hound as I'd feared.

She showed up with two press agents, publicity stills, a press release, and wearing an outfit so tight it was guaranteed to stop traffic all over town.

One of the exchanges with her went like this:

McKAY: Isn't it scary driving a cab by yourself?

GAYLE: No, I find the people I pick up are all very friendly and helpful.

McKAY: How about at night? I mean would you drive a fare to Harlem at night?

GAYLE: Harlem? No, I don't go to Harlem. I don't leave Manhattan.

McKAY: Uh—Harlem is in Manhattan.

GAYLE: Oh, right.

Needless to say, that didn't survive the editing room.
The final product that went on the air came out something like this:

McKAY: First, there was Robert De Niro in *Taxi Driver*. Then Marilu Henner as Nardo on the streets of Manhattan. But this is different—this is not just an actress playing the part of a cabdriver. This is an actress who actually is a cabdriver.

Yes, for Carlotta Gayle, "all's fare" when she gets behind the wheel of . . .

After the show was over, I dialed the number of a lawyer I knew named Clare Lefferts. Clare worked for the Legal Aid Society. She could have made ten times as much in private practice, but she didn't want to.
"I need some information," I told her.
"What kind of information?"
"Legal."
"It's going to cost you then."
"Huh?"
"I don't give out legal advice for free. How about you make a twenty-five-dollar donation to the House the Homeless Coalition?"
I sighed. "Still trying to save the world, huh, Clare?"
"Still fighting it, huh, Jenny?"
"Okay, twenty-five dollars for the homeless. Tell me what you know about Elliott Carson."
"The District Attorney? Why?"

"I have a thirst for knowledge."

She went through a brief biography of him. Most of it I already knew. Ambitious. Publicity-hungry. Touted as a real political comer.

"Look, I don't really have much contact with him though. You should talk to someone who does. Maybe some of the reporters who cover him regularly. He's real chummy with a lot of them. Likes to pal around with the media."

I thought again about my conversation with him. "So I hear."

"There's one guy in particular," Clare said, "from the *Daily News* . . ."

"Who?" I asked hopefully. I had a lot of friends at the *Daily News*.

"Jim Brantley."

"Oh, shit!"

"You know him?"

"We sorta dated."

"And?"

"Well, we sorta slept together."

"It didn't go well?"

"I sorta threw his clothes out the window of my apartment and locked him out in the hall stark naked."

"Wow!"

"Yeah, he started talking about his girlfriend after we made love and one thing led to another and . . . and eventually the cops came and arrested him when he went down to the street to get his clothes. I haven't talked to him since."

"Boy, I'd love to eavesdrop on you two when you meet."

"Maybe we won't have to. Thanks, Clare."

"No problem. Hey, Jenny—you know you really ought to try to get your life together."

"I'm paying you twenty-five dollars for legal advice—not personal advice."

"The personal advice is free," Clare said.

6

Let's Go to the Videotape

To make it big in TV news, you need a shtick.

A shtick is a shortcut. A gimmick. An attention-getting device. It can be a catchphrase or a way of speaking or something you wear or even some physical characteristic.

It's Linda Ellerbee saying, "And so it goes." Or Warner Wolf yelling, "Let's go to the videotape." Or Willard Scott wishing senior citizens around the country a happy birthday. Or Sam Donaldson's bushy eyebrows or Tom Brokaw's little wink when he says good-bye or even Diane Sawyer posing in her negligee for *Vanity Fair*.

The point here is that you can look strange and possess no journalistic ability and have an IQ with only two digits, yet still be a success in the TV business as long as you come up with the right shtick.

Me, I got no shtick.

I was discussing all this in the WTBK newsroom with the woman who did our weather, Stormy Phillips. Stormy Phillips had a shtick. Her shtick was to dress provocatively in front of the camera in an outfit based on her forecast—a bikini for a sunny day, a slinky raincoat for thunderstorms, a tight ski-bunny sweater and pants for snow, etc.

"You know, when I was a kid, I used to have a cheap toy for predicting the weather," I told her. "It was a barometer or something in the shape of a little house with a door in front. When it was going to rain, a guy in a fisherman's rubber hat would come out the door. For sun, you'd get some bozo in a Hawaiian shirt. That's just like you."

"Exactly," she said.

"I didn't mean that as a compliment," I pointed out.

Stormy was no dummy. A political science major from NYU. Graduated Phi Beta Kappa. Even had worked two years toward a law degree. Which made what she was doing in front of the camera each night even harder to understand.

"I mean I can see it from Liz St. John," I told her. "She has a legitimate excuse. She's an idiot. But you . . ."

Stormy chuckled. "You take this all too seriously, Jenny."

"Do I?"

"Sure. You yourself said you were looking for a shtick. So what am I doing that's so bad? I'm just giving people what they want. Is there anything wrong with that?"

"I don't know," I said thoughtfully. "Maybe we should aim higher than just giving people what they want. Maybe we should try to elevate their consciousness and—"

"Jesus Christ, Jenny, this isn't brain surgery we're doing here. It's fucking TV."

"I guess." I thought for a minute. "But maybe people are smarter than we think. How do we know people like you doing all that crap when you give the weather?"

"Because," she said, "if they didn't, the ratings would go down and I wouldn't be on the air anymore. That's the way TV works."

I couldn't argue with that.

Bill Hanrahan, the sports reporter and resident woman chaser, sat down next to us. He ignored me and turned to Stormy.

"Hey, Storm, look what I got here. Two tickets to a Bruce Springsteen concert. You interested?"

"In Springsteen, yes," she said. "Who gets the second ticket?"

"Me. I can't think of anyone I'd rather go with than you. It would make a perfect evening."

"Gee, I'm busy."

"I didn't tell you what night it was yet."

"Okay, what night is it?"

"Saturday."

"Busy."

"Okay." Hanrahan shrugged. "Maybe some other time then."

"Probably not in my lifetime," she told him.

Hanrahan turned to me now. "Hey, Jenny, you want to go see Springsteen on Saturday night? I can't think of anyone I'd rather go with than you. It would make a perfect evening—"

"Get out of here!" I screamed.

Bob Carstairs walked by and patted me on the shoulder. "McKay. My office. Now." He walked away. I stood up to follow.

"What's that all about?" Stormy asked.

"Maybe I won an Emmy," I suggested.

"Or you're getting fired," Hanrahan said.

"I like to think it's something in between those two options."

Carstairs was waiting for me when I got there. A woman was with him. She was dressed like and looked a lot like a fashion model. Carstairs introduced her to me as Linda Fairmont.

"Linda's with Collins, Strach, and Collins," he explained.

"No kidding?" I sat down next to her. "Does David Crosby still sing lead for you?"

Carstairs rolled his eyes. "Collins, Strach, and Collins isn't a singing group, Jenny. It's a consulting firm. The media consulting firm we've been using for advertising and overall product development. Linda here is going to be working with us for the next few days to try to improve the way we all come across on camera."

"Hey, that's great," I said. "I was just talking about how I needed a new look or something."

I related my conversation about having a shtick.

"Well, that's a valid point," Carstairs said. "Do you have ideas?"

"How about I shave my head into a Mohawk and appeal to all our Native-American viewers?"

"We don't have any Native-American viewers," Carstairs said.

"My point exactly," I told him. "Maybe if I did that, we could attract some. It's a really untapped demographic group. . . ."

Carstairs sighed loudly and turned to Linda Fairmont. "Miss McKay here likes to think of herself as a bit of a comedian," he explained. "She is a good newswoman though. Do you think you can do anything with her?"

"Well, I'm sure we can start by sprucing up her look quite a bit," Fairmont said.

They were talking about me in the third person, as if I wasn't there.

"Wait a minute," I told Carstairs. "I want to talk to you about a story."

"So we'll talk after you've spent some time with Miss Fairmont."

"How much time?"

"Oh, it shouldn't take too long." She smiled.

It took two hours. The first hour was spent watching videotapes. This Fairmont woman's idea was that I could improve myself by watching the tapes of other newswomen from around the country. So I sat there doing that. Blondes from Boston. Brunettes from Des Moines. Redheads from Fort Worth. The only problem is that they all looked the same to me. Same delivery, same voice patterns, same gestures. It reminded me of that old TV show, "To Tell the Truth." You know, the one where each contestant would stand up in turn and say, "I'm the real anchorwoman from Fort Worth." "No, I'm the real anchorwoman from . . ."

Or maybe it was even something more sinister.

Linda Fairmont shut off the videotape machine and turned to me. "So what do you think?"

"The Stepford Wives."

"Pardon me?"

"It's just like in the movie. Some evil men's organization has replaced the real women with these robot mechanisms. Most of them just learn how to do things like wash dishes and clean house, but some of them become TV anchorwomen too."

Linda Fairmont grimaced. "Look, I realize there is a certain similarity to some of these women . . ."

"Boy, that's an understatement."

"Nevertheless that similarity can be a plus on TV. TV viewers like a certain kind of sameness to the people they watch. It makes them feel comfortable. Now, on the other hand, you have some very unique qualities that are good too—energy, pluck, a sense of humor. Sometimes you just take these things a bit too far. What we want to do is merge these two elements—in other words, take your strong personality and refine it a bit so that it comes across better on TV. Doesn't that sound reasonable?"

I nodded. I wanted to be reasonable. I really did.

"Now the first thing we should probably deal with is your attire."

"My attire."

"That's right. The proper clothing is very important. It creates a certain . . . a certain air, an atmosphere of sophistication that translates into the way you relate to people. Clothes do make the man, and the woman too. I'm sure you understand what I'm saying. . . ."

She glanced over at me. I was wearing a pair of blue jeans, lizard-skin cowboy boots, and a T-shirt which said SAVE THE WHALES across the chest. The boots and jeans didn't matter, since you couldn't see below my waist on TV. And when it came time to go on the air, I generally threw on some sort of blouse to cover the T-shirt.

"Then again," she said, "maybe I should go into it in a bit more detail."

Her idea was to give me a new look. It consisted of a preppy-looking blazer, a white blouse with ruffles and big bow at the neck, and a pleated blue skirt. I tried them on and looked at myself in a mirror. Linda Fairmont seemed pleased with the results. She said I looked perky. Me, I thought it looked like a uniform for a Catholic girl's school.

After that she went to work on my makeup.

"What kind of makeup do you generally wear now before you go on the air?" she asked.

"Not too much," I said. "I try to keep it to a minimum."

"Makeup," she told me solemnly, "can be your friend, Jenny. Don't be afraid of it."

"Okay."

Reasonable. Be reasonable, I told myself.

She took out a cosmetics kit and went to work on my face. Using pancake powder, cheek color, eyeliner, eye shadow, mascara, and lipstick, she attempted to transform me from Jenny McKay, everyday woman, to Jenny McKay, TV personality.

"What do you think?" She asked when she was finished.

I looked at myself in the mirror.

The pancake makeup was so thick I couldn't see my natural skin color. My cheeks were a bright pink. As for my lips, well the lipstick had created a pouting look to my mouth that made it seem as if I'd just sucked on a lemon.

"Great, huh?" Linda Fairmont said.

"You don't think it's just maybe a little too . . ."

"Pronounced?"

"Excessive."

"Nonsense. It'll make you stand out on camera. Trust me on this."

A few minutes later I walked out into the newsroom.

Sanders and Jacobson were there. I decided to try out my new look on them first. Maybe they wouldn't even notice.

"Jesus," Sanders said when he saw me, "I thought Halloween was over."

I looked over at Jacobson. "Is it really that bad?"

"It depends," he said, looking up from his crossword puzzle.

"Depends on what?"

"Depends on whether or not you want me to tell you the truth."

I marched into Carstairs's office.

"This isn't going to work," I said.

"What?"

"This goop on my face."

"Is there a problem?"

"Bob, the problem is I look like Lily Munster."

"You're overreacting. You need to exaggerate things for them to show up on TV. Linda Fairmont knows what she's doing. Trust her."

"Yeah, that's what she said too."

"You mentioned before you wanted to talk about a story. What story?"

"Rikki Stiles."

"The dead hooker?"

"Yeah, I'd like to do a kind of documentary on her. You know, the life and death of a Sutton Place call girl. We could use the murder as a kind of springboard to look at the way people like Rikki live."

"Not bad. What gave you the idea?"

I could have said it was because Elliott Carson, the DA, seemed to be showing an abnormal interest in the case. Or that I thought there were still a lot of unanswered questions about her death. Or that I had this feeling that there was a lot more going on here than just the death of a prostitute. But I didn't say any of those things. Instead, I just shrugged and told him:

"It's a good murder. It'd make an interesting segment."

He nodded. "You think you can get enough information? I mean she's not going to be listed in *Who's Who* or anything."

"It'll probably take me a couple of days, but I think so. I'll try to get to Victor Galena—he's her pimp—and maybe this guy Johnny Camancho she told me about. Plus she must have family somewhere I can interview. Friends. People in her building. It should be pretty routine."

"Okay, go for it."

I went back to my desk. The first place I tried was the cops. They told me no family had turned up yet for Rikki Stiles. The only person they could find who knew her was Victor Galena and—like they'd said earlier—he'd been very uncooperative. "A pain in the ass" was the way they described it. I asked where I could find this guy Galena. They gave me a number for something called P & A Enterprises.

"That stands for the corporate office he's set up to handle his business," they told me. "The guy's a real operator."

"P and A?" I said.

"It stands for piece of ass."

Cute.

At first, Galena wasn't any friendlier with me than he was with the cops.

"A documentary on Rikki?" he said, when I got him on the phone. His voice was silky smooth, like a con man or a guy trying to sell you a used car. "Gee, I don't think so."

"Why not?"

"It could cause trouble, babe."

Babe?

"What kind of trouble?" I asked.

"You know, trouble with the law. In my business, it doesn't always pay to advertise."

"I can keep you out of it," I told him. "No cameras, no names or anything. I just want to find out more about Rikki. You could probably help a lot."

"Well, I don't have much time, ya' know? I'm booked. I don't think I can squeeze you in. . . ."

"Try."

"Well . . ."

There was a long pause at the other end.

"Okay," he said finally, "I'm supposed to have lunch with someone tomorrow at the Water Club. A business appointment of mine. Maybe if I pick you up, you can come along with us and I can find time to answer a couple of questions. Fair enough?"

"Fair enough."

"Where're you at?"

"Way down on South Street by the Brooklyn Bridge. Just before the South Street Seaport. Do you know where that is?"

"I'll find it. Let's say noon tomorrow, okay?"

"Okay. See you then."

Wow, I thought to myself as I hung up the phone, I'm going out to lunch with a real pimp.

Zowie!

I was doing a segment that night on cold-weather clothing tips for the approaching winter months. It's what they call a service piece. You know, you get some doctor or health official on the air to give out professional advice—don't wear Bermuda shorts in zero degree weather, try to get indoors if your toes and ears start turning blue or falling off. That sort of thing.

I was midway through it when disaster struck:

McKAY: So what you're saying, Dr. Palmerio, is the right selection of clothing can help you survive the coldest of winter days without undue discomfort?

DR. PALMERIO: Yes, I think common sense is the thing to remember when . . .

He suddenly stopped in mid-sentence.

DR. PALMERIO: And so . . . so . . .

McKAY: You were saying that common sense is the most important thing to remember when dealing with cold-weather dress.

I was trying to help him, but his mind seemed to be somewhere else. He was staring. Staring at something . . .

McKAY: Dr. Palmerio . . . ?

DR. PALMERIO: Yes, ah . . . that's right, you see . . .

I suddenly realized what he was staring at. Me. Or more specifically—my face. At first I wasn't sure why. Then I felt something wet on my face. My makeup! It was beginning to fall apart under the hot studio lights.

DR. PALMERIO: Now, a warm pair of gloves or mittens are the crucial element in this cold-weather kit. . . .

How bad was it? I felt something trickling into my eye and reached up to rub it off. When I looked down at my hand, it was covered with something black. Mascara. It was running all over my face. Not only that, but the pancake makeup felt like it was clogging up my pores and the lipstick was making its way down my chin.

DR. PALMERIO [He was struggling valiantly now.]: Many people wonder if leather or wool gloves are best. Or do they have to be fur-lined? Well . . .

I looked over at the anchor desk. Liz St. John was staring at me with eyes as wide as saucers. Conroy Jackson's mouth was hanging open. They'd never seen anything like this. Probably no one in the history of television had seen anything like this. It was time to end it.

McKAY: Thank you, Doctor, for that very helpful advice on how to survive old man winter. I'm afraid that's all we have time for. . . .

I looked at the camera and tried to smile. Only one eye was really open. The other one I had to keep blinking to keep the mascara out.

McKAY: And now back to the anchor desk. Liz and Conroy?

LIZ ST. JOHN: Thank you, Jenny, for that . . . uh, fascinating report. In other news . . .

I stalked off the set and confronted Carstairs.

"Trust her! Trust her, you said!"

"Now Jenny . . ."

"Don't 'now Jenny' me."

"There's nothing to get that upset about. . . ."

"I made a fool of myself out there on live TV."

"Oh, it wasn't that bad."

"Not that bad? Are you crazy?"

"I mean it. I'll bet hardly anyone even noticed anything was wrong."

That calmed me down a bit. "You really think so?" I asked.

"Sure, stuff like that always seems worse when it's happening to you. But you probably couldn't even see it on TV. I doubt that anyone in the audience . . ."

My telephone rang. Bill Hanrahan reached over and picked it up. He listened for a second, laughed, and then hung up.

"It was for you," he said. "Some guy said he saw you on the air and wanted to leave you a message. He didn't give his name."

"What was the message?"

Hanrahan smiled broadly. "Trick or treat," he said.

I whirled around to Carstairs.

"Linda Fairmont comes near me again, she's a dead woman!" I screamed.

Then I marched off to the ladies' room where I washed my face until every bit of the makeup she'd put on me was gone. After twenty minutes of furious scrubbing, the old me was finally back. Fresh-faced. Wholesome. Natural.

Out, out damned makeup!

Me and Lady Macbeth.

7

The Oldest Profession

Victor Galena picked me up for lunch the next day in front of the WTBK building.

He was driving a tan, four-door Mercedes, and there was another passenger—a woman—in the front seat with him. Galena was a tall, swarthy-looking man who appeared to be in his mid-thirties. He was wearing a three-piece, pin-striped suit, designer dress shirt, and a silk tie. He opened the back door and let me into the Mercedes, which had leather seats, thick carpeting, and an elaborate stereo system. Hanging from the rearview mirror above the stereo controls was one of those deodorizers you can get at car washes with a Playboy bunny emblem on it. Class, it always tells.

"This is Belinda," Galena said, nodding toward the woman in the front seat. "Belinda, Jenny McKay. She's on TV, and she wants to do a documentary on Rikki."

"Hi, Belinda," I said.

"Oh, about Rikki?" She smiled. "Isn't that interesting?"

There was a gap between her teeth when she opened her mouth, but I guess that's in, in some circles. The Lauren

Hutton look. She had short brown hair, cut in a sort of pageboy style, with bangs hanging down in front. Her blouse looked like pure silk, and she had on chocolate-brown leather slacks and an ermine fur jacket. Business appointment, huh? Well, maybe she was his accountant.

Galena shifted the Mercedes into gear and pulled out into the traffic heading north.

I started to say something to Belinda again, but I noticed she was busy. She was moving her hand up Galena's leg toward his crotch. I watched through the opening in the bucket seats as she slowly began massaging him there.

"So you want to know about Rikki?" Galena said, as if nothing was going on. "Poor ol' Rikki. Terrible thing to happen. I can't tell you how upset I was when I heard."

"Well, I . . ."

Belinda hit a sensitive spot and giggled when Galena responded.

"I'm sorry, what were you saying?" he asked after he regained his composure.

"Listen, I didn't catch you at a bad time or anything, did I?"

"Huh? What do you mean?"

"I mean I hate to intrude on somebody during their time of grief for a loved one. Maybe I should come back later when you're not so deep into bereavement."

"C'mon, what are you talking about?" he said, half turning around from the driver's seat to look at me. "I feel awful about what happened to Rikki."

"Okay."

"Believe me," he said, "Rikki was very special to me. You might not think so, but I really cared about her. No one will ever be able to take her place in my life. She was always number one. Understand?"

"Oh, sure, you're true-blue," I said, looking at Belinda working on his crotch again. "Anybody can see that."

The Water Club is a posh restaurant on the East River near 30th Street where the rich and powerful like to dine.

I guess Galena qualified on both counts. We were led to a table along the window with a scenic view of the river and the Brooklyn skyline on the other side. Galena and Belinda ordered crabmeat salads and white wine, while I went for some fried clams and an Amstel Light. We chatted about Rikki Stiles as we ate.

"I met her one night at a little bar down in the Village, near the NYU campus," he said. "She was drinking with some other people, students and stuff, but she stood out from the rest of the crowd. Really beautiful. So I went over and introduced myself, we talked for a while, and eventually she came to work for me."

"Sorta like a campus recruiter, huh?"

He smiled. "Something like that."

"What was she doing?" I asked. "Where did she come from?"

"Somewhere in the Midwest. Came to New York to try to make it as an artist or something, pounded the pavement for a while trying to sell her stuff to galleries without any success, took a few classes at NYU, and was running out of money. She was shacked up in some loft down near SoHo with about eight other kids, all of them struggling artists waiting for the big break to come their way. It's an old story."

"So are you," I told him.

"I suppose so."

"Yeah," I said. "She's nearly at the end of her rope, broke and desperate. And then you ride in like a knight on a white horse to rescue her. Take her away from it all."

"Something like that. She was a gorgeous girl, no question about it. You know that, you met her. I knew from the moment I laid eyes on her in that NYU bar she was quality goods. Hell, if she'd stuck with it, maybe she'd even have made it with the art thing. But that's an awfully iffy business. I offered her a sure thing."

"And she took it."

"That's right."

I looked down at my clams. I wasn't hungry anymore. Galena had done the impossible—ruined my appetite.

"So basically," I said, "you took a young, aspiring artist and turned her into a whore."

"Not fair." Galena picked up his napkin and dabbed at some dressing that had dribbled down onto his bottom lip. "I gave Rikki a beautiful apartment, the finest clothes, a job— what's wrong with that?"

"But she was still a whore."

"Not like you make it out. I mean I didn't have her out hustling herself down on 8th Avenue. She worked only for an elite clientele. My customers—most of them distinguished, well-heeled people—paid a lot of money for her company during an evening. There was nothing sleazy about it. Maybe they'd go, you know, to a show, dancing, or dinner at the Windows on the World or Four Seasons. And then, when it was over, uh, if the client wanted a little sensual satisfaction as a reward for everything he'd done—well, you know, what's wrong with that? I mean, don't you know women who go to bed with a guy as a sort of, uh, thanks for a nice evening out on the town? Didn't you ever do it?"

"We're not talking about me."

"Anyway, you get my point."

"I understand Rikki's fee was two thousand dollars a night," I said. "How much of that did you let her keep?"

Galena chuckled. "Now you're asking me to divulge business secrets. I can't do that."

"Just an estimate. Did she get . . . oh, let's say ninety percent of it? Sixty percent?" I paused and looked at him. "Nothing?"

"I don't know what you're trying to get at, Miss McKay. Rikki was well taken care of. I told you that."

"But she never got any of the money, did she?"

"I'm not going to answer that."

"I think you just did." I smiled.

The waiter asked us if we wanted dessert. I didn't, but Belinda did. She went for the chocolate fudge cake with whipped cream topping. Galena ordered a coffee and brandy; I just had a plain coffee. As the waiter was serving it, I suddenly realized that Belinda had hardly said a word during the entire meal. Galena seemed to have his women well trained.

"You said Rikki came from somewhere in the Midwest," I said. "Do you know where?"

"I'm not sure . . . Pittsburgh or Cleveland, something like that. Cleveland, I think. All those cities sound the same to me, you know."

"Any family?"

"Just a mother, she told me once. Her father died or left when she was a kid."

"Does her mother know what happened?"

"I don't think so. I don't know how to reach her."

"There's probably not that many Stileses in the Cleveland phone book," I said. This guy was talking. "The mother shouldn't be that hard to find."

"Her name isn't Stiles," he said, sipping at his brandy.

"Huh?"

"Rikki Stiles wasn't her real name. I gave her that. Thought it sounded classy. Her name was Susan. Susan Callandro, I think. Or something pretty close."

"Do the cops know this?" I asked.

Galena shrugged. "Not from me. I don't tell cops anything."

"Did you try to contact the mother to tell her what happened?"

"Sure. Spent hours calling long-distance to Cleveland and Pittsburgh and all over the Midwest. Trying to find someone with a last name something like Callandro who might have known her. No luck though. It was like looking for a needle in a haystack. Believe me, I really tried too. Exhausted every possibility."

"How about friends?"

"There was one woman she was very close to," Galena said. "Her name was Donna Willis. She worked for me too, had her own apartment. But eventually I had to let her go."

"Why?"

"She got involved with drugs, very heavily involved in drugs. That's bad for business. My clients don't want to go to bed with a junkie."

"Do you know where she is now?" I asked. "If she was friends with Rikki, I might want to talk to her."

"God, the last I heard she was working out of some escort service on the Upper West Side. I think it had some really raunchy name . . . like 'Cum Again' or something. Like I said, she really went downhill in a hurry."

Galena took another sip of the brandy and smiled. "This is quite nice actually, isn't it?" he said. "The restaurant, I mean."

I looked around. The place obviously attracted the executive crowd for lunch. Bankers, stockbrokers, corporate lawyers. Everyone looked like big money. I felt a little out of place. I hoped no one asked to see my bank account.

"I guess I must surprise you a bit, Miss McKay," Galena was saying. "I'm probably not what you expected at all."

"What do you mean?"

"Well, I suppose you were expecting someone who looked like a pimp. Maybe pick you up in a pink Cadillac, wearing loud clothes and jewelry. You may see pimps like that in the movies or up on One hundred and twenty-fifth Street, but I'm not like that."

"Oh no?"

"Of course not, I'm just a businessman."

I shook my head. "Funny, you still look like a pimp to me."

Galena stared at me for a second, then finished off the last of his brandy and turned toward Belinda.

"Go fix your makeup for a while, babe," he said, snapping his fingers at her.

Belinda looked up from her chocolate fudge cake.

"But it doesn't need fixing."

"Then go fix something else. Get outta here."

Belinda got up and headed for the ladies' room.

"Nice kid," Galena said as he watched her walk away.

"Terrific," I said. "Didn't I catch her on College Bowl a while back?"

He laughed loudly. "You're funny, McKay."

I didn't say anything.

"And cute too," he added.

"My, my. You flatterer, you."

He reached over, patted me on the top of my hand.

"Be still my heart," I said.

"Huh?"

I pulled my hand away, drank the last of my coffee, and stood up.

"You can put your little seduction kit away now," I said. "It's not going to work. I really don't need compliments from someone like you."

"You're not leaving, are you?" he asked.

"Yeah, I'm leaving," I said. "Thanks for lunch."

"You could stay awhile. Have a drink. . . ."

"I have to get back to the office. Working girl and all."

"I'm not used to having women run away from me, Miss McKay. Most women find me very attractive."

I shrugged. "Maybe you're losing the old sex appeal, Victor. It happens to all of us as we get older. I'd think about that if I were you."

I walked down to 23rd Street to hail a cab to the office. It was nice outside, one of those late Indian summer days you sometimes still get in November that makes you feel good just to be alive. Suddenly I got sad that Rikki Stiles wasn't around to see it. Her last day on this earth was probably that rainy, miserable day when I met her. I wondered how she spent those last hours.

Somehow I hoped it wasn't holed up in her East Side apartment with someone like Victor Galena.

Back at my desk, I pulled the phone close to me and dialed the information number for the 216 area code which covers Cleveland.

"How many Callandros are there listed in the Cleveland directory?" I asked.

There were nine. The first didn't know what I was talking about. The second's line was busy. I hit it on the third try. A woman's voice answered.

"Mrs. Callandro?" I asked.

"Yes."

"Mrs. Callandro, do you have a daughter, Susan, who lives in New York City?"

"Yes . . . that's right. Who is this?"

Jeez, Victor, you really tried hard to find her, didn't you?

"Is anything wrong?" Mrs. Callandro asked.

There was tension in her voice. She knew something was wrong. She was just waiting now to find out how bad it was. In the background I could hear a baby crying. This was the part of the job I hated the most. I took a deep breath and plunged ahead.

"Your daughter's dead," I said quietly. "I'm sorry."

There was a gasp on the other end of the line, then silence. It probably lasted for only a few seconds, but it seemed like an eternity. Somewhere in the background a baby was still crying.

"Look, Mrs. Callandro, if you call the New York City Police Department—"

"Tell me about it," she said.

I told her. I didn't make it any worse than it was, but I didn't hold too much back either. I figured she had a right to know. When I was finished, I asked her some questions about her daughter. She answered them patiently, almost as if she was talking about someone else, and gave me a pretty good picture of Susan Callandro, aka Rikki Stiles. Then I told her again how sorry I was, she thanked me for my kindness, and we hung up.

All in a day's work, I told myself, all in a day's work.

8

Jenny Does Manhattan

I tracked down Donna Willis, Rikki's girlfriend, a few hours later that afternoon.

It was a snap really.

First, I bought a copy of *Screw* magazine, which runs ads for escort services, massage parlors, phone sex, and all the other assorted trappings of twentieth-century civilization. That was fun. The guy at the newsstand I bought it from was an Arab with a three-day growth of beard, wearing a T-shirt that smelled like a clothes hamper. He leered at me when I took it off the rack and handed him $2.25.

"You like to look at the pictures in there, lady?"

"Yeah," I told him, "this and *National Geographic* are my favorites."

"I can show you something better." He leered again, or maybe it was supposed to be a smile. Several of his front teeth were missing. The ones he had appeared to be some color other than white. "My name's Ahmad. Are you interested?"

"Only if you can promise me it will be a meaningful relationship," I said.

"Huh?"

"You know—long walks in the moonlight, trips to museums, reading love sonnets together. . . ."

He scowled now. I think he was beginning to doubt my sincerity.

"Get outta here!" he shouted.

I left with the copy of *Screw* under my arm. Another dashed romance. Just two ships passing in the night. Oh, well—it never would have worked out anyway. He probably liked his women to wear veils or something.

I found a park bench, sat down, and began paging through *Screw*. This was difficult to do without attracting attention from people passing by. I guess they'd never seen a woman sitting on a park bench, reading a dirty magazine before. Actually I'd drawn quite a few stares walking down the street with it too. Maybe I should have asked Ahmad for a plain brown wrapper.

The ad for "Cum Again," the escort service where Galena said Donna Willis worked, was on page thirty-six. Right between "Madam Lily's House of Geisha Delights" and something discreetly labeled "Girls! Girls! Girls!" I called the number listed with the ad. It took a bit of doing, but I finally got the address from the woman who answered the phone. Only when I got there, it turned out Donna Willis had left months ago to work out of a place in Murray Hill.

"Was there a problem?" I asked.

"Do you know her?" the woman asked me.

"Yes," I lied.

"Well, she needs some help."

"Help?"

"Get her off the drugs."

She wasn't at the Murray Hill address either. Same story. They'd heard she caught on with a place in Chelsea, but that only lasted a few weeks or so. Why didn't I try something called Helena's Hideaway on 14th Street?

The first two places I'd gone to were in high-rise apartments with doormen. The place in Chelsea didn't have a doorman. By the time I got to 14th Street, it wasn't even a real apartment building. Just a couple of rooms on top of a doughnut shop a few blocks east of Union Square Park.

I told the woman who answered the door that I was looking for Donna Willis. She said Donna was busy with a client. I said I'd wait. The woman let me in, and I sat down on a decrepit old couch across from a middle-aged man sitting in a chair. I tried to avoid eye contact. But after a few minutes, he came over and sat down next to me.

"I'm Leonard," he said.

"Hi."

"What's your name?"

"Jenny."

"You work here, Jenny?"

I shook my head.

"That's too bad. I'd really be interested in a session with you if you wanted to. . . ."

"A session? What are you talking about?"

"Well, you know . . ."

I looked around the room. "Isn't this the free AIDS clinic?"

"What?"

"They told me when I picked up my AZT that this was where the free AIDS clinic was supposed to be."

He got up and went back to his chair on the other side of the room. A minute later, the door to the other room opened and a woman came over to me.

"I'm Donna Willis," she said. "You're looking for me?"

"Yes, you see—"

"Why?"

Her tone was impatient. I figured her to be about thirty, but she looked at least ten years older than that. There was a hard quality to her face too, like she'd packed a lot of living into those thirty years and there wasn't going to be much more to come. She was wearing a black V-necked sweater, red miniskirt, and Western-style boots. Her hair was done up in a kind of beehive style, and a cigarette dangled from her lips.

I handed her a card with my name and the Channel Six logo on it. She glanced at it and shrugged.

"So?"

"I'm doing a story on Rikki Stiles," I said. "I understand you two were very close."

"Rikki's dead," she said flatly.

"I know. I'm trying to find out more about what happened. Maybe find the person who did it."

"Oh yeah? Why are you so interested?"

"I met Rikki a few days ago. We talked about some things."

Donna Willis took the cigarette out of her mouth and ground it out in an ashtray next to me. "Were you a friend of hers?" she asked.

I thought about it for a minute, then said: "Yes." I wasn't sure why.

"Okay," she said, "I'm due for a break anyway. Let's go somewhere and talk."

We went to a bar down the block. It looked run-down, but it was nearly empty at this time of the afternoon. The only people in it were two seedy-looking men at the bar watching a "Gilligan's Island" rerun on TV. When the theme song came on, they sang along with it: ". . . for a three-hour tour. A three-hour tour." They seemed to find this extremely funny. Donna Willis and I ordered a couple of Amstel Lights and sat down at the table.

"I almost stole one of your clients back there," I told her.

"You mean Leonard?"

"Yeah, he was crazy about me."

She smiled. "But you weren't crazy about him. Right?"

"Let's just say I began to suspect he wasn't going to be able to fulfill me as a woman."

"Leonard's easy," she said.

"Easy?"

"Sure. You don't have to really do anything with him. Just dress up in something that looks like a cheerleader's outfit, do some jumping jacks, and let him look under your skirt."

"That's easy?"

"Hey, honey, you should see the hard ones."

She took a swig of her beer.

"Damn, this business with Rikki sure beats all, doesn't it? I mean her buying it like that at the end. Here I'm working in this dump day after day and dealing with the dregs of society and I'm still alive. Rikki's got that nifty apartment, nothing but high-class clients, and she's dead. Hard to figure, isn't it?"

"Murder often is," I said. "Did you talk to her a lot?"

"A lot? No, we sorta traveled in different worlds after a while."

"But you did keep in touch?"

"Yeah, we tried to anyway. So what do you want to know?"

As it turned out, she talked very easily about Rikki. They really did seem to be friends. Well, as close to friends as someone could be in their business. She recalled how they'd met soon after Victor Galena had recruited Rikki from the bar near NYU. Donna was already in another apartment on Sutton Place then, and they got together a lot, she said. Victor would get them tickets for the opera, the ballet, concerts. He wanted them to be refined and was real good about helping them with stuff like that, she remembered.

Donna said she was even the one who helped come up with the name of Rikki Stiles. "She needed something classy, something stylish. So I came up with the idea of Stiles. Then the double K in Rikki. That's classy, don't you think?"

I said I thought it was classy.

"How did the money work?" I asked. "The two thousand dollars a night Rikki got from her clients—did she get to keep any of it?"

Donna threw her head back and laughed. "Keep it? That's funny. A working girl never gets to keep much of her money in this business. Not at Rikki's level or"—she paused and looked around the room—"at my level."

"Rikki was getting some outside money from somewhere though, wasn't she?" I asked. I thought about Gallagher telling me how she'd made a few thousand dollars from being a snitch.

Donna Willis looked at me funny.

"You say you were a friend of hers," she said slowly, "and you seem okay. So I'll believe you. I may be making a mistake, but I will. You got to trust somebody sometime in this world, don't you?"

She poured some more beer into her glass. I noticed some smudges on it. My glass was dirty too. I started to call the bartender over to complain, but then decided it was the kind of place where it was best to let stuff like that slide.

"Rikki came to me last week," she said. "Told me she'd been saving some money over the past few months, trying to build up a nest egg. She was getting out of the business, she said, wanted to do something with her life. Maybe go back to school or something. But then she lost it."

"The money?"

Donna nodded. "Nearly ten thousand dollars. She told me someone took it from her, and she was really upset. Said she had to get out, she couldn't wait any longer. She'd been counting on using this money for some time."

"You think it was Victor Galena who took the money?" I asked.

"Who else?"

I brought up the bruise I'd noticed on the side of Rikki's face that day at the office. Donna said she'd seen it too.

"Did you ask her who did it?" I said.

"Nope."

"Why not?"

"I figured it was none of my business."

"But you said she was your friend. Weren't you concerned?"

She shrugged. "Hey, that stuff happens. It didn't seem like any big deal."

"I guess it comes with the job, huh?"

"Something like that."

There was silence between us for a few seconds. In the background, I could hear the sound of the TV. "Gilligan's Island" was over now, and "The Brady Bunch" was on. Jan was asking for an increase in her allowance. Fascinating fare, but I had to work.

"You say Rikki told you she wanted to get out of the business," I said. "Do you know if she ever tried to do that earlier?"

Donna thought for a minute. "Yes, I think so. Earlier this year. She disappeared from the scene for a while, then showed up again and said she'd gone home to her family in the Midwest. But after a few months, she came back and was doing business again on Sutton Place. I never knew what really happened."

"Do you remember exactly when that was?"

"Well, I think she left right after Christmas, sometime in January or February. Then she came back in the summer. I remember that. It was June, I think."

"Okay, so now she was ready to leave again," I said. "She'd accumulated this money on her own. But Galena took it away from her. So what was she going to do?"

Donna Willis bit her upper lip nervously. "She told me she was going to try to raise some more money in a hurry. She said she had a couple of ideas."

"Did she tell you what they were?"

"No, and I didn't ask." She paused. "If I did, I might be dead today too."

"The money might have had nothing to do with her death," I said. "She could have just been killed by some crazy. There's enough of them around."

"God, tell me about it." She looked down at her watch. "Speaking of crazies, I better get back to work. Leonard's still there."

"Leonard? Won't he be mad having to wait for you all this time?"

"No, I think he likes it."

"Listen," I said, "I'd like to come back later with a film crew and get some quotes from you about Rikki on camera. Is that okay?"

She shrugged. "Sure. Why not?"

"I mean we could alter the picture to conceal your identity if you want. . . ."

"You mean like Geraldo does sometimes?" She smiled.

"Well, yeah. . . ."

"No, I'd like to be on TV. Maybe it'll give my career a boost. You know, *A Star Is Born* kind of thing. What do you think?"

"Hey, you never know."

We left the bar and started walking back down 14th Street to Helena's.

"Can I ask you something?" I said. "You worked with Rikki. Had the same kind of setup on Sutton Place she did. How . . . ?" My voice trailed off.

"How did I wind up like this?" She threw back her head and laughed. Except it wasn't really a laugh. More like a bad joke on herself. "I got fucked up. I wasn't so young and beautiful anymore. And, well, you can't stay at the top very long in this business if you're not beautiful. There's always some other young chicks out there they can find to take your place. So you wind up moving down a notch on the ladder, so to speak."

"What was the problem?" I asked. "Drugs?"

She nodded. "Yeah, I'm a junkie. Look, spare me the lecture, okay? I know it all already. I'm okay now. Getting my life back under control." She smiled. "I have to or else Mickey will bounce me too."

We were standing in front of the doughnut shop again now.

"Who's Mickey?" I asked.

"He runs Helena's. You saw him back there. He was one of the guys sitting at the bar."

I remembered the two men watching TV and singing along with the "Gilligan's Island" theme.

"Is he your pimp?"

Donna Willis nodded. "My pimp. My lover. My boss. My father. Whatever I need him to be."

I shook her hand, thanked her for her help, and said: "Say hello to Leonard when you get upstairs."

"I'll give him a big cheer from you."

"Hip hip hooray!"

When I got home that night, there was a message waiting for me on my answering machine.

"Hello, Miss McKay, this is Mike Stoner from the Internal Revenue Service. I just wanted to remind you of our appointment for tomorrow night. I'll be over at nine. If there's any problem, leave me a message at my office tomorrow. Thank you."

Mike Stoner. Nice voice. Laughed at my jokes. Hmmm. Maybe if I played my cards right, I could parlay this audit business into some sort of meaningful relationship.

I walked Hobo, fed him, and was just starting to get my own dinner ready when the phone rang again.

"Jenny McKay?"

"Yes."

"Hi, it's Rick."

"Rick?"

"Rick Gallagher. From the police."

"Oh yeah. The cop who doesn't remember whether he's married or not."

"That's sort of what I wanted to talk to you about."

"How'd you get my home number anyway?"

"I'm a policeman, remember? A dogged investigator."

"I'm very impressed."

"Jenny, you're in the phone book."

"Oh, right."

"Look, when we talked about my . . . my domestic situation the other day at the station house, I think I handled it very badly. I'd like a chance to do better."

"There's really no need for that, Lieutenant, because I'm not—"

"Meet me for coffee someday."

"Gee, I don't think so. . . ."

"I'll buy."

I thought about it for a second. Okay, he was married—no question about it. But he was also cute. Plus it never hurt in my business to know another cop. Especially one who might be able to help answer some of my questions about Rikki Stiles. And it wasn't as if I was going to sleep with the guy or anything.

"We're only talking about coffee, right?"

"Just coffee."

"Not that crankcase oil you served me last time. . . ."

He laughed. "No, we'll do the real thing this time. Get it from a coffee shop or café or something. With cream too. And sugar, if you want it. The whole works. Price is no object."

"Okay, I should get out of work by seven-thirty or so tomorrow night. There's a coffee shop next door to the WTBK studios down on South Street. How about you meet me there?"

"See you then."

I hung up the phone and went back to cooking my dinner. This was not exactly a monumental task. My entrée for the evening was Chef Boyardee cheese-filled ravioli in a microwave container. Sixty seconds in the microwave, and it came out piping hot. Just like Mom used to make. Sometimes I wondered how frontier women lived before microwaves and VCRs and cordless telephones.

I ate in front of the TV set with "Wheel of Fortune" on. "Wheel of Fortune" is fun to watch with someone else you can play against. I had no one to watch with me except Hobo, and that was no fun. He never guessed one puzzle right. So I played against the people on TV. Won twenty-five thousand dollars and a trip to Disneyland too. Just my lucky day, I guess.

Actually it had been a big day for me—romantically speaking.

There was Gallagher, the married cop. Mike Stoner, the IRS guy who was probably going to put me in jail. Plus Ahmad, the hot-to-trot newsstand dealer. And Leonard. I couldn't forget about Leonard.

I decided to rank them in the order of their desirability. Gallagher was first. Stoner a close second, at least until I saw him. The battle for third place was a toughie—Ahmad or Leonard? I finally decided on Ahmad. Doing those jumping jacks for Leonard was just too much work.

Sorry, Leonard.

A cheerleader's outfit?

9

If It's Happening, We're There

ANNOUNCER: Live from New York City, it's the News at Six on Six—with the WTBK Action News team! Conroy Jackson and Liz St. John anchoring the news desk; Big Bill Hanrahan with *all* the sports; and our own Stormy Phillips with the S-E-X-I-E-S-T weather in town. Plus, live reports from all over New York—wherever there's news you need to know.

If it's happening, we're there.

That slogan—"If It's Happening, We're There"—didn't just come out of thin air. It was the culmination of hours of thought and hundreds of suggestions and lots of big bucks spent to Linda Fairmont's media consulting firm—which makes a living out of coming up with snappy stuff like that.

The idea was to try to capture the feel of what the news show was supposed to be. One model was WINS, the perennial number one all-news station on radio, which had a slogan of "All News—All the Time." Since on a given day much of our newscast consisted of celebrity interviews, cooking segments, and mindless banter, I suggested we go with "None of the News—None of the Time." This was not received well. My backup suggestion was "If It's *Not* Happening, We're Probably There." After that, they suggested I stop making suggestions.

Once they settled on a slogan, a massive promotional campaign was launched. Radio ads. Spots on our own station. Posters on subway station walls and the backs of buses. Imagine my shock the first time I saw a bus go by with "If It's Happening, We're There" and a big picture of Liz St. John on the back. Or Conroy Jackson. Or Bill Hanrahan. Or Stormy Phillips.

They didn't put my picture on any buses though.

Come to think of it, neither would I.

ANNOUNCER: And now here's Conroy and Liz with the news.

Liz was fluffing up her hair to get it just right. Conroy was going through his first story again to make sure there weren't any long words in it he couldn't pronounce. Then the camera turned in their direction and they both smiled at it. The red light flashed on.

It's show time, boys and girls. . . .

JACKSON: New student demonstrations swept across China today. . . .

The China story took three minutes. After that, there was a Con Ed explosion in the Bronx. Then a fight in the City Council about rent control, a drug murder on Staten Island, and a bomb scare at LaGuardia Airport. It was nineteen after six when Liz St. John got to me.

ST. JOHN: Last week, an East Side call girl—Rikki Stiles—was found murdered in her posh Sutton Place apartment.

Since then our own Jenny McKay has been looking into the baffling murder and circumstances surrounding it.

Here is her report on "Life and Death on Sutton Place." Jenny?

She turned to me and smiled. I smiled back. A mutual admiration society. Bet the viewers would have been surprised if they found out we came close to a knockdown battle just before we went on the air.

I was getting ready when she came by and asked if I wanted any advice on my makeup.

"What's that supposed to mean?" I asked.

"I just thought that after the—uh, incident on the other night's show you might want some help. . . ."

"That wasn't my fault!"

"Okay."

"Go take your makeup tips to Linda Fairmont."

"Jenny, I just happen to have some expertise in this particular area so—"

"Expertise? Expertise in makeup? Jesus, this is supposed to be a news show. Not one of your goddamned beauty contests."

"Look, I—"

"Why don't we forget about the news and just elect one of us Miss Congeniality while we're at it?"

Someone broke up the argument by telling us we only had a few minutes until airtime. I had a feeling it wasn't over though.

I'd worked all day on the story. We'd gotten a Cleveland station to shoot some footage of the neighbourhood where Rikki grew up, get some on-air quotes from the mother, and pick up some still photos of Rikki as a child. Plus I had the stuff from Galena, some videotape we'd shot of Donna Willis, and a few interviews from people in the Sutton Place building.

Now I looked into the camera and said:

McKAY: Who killed Rikki Stiles? Well, we may never know the answer to that question. But perhaps just as baffling is how she wound up in the life she did. How did an art student named Susan Callandro from Cleveland, Ohio, become Rikki Stiles—a high-priced East Side prostitute?

There was a logo behind me which said "Life and Death on Sutton Place."
Then the picture cut to a scene of Times Square at night. Women in hot pants and see-through blouses patrolling the streets, standing on corners, getting into cars cruising by looking for action.

McKAY: When we talk about prostitutes, this is what we think of. Times Square. Streetwalkers. Seedy hotel rooms.
   Rikki Stiles was a prostitute, but you didn't find her in Times Square.

Cut to a shot of her apartment house.

McKAY: Rikki Stiles lived here—in this posh East Side high rise on Sutton Place where she entertained her clients in a two-bedroom apartment on the eighteenth floor with a view overlooking the East River.
   Her fee: Two thousand dollars a night.
   And it was done so discreetly that most of the residents of the building never suspected what the tenant living in Apt. 18B did for a living.

The picture went to a shot of a woman neighbor who lived on the same floor, an advertising copywriter in her mid-thirties named Rita Butler.

McKAY: Miss Butler, did you know Rikki Stiles?

BUTLER: We talked a few times. Once at a tenants' meeting. Once when my cat got loose in the hall and she helped me catch it. Maybe a few times in the elevator.

McKAY: What was your impression of her?

BUTLER: She seemed . . . nice. A very nice person.

McKAY: Did you know she was a prostitute?

BUTLER: No. She said she was an art student.

McKAY: Didn't you ever wonder how a struggling artist could afford to live in a two-bedroom apartment in this expensive building?

BUTLER: Hey, this is New York. Everybody minds their own business.

When the piece was over the camera came back to me.

McKAY: One final personal note here. I met Rikki Stiles once. Just before she died, she came to me and told me something in confidence.

What she told me or whether it's true or not isn't really important. What is important is that I was never able to discuss it with her again before she died. So I'm left with this unfinished business.

The only way to close the book is to find Rikki Stiles's murderer and the reason why she was killed.

We'll keep you informed on the progress of that investigation.

Later, after the newscast was finished, Carstairs came by my desk.

"Good," he said. "I liked it."

"Thanks."

"Except for the personal tag line at the end."

"What was wrong with it?"

"I just thought you injected yourself a little too much into the story."

"It's called advocacy journalism."

"Let's just stick to regular journalism, okay?"

"Regular journalism? Around here? You've got to be kidding."

Liz St. John came by next.

"Jenny, do you dislike me for some reason?"

"Huh?"

"All I did before was try to offer you some makeup tips and you started yelling at me. I want to know if you dislike me."

I shook my head. "I don't know you well enough to truly dislike you."

"Well, then why . . ."

"Because," I said, "and please don't take this personally, you stand for everything I detest and loathe and have utter contempt for in this business."

"I'm not supposed to take that personally?"

"It's not your fault. They take someone with no experience and no journalistic ability and no idea what she's reporting on and put her on the air. . . ."

"Not fair," she said. "I've paid my dues around here."

"Paid your dues? I've worked twenty years in this town. You've been here six months, and you make more money than I do."

"Well, maybe I'm just better at it than you are."

"Liz, you're supposed to be reporting to people what you know about New York City. You don't know anything about New York City."

"Hey, I know a lot about this town."

"Oh you do? How do you get to Red Hook, Brooklyn?"

"Uh . . ."

"Okay, how about Pelham Park? That only happens to be the biggest park in New York."

"Well . . ."

"How many people are there on the city council?"

She shrugged.

"Tell me the difference between a fire marshal and a fire chief."

Another shrug.

"A police captain and a police inspector."

Still nothing.

"Here, I'll help you out, I'll give you a little verse to remember," I told her. "You might want to write it down.

> "Fire engines are red
> Police cars are blue
> The Bronx Zoo is in the Bronx
> Yankee Stadium is too."

She stalked off angrily. I looked around the newsroom. Everyone was staring at me. Sanders—who'd been watching the whole thing—came over and sat on the edge of my desk. There was a long silence.

"So did I just make a complete ass of myself?" I asked finally.

"Well, probably—but it *was* kind of fun."

He smiled.

"Just out of curiosity, Jenny, do you know how many people there are on the city council?"

"Of course. That's an old lawyers' rule for debating someone—never ask a question you can't answer yourself."

"So how many people are on the city council?"

"Forty-five," I said.

Sanders stared at me.

"Jenny, there're fifty-one."

"Really? Are you sure?"

"I'm sure."

"Oh." I thought for a second. "So maybe the old lawyers'

rule is never ask a question unless you know the answer or you can make the other person think you do."

"Sounds good to me."

It was seven-thirty now. Time to go downstairs to the diner and meet Rick Gallagher. Jesus, Rick Gallagher! Why was I doing this? And then it came to me—I didn't have the slightest idea. So what else is new?

Gallagher was sitting in a corner booth waiting for me. There was a cup of coffee in front of him and another on the other side of the table waiting for me. I slid into the seat.

"Been waiting long?"

"About five minutes," he said. "I ordered you coffee in advance. Just to show you I meant business. If it's cold, we can get more."

"Thanks, big spender."

I took a sip.

"It's fine. So what's the deal with you being early—no big crime waves tonight?"

"No, I spent most of my day doing what we refer to as administrative work. Paper shuffling."

"On?"

"The Lancaster Hotel robbery."

"How's that going?"

"We're at a dead end."

"You still think Rossiello was behind it?"

"We're sure of it. We just can't prove it, that's all. Plus he's already indicated by the Manhattan District Attorney on racketeering charges."

"Elliott Carson."

"The highly esteemed and highly quotable Elliott Carson."

"You don't think much of him, do you?" I asked.

"Not as much as he thinks of himself."

I wondered if I should tell him about my strange conversation with Carson. I decided not to.

"How about Johnny Camancho and his brother?" I asked. "Anything more on them?"

"Don't know. Can't find them."

"They're still missing?"

"Yeah, since last week sometime."

"When Rikki Stiles died."

"I guess so."

"There could be a connection, you know."

"Or they could have stiffed some loan shark in Benson-hurst. There's a million reasons why these guys could have taken it on the lam. Don't read too much into it."

We talked some more about the case. About people we knew. Finally I got down to it.

"So why are we here?" I asked.

"It's like I told you, I want to explain to you about my personal situation. I think I owe you that. Then you can decide what you want to do. Okay?"

"Sounds fair enough."

Gallagher took a deep breath and plunged ahead.

"I'm married," he said.

"Surprise, surprise."

"Got two kids. A boy and a girl."

"Congratulations."

"A cute little house out in Rockville Centre. Three bed-rooms. Nice neighborhood. Fenced-in yard. A little barbecue in the back. . . ."

"Very nice."

"Got a dog and a cat too."

"Christ, this sounds like something out of a Norman Rockwell painting. . . ."

Gallagher held up his hand. "Wait, there's more."

He looked down at his coffee.

"My wife is dying of cancer."

I wasn't sure what to say.

"I'm sorry."

"Yeah, well . . ."

"How . . . how long does she . . ."

"Hard to say. The doctors tell us it could be months or it could be a year. In the meantime, she's not very strong and hardly ever leaves the house. Has to use a wheelchair. . . ."

"That sounds rough."

"There's more. My son is retarded. He's fifteen now, but mentally he's about four."

I shook my head sadly. "Look, I don't know what to say. . . ."

"There's nothing to say. You see, my wife and I grew apart a long time ago. Maybe it was the pressure over Ben—that's my son—and maybe we just never really loved each other very much. Anyway, I was all set to go ahead with a divorce when this cancer thing came along and . . ."

"So you can't really leave her and a disabled kid too."

"It'd make me seem like a real shit, wouldn't it?"

"Yeah," I said. "I guess it would."

"So I live at home and take care of her and support the family. And each day I go a little more crazy. But it's the right thing to do."

"And on the side, you pick up strange women in police stations."

Gallagher sighed. "My wife and I are married in name only," he said evenly. "There's nothing else there. She knows that. And she knows I have a life of my own on the outside. There's no deceit there."

He gazed across the table at me.

"I guess you can see why I couldn't explain this all the first day we met."

"It is a real conversation stopper," I admitted.

"So what do you think? Can we do something together?"

"We are doing something together," I told him. "Drinking coffee."

"I was thinking about moving up to a regulation date. A real dinner or something. Maybe we can even do it tonight. I know a place in the Village. . . ."

I looked at my watch. Eight-fifteen.

"Listen, I've gotta get home. Someone's supposed to meet me there at nine."

"A hot boyfriend?"

"Nah, I'm being audited."

"You're kidding."

"Would I kid about something like that?"

"What happened?"

I told him the story of Murray, the singles-bar accountant.

"So how about some other night then?"

"I don't know. . . ."

"Why not?"

"You just seem like you're going to be more trouble than you're worth."

"Yeah, you're probably right," he said in a resigned tone. "Sorry to have wasted your time."

I looked across the table at him and smiled.

"Hey, don't give up that easy."

"Meaning?"

"Meaning give me a call someday and we'll see."

10

Uncle Sam Can
Be Your Friend

Someone buzzed me from the lobby of my apartment at about 8:45.

I assumed it was Mike Stoner. Arriving just a little early to get a head start on the audit. That was my first mistake.

I buzzed open the front door without checking. That was my second mistake.

A minute later there was a knock on my door. I opened it up a crack, leaving the chain on, expecting to see Mike Stoner for the first time. Instead, there were two guys wearing work jackets of some sort.

"Sorry to bother you this late," one of them said, "but we're from Manhattan Cable. There's been some problems with reception reported in this area. Can we come in and look at your connection?"

I looked at my TV. It was on and the picture was clear.

"No problem here," I told them.

"Yeah, I know," the guy said, "but sometimes a loose connection in one apartment can screw everyone else up.

We've got to check them all. A real bitch, huh? It'll only take a second."

I looked at the two of them again standing there in the hall. Now, Manhattan Cable spends a lot of money on a public awareness campaign so that customers know what its employees look like. The ads tell you that every Manhattan Cable repairman has an authorized ID he will show before coming into your apartment. I've seen these ads a hundred times.

But it was late and I was in a hurry and I wanted them to be done and gone. So I unchained the door and let them in.

That was my third mistake, and it was a beaut.

I knew there was a problem right off when they plopped down on my living room couch.

"Sit down," the guy who'd done all the talking so far told me.

"The TV set's over there," I pointed out.

"Terrific. Sit."

He took a gun out of his belt and pointed it at me.

I sat.

The guy holding the gun was about fifty, with a heavyset face and short cropped blond hair. He was chewing gum, had his feet up on my coffee table, and in general acted as casually as an old friend who'd dropped by for a chat. The other one was thin and wiry, with oily black hair, and looked a lot younger—probably no more than thirty. He seemed very nervous.

Hobo was barking at both of them.

"Cute dog," the big guy said.

"Thanks. I think the gun makes him nervous. I know it makes me nervous."

"It'd probably be better all around if you put him somewhere else, like in another room, until we're finished. You know what I'm saying?"

I picked Hobo up and carried him into the bedroom. While I was there, I looked out the window at the drop three floors below to the street. Should I make a try for it? I didn't know if I could do it without breaking a leg or possibly something more important. I put Hobo down, closed the bedroom door, and went back out into the living room.

"I don't have much money," I told them. "A little jewelry. Take whatever you want, but . . ."

"We're not burglars," the guy with the gun said.

"You're not Manhattan Cable TV repairmen either," I pointed out.

"No, we're not." He leaned forward. "Miss McKay, we're just here for some information, that's all. You give it to us and we're gone. No problem."

He smiled. Friendly. Fatherly-like. Just a guy who dropped in to ask me a couple of things. Only there was something scary about him. A look in his eyes . . .

"Information?" I said. "Hey, news is my business. Tell me what you need to know."

"Good. Very good." He leaned back now and looked around the room. He was making himself very much at home. "Do you think I could trouble you for something to drink?"

The little guy spoke for the first time now. "Jesus, Leo, let's get this done . . ."

Leo, huh? Leo froze him with a stare from those eyes. "Now, Albert, we're guests in Miss McKay's home. I think a nice social drink would be good for all of us. Help us to relax."

"I have some scotch," I said.

I went over to a cabinet, took out the bottle, and poured some scotch into three glasses. Then I took them back to the living room. Leo rested his gun on his lap when he took the glass.

"To your continued good health, Miss McKay," he said, making a toast.

"I'll drink to that."

I took a gulp of the scotch.

"You mentioned something about wanting information?"

"Right. We're very interested in finding out more about something you talked about on the air."

"What's that?"

"Rikki Stiles."

Bingo.

"What about her?"

"You said she told you something before she died. What did she tell you, Miss McKay?"

I sighed.

"I don't think I can reveal that to you."

"Why not?"

"Well, you see, she was a source. In the news business, we have these rules. And one of them is you never reveal something a source tells you in confidence."

Leo took the gun out of his lap and pointed it at me again.

"Cut the crap, McKay."

"Well, of course, they're not really rules. I mean, they're not even written down or anything. Probably no one would even care if I was to break one now and then. . . ."

"What did Rikki Stiles tell you?"

I went through it all for them. Told them her theory about the Camancho brothers and the Lancaster Hotel robbery. I didn't see any point in holding anything back now. Rikki Stiles was dead. It wasn't going to hurt her any.

When I was finished, the two of them looked at each other.

"What now, Leo?" the little guy asked.

"I don't know, Albert. Maybe we give her another chance."

"We don't have time . . ." he said excitedly.

"Calm down, Albert. Miss McKay's going to cooperate with us." He turned to me. "Aren't you, Miss McKay?"

"What are you guys talking about? I told you all about the Camancho brothers and the Lancaster robbery. That's all I know. What else do you want me to say?"

Leo stared at me. "Tell us about Elliott Carson."

"Who?"

"Elliott Carson. The Manhattan District Attorney."

"What does he have to do with anything? I thought this was about the Lancaster Hotel robbery."

"I don't know anything about the Lancaster thing," he said. "It's got nothing to do with me. I want to hear everything you know about Elliott Carson. It's as simple as that."

"Okay," I said slowly, "his name is Elliott Carson. He's the Manhattan District Attorney. His office is at One Hogan Plaza. And . . . well, that's pretty much the extent of everything I know."

Leo sighed loudly. "Look, this is getting us nowhere. Let me refresh your memory a little. You went to see Elliott Carson the other day. You spent about forty minutes there. What did you talk about?"

"Okay," I said, "but you're not going to believe me."

"Try me."

"He wanted us to do lunch."

"Huh?"

"His office called me up and said he wanted to see me. When I got there, he said he'd seen me on TV, thought I was a hot commodity, and said he wanted to get to know me better. Talked about how he was trying to make friends in the media."

Leo looked over at Albert. He was still fidgeting nervously. His face was a blank. Albert's face was probably always a blank. But Leo was different. He seemed gregarious and friendly on the outside, but I was afraid of him. . . .

"And?" Leo asked me now.

"We talked for a while. I said I'd get in touch with his office to make a date for lunch, and that's all that happened."

"You could be telling the truth," he said.

"Of course I am. Would I lie to you in a situation like this?"

"No, probably not. I guess you really don't know . . ."

The buzzer from the lobby rang again. They both looked startled. Mike Stoner, I thought.

"You expecting someone?" Leo asked.

"Uncle Sam."

"What?"

"An investigator from the IRS. I've got an appointment with him for an audit."

"Just let it buzz," Leo told me. "He'll think you're not here."

"No, he won't." I thought fast. "I told him I might be late. Said he should wait for me until I got back."

Leo stood up. So did Albert. They moved toward the door.

"We're going to walk out of here quietly," Leo said. "No trouble, no fuss."

He took me by the arm and pointed to the intercom.

"Tell him to come on up. Nothing else, McKay. Got that? Don't do anything stupid."

I nodded. After I delivered the message down to the lobby, they walked out and made their way down the stairs. A minute later, another man emerged on the third floor landing and headed for my door.

"Hi, I'm Mike Stoner. . . ."

"Did you see two guys on the steps?" I asked.

"Yeah. They just walked out the front door."

"You're sure?"

"I saw them go. What were they—workmen or something?"

"They were armed intruders," I said.

"What?"

"C'mon inside. I gotta call the cops and then I'll explain."

He walked into the apartment.

"Oh, by the way, I'm Jenny McKay."

He stuck out his hand in greeting. I started to shake it, then put my arms around him instead and gave him a big kiss.

"You don't know it," I said, "but I think you may have just saved my life."

"Wow," he said, after recovering from his surprise, "we IRS investigators don't usually get this friendly a reception when we arrive to audit someone's taxes."

"God bless the federal government," I told him.

Two uniformed cops from the Elizabeth Street station showed up about thirty minutes later.

This didn't exactly seem to be a high priority case for them. They asked me a few perfunctory questions, poked around a little, and generally seemed bored by the whole business.

"So you're saying these two guys didn't take anything or harm you in any way, right?" one of the cops said.

"Well, they pointed a gun a me."

"But they didn't shoot you."

"No. Sorry to disappoint you."

"So all we really have here is a slight case of breaking and entering. And it's not even really breaking and entering. I mean you did open the door and let them in voluntarily. . . ."

"Under false pretenses."

"Okay. Still . . ."

"Look, I'm not a trained professional investigator like you, but if I had to make a wild guess, I'd say this pair was really mobbed up."

"So why come to you?"

"They wanted to know about a dead prostitute named Rikki Stiles."

"What's your connection?"

"I'm a TV reporter and I'm working on the story."

"You're on TV? What's your name again?"

"Jenny McKay."

"Never heard of you."

"I'm on Channel Six. You know—the News at Six on Six."

"I watch Michelle Marsh on Channel Two," he said. "I like Michelle Marsh."

Fame is so fleeting.

He turned to his partner. "Hey, Benny, this woman says she's on the six o'clock news. You recognize her?"

"No," Benny said, "I watch 'Diff'rent Strokes' at six."

"A shrewd choice," I told him. "Look, both of these guys drank out of the glasses on the table there. Maybe there's fingerprints on them. Why don't you take them into the crime lab or whatever and find out?"

"Okay," the first cop sighed, "but like I said before, this isn't exactly the crime of the century. All that happened is two guys asked you questions about some prostitute . . ."

"They wanted to know about Elliott Carson too," I said.

The cop did a double take.

"The District Attorney?"

"No, Elliott Carson, the taxidermist. Of course, the District Attorney."

"There's no need to be sarcastic about it, Miss McKay. It just seems a little unusual . . ."

"I know it seems unusual. Maybe you should look into it. . . ."

"What did they want to know about Elliot Carson?"

I told him the story.

"Well," he said when I was finished, "you said yourself these two guys acted like they were from the mob. And Carson just indicted Jerry Rossiello. It's natural they'd have him on their minds. Carson might just break up that whole goddamned family before he's through."

"It was something more than that," I said. "Something specific they were looking for from me."

"Like what?"

"I don't know. Why not ask Elliott Carson?"

The cop looked at me strangely.

"What *are* you going to do with this stuff I'm telling you?" I asked.

"I'm going to write it up in an official report," he said evenly. "That's procedure. And when I'm going to pass it on to my superiors. That's procedure too. Okay with you?"

He didn't say any more, but he didn't have to. Pass it on to your superiors. That's the way you do it. Elliott Carson is the DA and his name pops up somewhere it shouldn't be. So what do you do? Pass it on to your superiors. Hell, you tell yourself, I'm not making enough money to make a decision about something this sensitive. Then your superior passes it on to his superior, who passes it on up the ladder. Pass the buck, keep it moving. When it stops, nobody knows. But everyone makes sure their ass is covered. That's what makes the world go round.

"Do me a favor," I said. "You know a lieutenant named Gallagher? Works out of the Seventeenth Precinct?"

"Rick Gallagher? Yeah, I know him. Why?"

"Tell him about this. Mention my name."

"He knows you?"

"We have a passing acquaintance."

And that was it. They gave the place another once-over, took the two glasses, and walked to the door. Both of them wished me a good evening and said I should call if there was any more trouble.

"Well, there go two of New York's finest," I said after they were gone.

Stoner smiled. He was sitting at my kitchen table going over my records. Hobo was lying quietly at his feet, no worse for wear after the excitement of the night. Not much of a guard dog, but then what was he supposed to do? Attack a man with a loaded gun? He got up now and licked my face excitedly. Just a lover, not a fighter.

"So how does it look?" I asked.

"You'll love Leavenworth in the spring."

"That bad."

"Nah, not really. Of course, your friend Murray did take some rather questionable deductions for you. I mean, claiming the corner of your room where you have your TV as a home office because you're a broadcaster . . ."

"Yeah, I kinda thought that one might be a bit of a reach."

"On the other hand, he overlooked some legitimate deductions. I think I can go over this and make it balance out so you really don't owe very much at all."

"Wow, that's great. I didn't know you IRS guys were so nice."

"We're a very misunderstood group."

Mike Stoner looked a little like a young Woody Allen to me. Fortyish, with glasses, balding slightly in the back. And he had a slight nervous twitch sometimes when he talked. Not exactly Robert Redford. But sort of likeable. I liked him.

"Are you going to be all right by yourself tonight?" he asked now.

"Oh, I don't think they'll be back. Anyway, I don't have much of a choice. The Keystone Kops didn't exactly offer me twenty-four-hour police protection."

"I could stay if you want."

His twitch grew more pronounced when he said it and his face turned a bright red.

"Uh, I didn't mean that the way it sounded. I just meant if you wanted someone here . . . that is, I could sleep on the couch and . . ."

"Thanks for the offer." I smiled. "But won't Mrs. Stoner be upset if you don't come home?"

"There is no Mrs. Stoner."

"You're divorced?"

"No."

"Widower?"

"I've never been married."

"Really?"

Ah, McKay, you sly devil, you.

"If it makes you uncomfortable, I'll just leave now and—"

"I'd love for you to stay," I told him. "It would make me feel . . . safe."

I took out some extra sheets and a pillow and fixed up the couch for him. I thought he might make a pass at me, but he didn't. So I just gave Hobo his last walk, went into the bedroom to get undressed, and crawled under the covers.

There's a TV in the bedroom. I clicked it on and watched a rerun of "Taxi." Jim had just burned down Louie's apartment, and Alex was trying to fix things up. After that was over, "Kojak" came on. Maybe I should go out to the living room and make a pass at him, I thought. The guy did come to my rescue. And he seemed so nice. . . . Of course, that didn't mean he wanted to make love to me. Maybe he had another girl. Maybe he was gay. Maybe . . .

I shook my head and tried to forget about Mike Stoner lying in the other room. It was getting me nowhere. I lit a cigarette and changed the channel. "Star Trek" was on now. Captain Kirk and Spock and the rest of the *Enterprise* crew were in a big battle with the Klingons and they were losing. The Klingons had discovered a new cloaking device that made their ships invisible. Captain Kirk had to get it away from them to save the Federation. That's all I remember. Sometime soon after that, my head hit the pillow and I drifted off into unconsciousness.

I slept a solid eight hours without anyone trying to kill, kidnap, or molest me.

11

Nicky Camancho

Things were beginning to happen quickly now.

It's funny how a story like this sometimes gets a life of its own. You think you're in control—that you'll decide what to do, how far to take it, and when to stop. But in reality a series of events has already been set in motion, and now you're just along for the ride. It's like being on a roller coaster and heading for the top of that first hill. You might be scared to see what's on the other side, but it's too late to change your mind. That's what happened with Rikki Stiles.

Rick Gallagher called me at the station the next afternoon.

"I'm at Kennedy Airport," he said. "Parking Lot D. You might want to get out here with a film crew right away."

"What's happening?"

"We've got a body in the trunk of a car."

"Who?"

"Nicky Camancho."

"Johnny Camancho's brother?"

"One and the same."

Sanders, Jacobson, and I got in the mobile van, headed across the Williamsburg Bridge, and made it onto the Brooklyn-Queens Expressway before the worst of the evening rush hour.

"Boy, this is different," Sanders said as he drove. "A cop calls us and tells us about news. What gives?"

Jacobson looked up from his ever-present crossword puzzle. "I think Lt. Gallagher is sweet on our lil' Jenny."

Sanders swiveled his head around and looked at me. "Really? Is that right, Jenny?"

"Nah," I said, "he's probably just looking to collect that twenty-five-dollar fee we pay viewers for hot news tips."

"Oh, he's looking for something hot, all right." Sanders chuckled.

"Only it isn't news," Jacobson added.

They both laughed uproariously.

"Get a life, you guys," I said.

It took us thirty-five minutes to get to JFK. Then we spent another ten minutes driving through airport parking lots until we got to D. There was a circle of police cars with flashing red lights converged in a corner of the lot, near the water. Some uniformed cops and a few in plainclothes were milling about. One of them was Gallagher. We parked the van, got out, and walked over to him.

"Where is he?" I asked.

He nodded toward the open trunk of a 1991 Oldsmobile Cutlass that was at the center of all the cops' attention. Next to the car lay a plastic bag. A body bag.

"R.I.P., Nicky Camancho," he said.

"What happened?"

"Well, you know we haven't been able to find the Camanchos since the Rikki Stiles killing. Their bodywork shop was closed up tight when we went out there. No sign of them. So we put out an APB that they were wanted for questioning. . . ."

Gallagher took out a cigar, unwrapped it carefully, and lit it.

"Anyway, today I get a call. It seems the Port Authority cops checked out this car that's been sitting here for a few days. They open up the trunk, find our friend here sleeping like a baby inside. Two bullets to the head, and his throat cut from ear to ear. A little bit of checking turns up the fact that he's Nicky Camancho. They know I'm looking for him, so that's why I'm here."

I nodded. "How about Johnny Camancho?"

"Still missing," he said.

"You figure he might have done this?"

"You mean a falling-out among brothers? Tsk, tsk."

He took a puff of the cigar, blew some smoke in the air, and smiled.

"Or . . ."

"Or what?"

"Maybe someone else knocked off Nicky boy here and brother Johnny is next. Or maybe he's dead too."

I looked over at the body bag again. Sanders and Jacobson were shooting film of it and the Cutlass. When they were finished I'd put Gallagher on the air. It was still too early for a live interview on the six o'clock show, but we could send the film in and then do a remote setup from here in a few hours. You know, where I stand in an empty parking lot and say, "Just hours ago police found a body at this spot. . . ."

"You still think this has nothing to do with the Lancaster Hotel robbery?" I asked him now.

"Actually I was just coming to that."

"Yeah?"

"Let's take a little walk. Get some privacy."

We walked over to a corner of the parking lot. It was chilly out. We were getting into the heart of November now, and I was still wearing my lightweight trench coat because I thought it looked nifty on camera. Made me look like Leslie Stahl does standing in front of the White House. Pretty soon though I was going to have to switch to my winter parka. Then I'd look like *Nanook of the North*.

"I've got a scoop for you," Gallagher said. "Gonna make you a star."

"Terrific."

"You got to protect me on this one though. You can't quote me by name or as a source."

"They won't get it out of me with hot pokers and cattle prods. You want me to sign a blood oath or anything?"

He puffed on the cigar and smiled. "I sent some guys over to Nicky Camancho's house after I heard about the body," he said. "They found some jewelry there. Lots of jewelry. The pieces are identical to those taken during the Lancaster robbery."

"Jesus!"

"There's more. Remember the jewelry in Rikki Stiles's apartment? Some items we found underneath a drawer?"

"You mean they—"

"Not all of them. Just a couple. From the Lancaster job too."

"Don't crooks generally fence that kind of stuff?" I asked.

Gallagher made a snorting sound. "Like I said, these are the Camancho brothers we're talking about. They couldn't fence in a dog."

"So the Camancho brothers did the Lancaster heist after all."

"It looks that way. . . ."

"But you said it was so sophisticated and professional. How could they . . . ?"

"None of it makes sense, does it?"

The wind was getting colder now. I pulled up the collar of the trench coat around my face, but it didn't help much. Screw the Leslie Stahl look. I was freezing my ass off.

"Did a couple of cops tell you what happened to me last night?" I asked.

"I was just coming to that."

"I gave them some fingerprints on a couple of glasses . . ."

"We ran them this morning. Got a make on three people. All with records."

"Three?"

"Uh-huh. The first one appeared in court on 12-8-92 and was charged with nonpayment of $1347 worth of parking tickets. Suspect made restitution and promised to turn over a new leaf. But outstanding new fines now total $981."

"Wait a minute . . ."

"Suspect identified by computer as Jennifer Ann McKay, age forty-one, last known address . . ."

"Very funny. I get it—my prints were on the glasses too, so you ran them through the computer."

"You know you really ought to pay your parking tickets, Jenny."

"Not until I turn up on 'America's Most Wanted.' Who were the two guys?"

"One of them is a sweetheart named Albert (the Weasel) Girardi. Girardi's a small-time hood. Runs errands, drives, gets coffee and stuff for the big guys. He works for—"

"Jerry Rossiello," I said.

"My, my, what a smart little girl you are."

"And the other one?"

"Leo Kluge."

"He works for Rossiello too?"

"Nope. Kluge's based in Chicago. He's a free-lancer."

"Meaning?"

"He's a hit man, Jenny. One of the best. This guy kills people for a living."

I thought about his eyes. Cold, sinister. I believed it.

"You know about the Elliott Carson connection?" I asked him.

"The patrol guys told me about that too. So I called Carson today and laid out for him what happened. His response was that Rossiello's people were just obsessed with him because of the indictment. A reasonable enough answer."

"And?"

"And what? Elliott Carson's the District Attorney, Jenny. One of the highest law enforcement officials in the city. I'm a cop. I've done my duty. End of story."

"Yeah, well . . . I just think Elliott Carson knows a lot more than he's telling us."

We walked back to the crowd gathered around Nicky Camancho's body. Then Sanders, Jacobson, and I shot the interview with Gallagher. He detailed again how the cops found the body and the cause of death and about the search for brother Johnny. He did not mention the Lancaster Hotel connection. I'd do that as a "sources have told Channel Six News" when I delivered the report at six o'clock.

Later, when the cops were cleaning up and getting ready to leave, Gallagher came over and said to me: "You want to grab a bite to eat or something?"

"I can't," I told him. "Gotta work. Big story, remember?"

"Right."

"Maybe next week," I suddenly blurted out. "Monday night would be okay."

"Sure." He looked at me with surprise. "So why the change of heart about seeing me? Is this a little quid pro quo? A date in exchange for what I told you?"

I shook my head. "I don't work like that."

"Then why?"

"I just decided that maybe you were worth taking a chance on."

He smiled. "Good. You won't regret it, Jenny."

"Oh, I probably will."

"See you Monday night."

He started to walk to his car.

"Hey, Lieutenant." He turned around. "This guy Kluge . . ."

"Yeah?"

"He's really scary."

"I know." He sighed. "So what the hell is a hit man from Chicago doing in New York right now?"

"More to the point," I said, "what the hell was he doing in my living room?"

12

Killer Consultants
From Outer Space

Linda Fairmont was back.

Sitting in the newsroom as big as life when I came to work the following Monday. She was talking to Bill Hanrahan this time, working with him on his delivery and appearance. Hanrahan did not look particularly happy. That surprised me a little because he usually liked any type of contact with any type of female.

God, I hated her. She seemed so out of place in what was supposed to be a newsroom. Like an alien from outer space. A being from another world. Sort of like that old supernatural TV show, "The Outer Limits," which began: "Ladies and gentlemen, there is nothing wrong with your reception. We have taken control of your TV sets." Or like a bad science fiction movie playing late at night on cable TV. "You'll Scream! You'll Shake! You'll Die of Terror!" Now playing in the WTBK newsroom—"Killer Consultants from Outer Space."

I walked over to Sanders and Jacobson, pointed toward Linda Fairmont, and said in a squeaky voice like the little girl in the *Poltergeist* ads:

"She's b-a-a-a-ck!"

"Scary, isn't it?" Sanders said.

"How much are they paying this consulting firm anyway?" Jacobson asked.

"The word on the street is two hundred and fifty thousand dollars," Sanders said. "That's for an ad campaign, coaching of on-air personnel, and conceptual input."

"Conceptual input?" I said.

Jacobson made a low whistling sound. "Two hundred and fifty thousand dollars. That's not bad."

"Yeah, how do you become a consultant anyway?" I asked.

"If you have to ask"—Sanders smiled—"then you don't have what it takes."

I sat down at my desk and went through the weekend papers. For a change, this was fun. Everyone had picked up my story from the newscast. "SLAIN HOOKER, HOODLUM LINKED TO LANCASTER ROBBERY," the *Daily News* said. The *New York Post* screamed: "HOTEL HOMICIDE!" The story began:

Police believe a minor underworld figure murdered at Kennedy Airport helped carry out the six-million-dollar Lancaster Hotel robbery, a TV station reported.

The report—aired on Channel Six—quoted police sources as saying that jewelry from the Lancaster robbery was found among the belongings of Nicholas Camancho, thirty-nine, whose body was discovered in the trunk of a car yesterday in an airport parking lot.

The sources also said that jewelry from the spectacular heist was discovered in the apartment of Rikki Stiles, an East Side call girl found slain last week. . . .

I put down the paper and looked around the newsroom. Linda Fairmont was gone now. Probably off to do her mischief somewhere else. I walked over to Hanrahan.

"So how'd it go with the Dragon Lady?" I asked.

"It went."

He definitely did not seem happy. There was a full cup of coffee which sat untouched and getting cold on the edge of his desk. He kept staring down at it.

"Boy, you sure seem depressed," I said. "What's the matter?"

He looked up at me now.

"How much time did she spend with you?" he asked me.

"Who?"

"Who?" he grunted. "Linda Fairmont, that's who."

"I don't know. Two hours, maybe three. It seemed like a lifetime. Why?"

"She spent about ten minutes with me."

"So?"

"So what do you think that means?"

"I don't know," I said, "maybe she thought I needed more help than you did."

"It doesn't work that way, Jenny."

"I still don't . . ."

"Let me explain it this way. She spent a day each with Conroy and Liz, she's having dinner with Stormy Phillips, and you talked for two to three hours. Me, I got ten minutes."

"Oh."

"My contract's almost up, Jenny. You know what I'm saying?"

I knew what he was saying. Maybe someone—someone like Carstairs—had passed the word to Linda Fairmont. Don't waste much time on Bill Hanrahan. It's not worth it. He's not going to be around here much longer anyway.

I'd gone through the same thing the year before. My contract was winding down, and I wasn't sure if it would be renewed. As it happened, I broke a big story and I was riding high so they had no choice. I related that to him now.

"Timing is everything," I said.

"No, it isn't," he told me. "Race is."

"Uh yeah, that too. . . ."

He didn't say any more. He didn't have to, I knew what he meant. There's a sort of unwritten rule in broadcast news—

your news team has to have the right ethnic mix. A black guy, a woman, maybe even a Hispanic or an Asian person, and then a bland white guy to make sure you didn't scare away the Silent Majority. We had the white guy, we had some women—what we didn't have was a black. Oh, we had a couple of black reporters and people behind the scenes like Sanders, but that wasn't enough. All those smiling pictures on the backs of buses of our news team—Conroy, Liz, Stormy, and Hanrahan—were conspicuously white.

"I knew it was going to be a problem ever since Larry left," Hanrahan said.

Larry was Larry Travers, our weatherman before Stormy Phillips. He was a middle-aged black man with a family who simply got fed up with the craziness of the New York TV market. Now he worked for a small station in San Jose, California.

"I mean they can't get rid of Conroy Jackson," Hanrahan was saying, "because he's practically an institution in this town. They're committed to Liz St. John for a lot of money. And the viewer surveys show that half the men out there are in love with Stormy Phillips. So that leaves ol' Bill Hanrahan to put his head on the chopping block."

"Has anyone talked to you about this?" I asked.

"No."

"Well, then maybe they're not really going to . . ."

"C'mon, don't you think that's a message of its own?"

My telephone rang. I walked back to my desk and picked it up. It was the guard at the front door. Someone named Mike Stoner was there and wanted to come up to see me. Was that all right? I said yes.

A few minutes later he walked into the newsroom carrying a sheaf of papers under his arm.

"Boy, I didn't know the IRS made so many house calls," I said.

He smiled. "Well, it's no problem. You see, I work in the neighborhood anyway, so . . ."

"Really? Where?"

"On—on Church Street."

"Church Street isn't exactly in the neighborhood," I pointed out.

"Well, I mean it's downtown. . . ."

"Yeah, the other side of downtown. It's at least a twenty-five minute walk from here."

His face turned beet red. "Well, yes, it is. That is—I didn't really . . ."

"Hey, don't apologize," I said. "I'm glad to see you."

He took out the papers and spread them on my desk. Then he went into an explanation of everything he'd done. Something about depreciation and amortization and tax base rates. I nodded as if I understood what he was saying. Don't let him think you're shallow, kiddo.

"Now, I'd suggest you have your own accountant look this all over and then . . ."

"Well, that could be a problem," I told him.

"Oh, right. I forgot."

"Yeah. I think tracking down Murray's forwarding address might be a little tough."

"For whatever it's worth, I assure you that everything is in order. So if you trust me . . ."

"Implicitly."

"Then just look through them in the next day or so, sign the form, and that ought to do it."

"No problem," I said. "You guys do a pickup service too?"

"I could drop by tomorrow. I mean I'm—"

"In the neighborhood?"

Stoner laughed. "Well, sort of."

"How about tomorrow night?" I asked him. "My place. Say around nine?"

"I—I suppose I could do that."

"I'll cook you something for dinner to thank you for all your help. I'm a great cook. Hey, you think that could be construed as a bribe?"

"Possibly. But let's live dangerously."

"You remember how to get to my place, right? Just look for some guys with guns and you're probably in my living room."

Gallagher and Stoner, I thought after he was gone. Back-to-back dates. I was really on a roll. When you're hot, you're hot—when you're not, you're not. Most of the time I was not. But right now I was like a firecracker.

I headed down the hall toward the ladies' room. On my way I passed by Carstairs's office. He was alone. I stuck my head in.

"Got a second?" I asked.

"Sure. C'mon in." I sat down. "Hell of an exclusive," he said.

"It sure was, wasn't it?"

"My, aren't we modest?"

"Yeah, it's one of my many virtues. Listen, can I ask you something?"

"Shoot."

"What's the deal with Bill Hanrahan?"

Carstairs stared at me for a second before answering. "He's the sports reporter."

"I know that, but he thinks he might be on the way out. He's really down. I thought maybe if you talked with him . . ."

"About what?"

"About what a valuable member of the news team he is." I paused. "He is a valuable member of the news team, isn't he?"

There was a longer silence this time.

"Jenny, Bill Hanrahan has a contract to do the sports for this station. He will be doing sports here for the duration of that contract. At the proper time, we will make a determination as to whether or not his contributions to the station should be continued for another—"

"Jesus Christ!" I said. "You're really going to do it, aren't you?"

"What do you mean?"

"You're going to fire him."

"Jenny, I really don't think this is any of your business—"

"What about our ads? The ones that talk about how we're all one big happy family. All for one, one for all."

Carstairs sighed. "You know, not too long ago you came really close to getting fired yourself. Since that time, I guess I've changed my mind about you. I mean I've acquired a grudging respect for who you are and what you do. A realization that your plusses generally outweigh your minuses."

"Thanks."

"But don't push it," he said.

I didn't say anything.

"Get my message?" he asked.

"Loud and clear."

"Good. Very good."

More silence. I stood up to leave. End of conversation.

"So what are you doing right now, Jenny?"

"Well, I was on my way to the ladies' room."

"After that?"

"I thought I'd dig around some more on the Rikki Stiles story. I think there's a lot still there."

"Then go do it," Carstairs said.

13
Paper Trail

I decided to take stock of what I knew.

This did not take a great deal of time. I mean, I knew the Camancho brothers pulled the Lancaster job after all. And I knew Rikki Stiles and Nicky Camancho were dead. Maybe Johnny Camancho killed Rikki because she was talking about the robbery and then killed his brother in a fight over the loot. So far, so good. That all made sense. And it was nice and neat.

But then what about the hit man in my apartment? And Elliott Carson? And Jerry Rossiello? And how did a pair of small-time punks like the Camanchos ever get involved in something as big as the Lancaster heist? For that matter, how did I know Johnny Camancho wasn't dead too? These were all good questions. The trouble was I didn't have any answers.

I had an idea though. In fact, I'd spent all night coming up with the idea. I was going to do some digging and find out everything I could about Elliott Carson. Okay, it wasn't much of an idea, I'll grant you that. But it was the only idea

I had. So I decided to go with it.

One of the great things about working at a newspaper—
and there are many—is being able to use its morgue. I don't
mean a morgue with dead bodies. I mean a morgue with
newspaper clippings and old photos and volumes of bound
editions. TV has nothing like it. Maybe because a morgue
is something of real substance, and TV has no need for
substance.

The best newspaper morgue used to be at the old *New York
Herald-Tribune*. Then the *Herald-Tribune* merged with the
Journal American and the *World* to form something called
the *World-Journal-Tribune*. When that died, the *New York
Post* moved into its building on South Street, a few blocks
away from where WTBK is now. These days the *Post* morgue
was *the* place to do some research.

Of course, it was not open to the general public. The
only people who were supposed to have access to it were
Post reporters. Or maybe the occasional *New York* magazine
writer or author who got special permission from the paper's
top management. But in reality all you had to do to get in
was stay on the good side of Melvin Spellner.

Melvin Spellner was the *Post*'s head librarian—a crusty
old man who'd been with the paper for more than forty
years and ran his department like a dictatorship. A few years
ago, when the *Post* was going through one of its periodic
ownership changes, someone in the new management noticed
that Spellner was approaching the mandatory retirement age.
Only when they attempted to enforce the rule, they discovered to their chagrin that no one but Spellner knew how to
find seventy percent of the stuff in the morgue. It would take
thousands of dollars and hours and hours of manpower to
reorganize the place so it could function without him. So he
stayed.

"Hi, Melvin," I said, planting myself in front of his clut-
tered desk.

He looked up and smiled when he recognized me.

"Jenny! Long time, no see. What're you doing these days?"

"I work over at Channel Six."

Spellner harrumphed loudly. He didn't like TV. Most old-time newspaper people didn't. Hell, I wasn't wild about it myself.

"You should be working at a newspaper, Jenny," he said, shaking his head. "You're a newspaperwoman."

"They all died," I told him.

"Yeah." His face suddenly brightened. "Hey, how about coming to work here?"

I shook my head.

"I tried a year ago. But all they're looking for is reporters who are twenty-five years old and willing to work seven days a week for thirty thousand dollars."

"Hell," Spellner said, "you can't be much more than twenty-five."

"Melvin, I'm forty-one."

"No kidding? Damn, time sure flies, doesn't it?"

"Tell me about it."

"Anyway, what can I do for you, Jenny?"

"I want to see all your clips on Elliott Carson, the Manhattan District Attorney."

Spellner made a whistling sound. "All the clips? That's a ton of stuff. The guy likes publicity an awful lot. He's got a file the size of Madonna's."

"I know."

"Okay," he sighed, "you want 'em, I got 'em."

Five minutes later, he came back with two boxes filled with envelopes of newspaper clippings and laid them down in front of me. While I was waiting, I'd gone to a stand in the lobby and bought myself a buttered bagel and a black coffee. I laid them down now on a desk next to the clips. Then I sat there munching on the bagel, sipping coffee, and reading about Elliott Carson.

He'd grown up on Long Island, went on to Harvard and graduated with top honors from law school there. Went on to join a top New York City law firm; Feitzer, Jackson, and Evans; where he quickly moved up to become a junior partner. He left to run for elective office—a seat on the city council—and won handily. After a few years there, he was elected to the State Senate. Spent ten years there and was responsible for a whole slew of important legislation—criminal justice reform, tax cuts, aid to the elderly.

The Republicans approached him about running for Manhattan District Attorney last year. He agreed and upset the longtime incumbent to win the office. He'd been DA now for less than a year, but he'd already indicted many of the city's top mob figures. Nailing Jerry Rossiello the other day was his latest and greatest coup. The papers were calling him the biggest racket-buster since Tom Dewey, and already people were speculating on him running for governor in two years. Maybe even the White House after that.

As for his personal life, he lived in Larchmont with his wife and three children—two young girls and a teenaged boy. He was active in the community, a big contributor to charities, named Westchester Man of the Year three consecutive times.

I sighed and looked at my watch. Two hours I'd been at it. What had I accomplished? Zilch. I was looking for something to show me Elliott Carson was really Simon Legree. Instead I got Albert Schweitzer. Everything about him added up to one terrific guy. Almost perfect.

What now? I suddenly remembered what Clare Lefferts had told me about Jim Brantley at the *Daily News*. Brantley knows all about Elliott Carson, she'd said, they're pals. Only it might be kind of embarrassing to talk to him. The incident with him being arrested stark naked outside my apartment had become legendary in media gossip circles. On the other hand, it happened six months ago. Maybe everyone—even him—had pretty much forgotten about it by now.

"Hey, Melvin," I said, "you know Jim Brantley over at the *Daily News*?"

"Sure. I just talked to him the other day."

"Does he still work out of the Criminal Courts pressroom?"

"That's right. You going to see him?"

"I think so."

"Hope you recognize him."

"What do you mean?"

"Well," he said, "Jim usually likes to wear his clothes when he's at work."

He chuckled loudly to himself.

Yep, everyone's forgotten all about it, all right.

The Criminal Courts pressroom is on the first floor of the courtroom, which is attached to the DA's office at 1 Hogan Plaza. I'd worked there briefly about ten years ago, and it hadn't changed much. It was a dingy place, right out of *The Front Page*. The walls were covered with Page One headlines from the past thirty years. Son of Sam. The Mad Bomber. Alice Crimmins. Bernie Goetz. Reporters—when they weren't in court—sat around swapping stories or playing cards or sneaking a drink from a whiskey bottle someone generally kept in their desk. I didn't much like the atmosphere. Jim Brantley, he loved it. Just another example of our incompatibility.

Brantley was surprised to see me, but not unfriendly.

"Jenny McKay! What are you doing here?"

"I'm looking for some information. I thought maybe you could help me. Is that okay?"

"Sure. It's just that I haven't seen you in a while. Since . . ."

"Since I threw your clothes out my window."

"Uh, yeah. . . ."

He seemed more embarrassed than angry over it.

"Listen, I'm sorry about that," I said. I wasn't that sorry, but what the hell. Anything for a story. "I kind of over-reacted. I hope we can let bygones be bygones."

"Absolutely."

We made small talk for a few minutes. About mutual friends. The weather. The Giants' chances of making the football play-offs. Finally I got down to it.

"Tell me what you know about Elliott Carson?"

"Carson? Why?"

"It's for a story I'm working on," I said.

"On Carson?"

"No, it's not about him. But I think he might be involved somehow. That's what I'm trying to find out."

"What's the story?"

"I can't tell you that right now."

Brantley eyed me suspiciously. "What's going on here? Do you think Carson's involved in something shady? Illegal? A scandal? I know that look in your eye, Jenny. . . ."

"Just talk to me about him, Jim."

He shrugged. "What do you want to know?"

"I'm not sure. I mean, I went through the clips, and he seems to be Mr. Wonderful. Is there anything else? Does he kick puppy dogs behind closed doors? Molest little girls in school playgrounds? Trip old ladies trying to cross the street? Or is he as perfect as he seems?"

"Carson's a great guy," Brantley said. "I think he may be the best DA since Tom Dewey . . ."

"Like I said," I told him, "I've already read the press clips. Tell me something I don't know. Aren't there any skeletons in his closet?"

"Such as?"

"I don't know." I thought again about Rikki Stiles. "How about women? Does he like them?"

Brantley grinned. "Sure. Who doesn't?"

"I mean does he ever do anything about it? Does he ever come on to them?"

"Jenny, let me tell you something," Brantley said, shaking his head. "A guy like Carson's almost like a rock star. Look at him—good-looking, distinguished, plus that whole power image he conveys. Women get off on power. On politicians with power. I guess it's like the Kennedys or Henry Kissinger or something. All I know is Elliott Carson could have as many chicks as Mick Jagger. If he wanted them."

"Does he want them?"

"Sometimes. He's no monk, but so what? We all have our desires."

"Jeez, the two of you must get along great."

"Hey, that was a shot, Jenny. I thought we were letting bygones be bygones."

"Sorry."

Brantley smiled. "As a matter of fact, we do get along well. I've had a few pretty wild nights on the town with him. He likes a good time."

"Isn't he supposed to be married?" I asked.

"C'mon, this is the twentieth century, Jenny."

"Yeah." I thought about something else. "How about his assistant, Carrie Macklin? What's the story on her? Do you know her?"

"You mean old sourpuss?" He made a face. "Sure, I know her. Boy, there's somebody you don't have to worry about him playing around with, huh?"

"What's your opinion of her?"

"I thought we were talking about women."

"I'm serious. What's she all about?"

"Well, she pretty much runs Elliott's whole life. Schedules his appointments, writes his speeches, makes sure he's got clean shirts. Sort of like a mother. Carson says she's indispensable, he couldn't do without her. But personally . . . yecch."

I thought again about the organized, efficient way Carrie Macklin ran that office. What was it Elliott Carson said to me about her—something like "I couldn't do without that little lady."

"The truth is it's probably a good thing she looks the way she does," Brantley was saying. "I mean if she was any kind of a looker, there might be some sexual tension with them being so close and all. But this way it's all business."

We talked for another ten minutes or so about Elliott Carson.

"Thanks a lot for your help, Jim," I said finally, getting up to leave. "I'll let you know how it comes out."

"No problem." He checked me out, now that I was standing. "Hey, Jenny—you're looking real good."

"Thanks."

"You work out these days or what?"

"Only if you call walking back and forth to the Baskin-Robbins working out."

"You know, the last time we were together we sort of parted under . . . well, difficult circumstances." He cleared his throat nervously. "Maybe we could get together and have a drink or something sometime and . . ."

I thought about Rick Gallagher. And Mike Stoner. I wrinkled my nose.

"Jeez, I don't think so, Jim. My social calendar's pretty filled up these days."

"Right. Well, anyway it was worth a shot."

"Wouldn't Donna be upset if she found out?" I asked him.

Donna was the girlfriend we'd had the fight over in my apartment.

"Uh, Donna and I aren't together anymore."

"Really? What happened?"

"Actually the word got out about what happened and someone told her and she . . . she decided she didn't want to be with me anymore."

"Oh, that's too bad."

God, I loved this!

"Yeah, well, these things happen."

I started to walk toward the door.

"Jenny, one more thing," Brantley yelled after me.

I turned around. "What?"

"Are you serious about all this? I mean, do you really think Carson's mixed up in something bad?"

I sighed. "Yeah, Jim, I do. I really do."

"So how you gonna find out for sure?"

"I don't know," I said. "Maybe I'll ask him."

14

Elliott Carson Again

Carrie Macklin was wearing a shapeless grey dress this time. A belt or sash around the waist might have helped a little, but she wasn't wearing one. Probably thought it was too daring. Her hair was still pulled back in the same severe bun, and even the few hints of makeup she'd worn before were gone. No mascara, no eyebrow pencil, no lipstick.

"Hi, remember me?" I said. "I'm Jenny McKay. Is Mr. Carson in?"

She carefully laid down the pen she was writing with, made sure it was in its proper place, and then looked up at me.

"Why, of course, Jenny. How are you? Good to see you again. Is he expecting you?"

"No, I was in the neighborhood, so I just took a chance and dropped by. I hope that's all right."

"Well, certainly it's all right, Jenny. It's not like you're a stranger or anything."

Sure, of course it was all right. Why not? We were pals. I was aces in her book. One meeting with the boss, and I could have anything I wanted.

She picked up a phone, talked into it for a second, then hung up and smiled at me.

"Mr. Carson is busy with something now, but he says he'll be able to see you soon. Why don't you just have a seat and wait? I don't think it'll be too long."

I sat down in the same chair where I'd waited before. Without thinking, my hand went into my purse and came out holding a cigarette. I'd just started to light it when Carrie Macklin caught me.

"Uh-uh, Jenny," she said. "Remember the rules."

She pointed to the THANK YOU FOR NOT SMOKING sign.

"Oh," I said, putting the cigarette back in my purse. "I forgot."

"I'm sorry to have to say anything. But it does smell up a room something awful. I mean a few puffs on that thing in here and I wouldn't be able to get it out of my hair for days. You do understand, don't you, Jenny?"

"Sure." I smiled. "No problem, Carrie."

Pals.

It took a while for Carson to finish what he was doing. Every few minutes Carrie Macklin looked over at me and smiled, and I smiled back. I felt naked sitting there without a cigarette to smoke. To pass the time, I began watching a tiny spider that was trying to spin a web alongside the base of the wall next to me. The spider started it a half dozen times, but it kept breaking off before it was finished. Finally it made it on the seventh try. I wanted to cheer. Perseverance, that's the name of the game. Spider probably got up an hour early to start working on that web. Carrie Macklin would have been proud of it.

Finally Elliott Carson strode out of his office and came over to greet me. He was smiling and stuck his hand out.

"Well, well, this is a pleasant surprise," he boomed. "C'mon in, Jenny. Let's talk."

I followed him into his office and we sat down. The Man of

the Year awards were still there facing me. So was the picture of him sitting on the white horse and looking distinguished.

"I didn't mean to keep you waiting," Carson said, "but we're working on a big case. The Jerry Rossiello indictment, as I'm sure you know. You have no idea what a giant step forward this is for law enforcement, Jenny. I believe that now we've broken the back of the organized crime movement in this city by taking Rossiello out of action. And this is just the start. There's going to be some very exciting things happening over the next few months, and I—"

"Look," I said, holding up my hand, "why don't you save that stuff for the campaign trail. I'm sure it'll go over great on the rubber chicken circuit."

He stared at me for a second, still with the smile on his face.

"Ha, ha," he laughed. "Like I said before, Jenny, you certainly are direct. You speak your mind. Well, I like that. Yes, I like that a lot."

He didn't look as if he liked it so much, but I let that pass.

"So when are we going to have our little get-together?" he said. "I'm busy today, but if—"

"That's not why I'm here," I told him.

"Oh, I just assumed . . ."

"I need to ask you some questions."

"Questions?" He leaned forward now and watched me closely. The smile was gone. "Questions about what?"

"Rikki Stiles."

"Rikki Stiles?" He rubbed his chin thoughtfully. "Uh, refresh my memory again. She's . . ."

Boy, he had a lot of trouble remembering that name.

"The hooker I found murdered on Sutton Place."

"Right, right. So how can I help?"

"First of all," I said, "did you hear about what happened to me in my apartment the other night?"

He nodded. "A police lieutenant called me up. Said two men with guns or something broke in and terrorized you and mentioned my name. He seemed to take it as some kind of threat against me. But we get so many threats here, I can't get too excited over every little—"

"It's a little more complicated than that," I said. "The two guys wanted to talk to me about Rikki Stiles. Like I told you last time, she came to me with a story about who pulled the Lancaster Hotel robbery. I didn't believe her then, but I do now. After she left our newsroom, she was killed. When I reported it on the air, I simply said she'd told me something that day without saying what it was. The pair in my apartment wanted to know what it was we talked about."

"And did you tell them?"

"Yes. I had a gun pointed at me, so I went through everything I knew about the Lancaster heist. And then a funny thing happened. They didn't want to hear about it. Said they didn't care about that at all. I was surprised, because I thought that was what the whole thing was about. But they were interested in something else."

"What's that?" Carson asked.

"You."

"As I said before, many mob bosses are obsessed with my crime-fighting successes and . . ."

I shook my head. "It's more than that. They asked me specifically about our meeting last week. How did they know about that?"

"I—I don't know." He shrugged. "Maybe they were following you."

"Did the police tell you who they were?"

"Yes. One of them works for Rossiello and the other is from Chicago."

"He's a professional killer. A hit man."

"Miss McKay, if the Jerry Rossiellos of the world weren't unhappy with me, I wouldn't be a very good DA. Fortunately I have an excellent security team, so I'm not overly concerned."

Carson stood up from behind his desk and made a show of looking at his watch. "Now if there's nothing else, Jenny, I do have some other appointments so . . ."

I didn't get up. Instead I finally took that cigarette out of my purse and lit it. It felt good. Helped me steady my nerves a bit. I took a deep puff, blew out some smoke, and looked across the desk at him.

"It's not that easy," I said. "There's more."

"Huh?" He sat down again. "What are you talking about?"

"Look, it's not just that Rossiello and his men were so interested in you. It's also that there's a connection with the Rikki Stiles murder. I mean they came after me because she told me something. Something they thought involved you."

"But she didn't. . . ."

"Okay, but that's not the point. The Stiles woman is. She's the common thread here. The key to this whole thing. Why?"

He shook his head. "I have no idea. This is all very confusing to me."

"Me too. But I keep coming back to her."

I looked at him.

"Did you know Rikki Stiles, Mr. Carson?"

His mouth dropped open and he stared at me in surprise.

"Me? Know her? How would I know her?"

"I don't know. That's why I'm asking. Was there ever any connection between the two of you?"

He ran his fingers through his hair nervously. There was perspiration on his forehead now.

"What do you mean, connection? With my *office*? Not that I know of. Of course, I suppose someone in my office could have been involved with an arrest of hers at some point. . . ."

"I'm not talking about your office," I said. "I'm talking about you."

His face flushed a bright red.

"Me? How in the hell would I know her?"

I sighed. "That's my question. I don't know. Maybe you prosecuted a case against her. Maybe you used her as an informant. Maybe your paths crossed at a party. Maybe you decided to stop off at her apartment on Sutton Place one night before heading home to the wife and kids in Larchmont. You tell me."

"That's totally absurd," he snapped.

"Then your answer is no? You didn't know her?"

"Of course it's no."

"And that's the truth?"

"Of course it's the truth." He glared at me. "What kind of a chickenshit question is that anyway?"

"Mr. Carson, I'm only trying to—"

"Who the hell do you think you're talking to, McKay? I'm the District Attorney of New York County. You act as if you think I'm guilty of something."

I shrugged.

"Let me tell you something else, young lady," he said, "I'm getting real tired of your smart mouth."

"Jeez, you used to think it was cute. I'm heartbroken."

"McKay, I happen to be a very substantial person in this community. I know a lot of people in media circles. . . ."

"Meaning?"

"Meaning I don't think the people who run your station are going to be too happy to find out they've got some sort of a kook running around making wild accusations like this."

I arched an eyebrow at him. "Is this the part where I'm supposed to apologize?" I asked. "Where I say I'm sorry? Where I say please don't get me in trouble with my bosses? Please don't make me lose my job?"

"You ought to worry about your job," he snapped. "And you just threw away any chance you had to have a good working relationship with me and—"

"I don't want to have a good working relationship with you," I said. "And I don't think you care about having one with me. I think you just wanted to talk to me the other day to find out what I knew."

I took another drag on the cigarette and stood up.

"The truth is, Mr. Carson," I said, "I don't believe you. I think there was some sort of connection between you and

Rikki Stiles. Exactly what it was, I don't know. But I'm going to try to find out. And when I do, I'm going to put it on the air. Do you understand that?"

Carson looked as if he were going to jump over the desk and punch me.

"Get out of here!" he yelled. "Get out of here before I call security and have them throw you out!"

I got out of there.

On my way through the outer office I passed by Carrie Macklin at her desk. All her papers on top were still organized in neat little piles. Everything was sparkling clean. The THANK YOU FOR NOT SMOKING sign still sat on the edge of the desk. She looked up at me and frowned when she saw the cigarette in my hand.

"Jenny, I'm afraid I'm going to have to ask you to put that out until you get outside."

That one did it.

I walked over to Carrie Macklin's desk, leaned very close to her, and blew a big puff of cigarette smoke in her face. Then I carefully took the cigarette out of my mouth, flicked some ashes all over her neat little piles of papers, and finally ground the cigarette butt out on her THANK YOU FOR NOT SMOKING sign. It left a big burn stain on it.

"Jenny, Jenny!" She coughed. "What are you doing?"

"Oh, by the way," I told her, pointing toward Carson's office, "I think he's gonna need you any second now."

Then I turned and walked out.

Okay, okay—it was childish. I know that.

But it made me feel a helluva lot better.

15

Nothin' Says Lovin' Like Somethin' From the Oven

The doorman on duty at Rikki Stiles's apartment building was the same young guy who had been there the first time I came.

"Hi," I said. I gave him a big smile. The friendly approach. Get him on your side, McKay. You catch more flies with honey than vinegar. "I wonder if you can help me."

He eyed me suspiciously. "Help you what?"

"Good answer." I reached into my purse, took out a card with my name and the Channel Six logo on it and handed it to him. "I'm a reporter."

He glanced down at the card and nodded.

"Rikki Stiles, huh? Jeez, I thought we'd seen the last of you people. Isn't this story old news yet?"

"Some of us are a little more persistent."

"And some of you are bigger pains in the ass."

The honey approach didn't seem to be working too well, but I plunged ahead anyway.

"So will you answer some questions?" I asked.

"You guys paying for interviews?"

"No," I told him.

"Then what's in it for me?"

"Just the satisfaction of a citizen knowing he's doing his role in helping to maintain a free and independent journalistic watchdog."

He smiled. He seemed to like that.

I reached into my purse again and took out a picture of Elliott Carson I'd copied earlier at the *Post* library. I showed it to him.

"Ever seen this man before?" I asked.

He looked at the picture. "Maybe. Like in the newspapers or something. Should I know him?"

"Ever seen him here? At this building?"

He shook his head. This time he was definite. "No. Never."

"Are you sure?"

"I'm sure."

"Maybe he came to visit one of the women who live here."

"No way. I know all the women in this building. I know who comes to visit them. A doorman sees all this stuff."

"Did you know Rikki Stiles?" I asked.

"Sure. She was one fine piece of work. A real knockout. That was a terrible thing that happened to her. Terrible."

"Then there's no chance you ever saw this man in the picture coming to see her?"

"Never," he said. "And I'd know."

After I finished talking with him, I went to a coffee shop across the street from the apartment house. There was a small table near the window where I could watch the front of the building, so I sat there and ordered some coffee. I wasn't sure why. Maybe hoping for inspiration to strike.

Of course, Elliott Carson could have slipped up to Rikki's apartment without the doorman seeing him. I mean I did it the day I found the body. Or maybe Carson even disguised himself. Somehow I didn't think he'd been here though. I couldn't see him furtively sneaking past the security cameras wearing a wide-brimmed hat and holding a newspaper in front of his face. He was more the type to pull up in a limousine.

It was still the middle of the day, so most people who lived in the building were at work. But a few tenants wandered in and out. I grabbed a couple of them and showed them the picture of Carson. No one recognized him. No one had ever seen him in the building. No one linked him to Rikki Stiles. No one knew anything.

Okay, so Carson never met Rikki Stiles at her apartment, that seemed apparent. Then what about someplace else? Not his place. That was up in Larchmont, with family and friends around. So it was out. What else was there? Maybe nothing. Maybe the whole thing was just a figment of my imagination.

I suddenly remembered somebody who might know the answer. Victor Galena. I found Galena's number in my notebook and called him from a pay phone.

"If Rikki Stiles ever slept with somebody important," I asked him, "would you know about it?"

He laughed. "Of course. I knew about everyone she slept with."

"Were there any important people?"

"Of course, dear. At the prices we charge, you have to be important to be able to afford them. You have no idea of the kind of people who spent time in that apartment. A real *Who's Who* of names."

"I don't care about the whole list," I said. "I want to ask you about a specific name."

"Can't help you," he said.

"Why not?"

"Professional ethics."

"Oh yeah, I'm sure that ranks real high in your list of priorities."

"I'm serious. I can't go around telling who sleeps with my girls. It's bad for business. Confidentiality is very important. If that's broken, I lose customers. No way."

"How about if I give you a name?" I said. "You just answer with a simple yes or no."

"I don't know. . ."

"Elliott Carson," I said.

He erupted in a fit of laughter. "The District Attorney? Oh, that's great. No, I can honestly tell you that Elliott Carson was not a customer of Rikki Stiles."

He was still laughing.

"That's really a riot. The District Attorney as one of her clients. You're a funny lady, McKay."

"Yeah," I said, "real funny, that's me."

When I got back to the office, everyone was waiting for me.

"Bob Carstairs wants to see you right away," Liz St. John told me.

She smiled broadly.

"He looks real mad."

"I'm glad you're so pleased by it," I said. "If he fires me, it'd probably make your day."

I walked into Carstairs's office. He was pacing around it with a kind of angry energy. Like a hungry lion just before feeding time at the zoo. When he saw me, I suddenly realized I was the red meat.

"You had to do it, didn't you?" he screamed.

"Do what, Bob?"

"You just couldn't leave well enough alone."

"Look, if you'll just tell me what it is I did, maybe—"

"You went to see Elliott Carson today."

"Oh," I said. "That."

"Yeah, that."

"He called, huh?"

"Yes, he called. Not me. Not even Andrew Cafferty, who runs this station. No, Carson called Andrew's father, Edward R. Cafferty, chairman of the board and president emeritus. Following that phone call, Cafferty called his son and yelled at him. Then Andrew Cafferty called me and began yelling. That's the way a chain of command works. The people at the bottom get all the grief from the top. Now I've only got one person below me I can give grief to over this. Starting to get the picture, McKay?"

I nodded. "What did Carson say?"

"That you called him a liar. Questioned his integrity. Threatened him. He said you acted irrational, unstable— suggested you might be on drugs or alcohol or something."

"Did he tell anyone exactly what we talked about?"

Carstairs shook his head. "No, I don't think so."

"Interesting," I said.

I told him everything I'd found out about Rikki Stiles along with my suspicions.

"So you decided on your own that Elliott Carson had some sort of affair with this dead hooker?" Carstairs said when I was finished. "What did you think he was going to do when you marched into his office and told him all this? Confess?"

"I don't know—I guess I wanted to shake him up. Make something happen. Maybe I did."

"Well, it doesn't matter because you're off the story. In fact, you're off any story."

I stared at him. "You mean I'm suspended?"

"Sure. Why not?"

"You can't suspend me. You just suspended me the week before last. And then you reinstated me last week. This is getting ridiculous."

"Okay, you're not suspended. Not officially. But you're not doing any news either until further notice."

"What am I doing?"

"Well . . . well . . . today you can fill in for Rebecca James. She called in sick a few hours ago."

"Rebecca James? The woman who does the 'At Home With' segment?"

"That's right."

"At Home With" was a segment of consumer tips for housewives. Stuff like how to bake a casserole, keeping your house clean—some of the real issues of our times like that. The last time I'd watched it, Rebecca demonstrated the proper way to defrost a refrigerator. The key, as I remember it, was to not let your frozen dinners thaw out. We're not exactly talking "60 Minutes" here.

"Bob, I'm not the Happy Homemaker type. I need a cookbook to boil water. I got dust bunnies in my apartment so big I could put a leash on them and walk them with my dog. My kitchen and bathroom are on the EPA's list of top ten toxic hot spots. . . ."

Carstairs waved me off with an angry shrug.

"I don't want to hear this," he said. "Now, your guest on tonight's show is going to explain to you how to make a lemon meringue pie. She'll go through all the steps in the baking process—from getting the ingredients together to the finished product." He paused. "I hope you won't find the need to consult with the District Attorney of New York over this assignment."

"Lemon meringue," I muttered.

"And don't forget the homemaker tip at the end."

"Oh, Jesus, Bob. . . ."

The homemaker tip was a little slogan or verse or phrase Rebecca James always gave to the audience as she was signing off. It was sort of her trademark. Her own little shtick, I guess. Like I said, everybody but me has a shtick. Even the Happy Homemaker.

"How about 'home is where the hell is,' " I suggested.

"Just get out there and get to work, McKay."

I went back to my desk, picked up a newspaper, and paged through it to the TV listings. Lemon meringue pie, huh? "48 Hours" was doing a special tonight on Colombian drug dealers. Peter Jennings was interviewing East Germans at the site where the Berlin Wall used to be. Me, I was giving housewives a recipe for lemon meringue pie.

Yep, you've come a long way, baby.

I looked through the rest of the TV listings. There was a movie on Channel Eleven at 2 a.m. called *Chicago Deadline*, starring Alan Ladd and Donna Reed. It was about a reporter investigating the death of a call girl. Hmmm. I made a note to set my VCR to tape it before I went to bed. Maybe I'd pick up some tips.

Carstairs came into the newsroom to consult with Conroy and Liz over the opening of the show.

"Hey, Bob," I said, walking over to him, "I got a great idea for a real ratings grabber. How about I come out on camera dressed in a skimpy bikini like Stormy Phillips? Then, after the pie is finished baking, I stick my fingers into the lemon meringue and begin spreading it all over my body. We could even run a contest—you know, the winner gets to come on the air and lick it all off of me. Finally I wrap it all up with my homemaker tip for the day. . . .

" 'Nothin' says lovin' like somethin' from the oven.' "

Carstairs didn't like that slogan either.

There's just no pleasing some people.

16

John Gotti Doesn't Eat Here Anymore

I was supposed to meet Gallagher at eight o'clock at a restaurant called Sparks Steak House.

By the time I got there, it was closer to eight-forty.

"Jeez, I was starting to wonder if you were going to show up," he said, as I slipped into the seat across the table from him.

"Sorry. I got tied up at work."

"Big story?"

I shrugged.

"So what was it?" he asked. "Triple homicide? A four-alarm fire? A kidnapping?"

"My piecrust was underdone."

Gallagher stared at me.

"Don't even ask," I said.

Sparks is a lavish restaurant in Manhattan's Steak Row with dark wood paneling, elegant chandeliers, and a menu specializing in sirloins, filet mignons, and huge lobsters. It gained a measure of fame a few years ago when a big mobster named Paul Castellano, the New York "boss of bosses," was gunned down outside the front door as he was coming in for dinner. Everyone always figured his arch rival, John Gotti, did it, and the feds finally got enough evidence to send him away to prison.

The mob rubout led to a spate of Sparks Steak House jokes. I mean people would talk about calling up the restaurant and saying stuff like, "Can I have a reservation for a party of six in the no-shooting section?" Or else some guy would order duck and everyone around him would dive under the tablecloth. Frankly, I thought the owners should have paid off John Gotti for all the free publicity.

"So how come we're eating here?" I asked Gallagher. "You on stakeout in case someone else gets rubbed out?"

"Nah, the food's just real good. Mob guys know how to eat, I'll say that for them."

"Yeah, I know," I told him. "You've heard of the Gotti List, right?"

"Sure. It's a list of all the Italian restaurants around town that John Gotti's people frequent these days. Nobody from the force is supposed to eat in them—even while off duty. Fraternizing with the enemy or something. It's a long list too."

"A friend of mine at the police shack got ahold of a copy of it," I said, nibbling on a bread stick, "and we started making the rounds. Best Italian food I've ever eaten. Got halfway through it before we stopped."

"Only halfway? What happened?"

"I put on twenty pounds," I said.

The waiter brought us drinks and menus.

"So what's good?" I asked Gallagher.

"Try the sirloin steak. Very rare. It makes you feel like an animal eating it."

"Like an animal. That's good?"

"Well, sometimes." He smiled at me. "I can think of one place where it's really exciting to be an animal. . . ."

"Don't do this," I said.

"Do what?"

"Come on to me."

"I'm not coming on to you."

"Sure you are."

"Okay, I am."

I put down my menu and looked at him.

"You know, we're just here to have dinner," I said.

"Dinner," he repeated.

"Yeah. No romance. No sex. No innuendos across the table. Just dinner."

"Is it okay if I fantasize quietly to myself about you nibbling on that bread stick?"

"You're doing it again."

"Sorry. Lost my head."

"Look," I told him, "the last thing in the world I'm going to do is get involved with a guy who's got a sick wife and two kids—one of them with very serious problems too—waiting at home. What kind of a woman do you think I am?"

I didn't get an answer to that one. The waiter showed up for our order. Gallagher went for the steak. I decided to try the lobster tails. That was as animalistic as I was going to get.

"So let's change the subject," he said after the waiter was gone.

"Sure. What do you want to talk about?"

"How about your friend Elliott Carson?"

"I think he's dirty," I said.

"Dirty? Dirty how?"

"Dirty in that he was doing something with Rikki Stiles, the dead call girl."

"You mean like sex?"

"Well, I don't think he was giving her art lessons."

"Elliott Carson, Mr. All-around Wonderful, in the sack with a call girl." Gallagher chortled. "Boy, that would really put a crimp in his campaign bandwagon, wouldn't it?"

"I'm sure that thought has crossed his mind too," I said.

"So how do you know this?"

I told him everything that had happened.

"You don't have much there except a lot of speculation," he said somewhat dubiously when I was finished.

"Yeah, but it's solid speculation."

"Still—the pimp didn't know about it, and neither did anyone at her building. So how and where did these encounters between Carson and the Stiles woman take place?"

"I'm still working on that."

"You're still working on that," he muttered.

The waiter brought our food.

"How about Johnny Camancho?" I asked, slicing off a piece of my lobster and dipping it into a huge cup of melted butter. I popped the butter-drenched lobster into my mouth. Succulent. Definitely succulent. Between the teeth, over the gums, look out thighs—here it comes.

"Still missing," Gallagher said.

"Any leads so far in tracking him down?"

Gallagher cut off a big piece of his steak and chewed on it without saying anything.

"That was a question," I pointed out. "It's meant to elicit a response."

"Yeah, well . . ."

"There is something new!" I said.

He shrugged. "I was trying to keep it quiet. I was afraid you'd start speculating and . . ."

"So let me speculate."

"Okay, they found Camancho's car early this morning on the Tappan Zee Bridge. The motor was running, his wallet left behind on the front seat, and someone said they thought they saw somebody go into the water."

"You think he jumped?" I asked.

"Maybe."

"Or else he just wanted to make it look like he did to throw people off his track."

"That thought crossed my mind too."

"You say his wallet was on the front seat?"

"Yep. Just sitting there for us to find, all nice and neat. And then, of course, there was the phone call I told you about.

Someone called the state troopers and said they thought they saw a man jumping off the bridge."

Gallagher shook his head. "We're officially listing it as a possible suicide, but it seems a little too pat, doesn't it? I mean everybody in the world is looking for this guy Camancho. You. Us. Probably whoever knocked off his brother, unless he did it himself. So why suicide? He wanted to stay alive, that was his problem. So that leaves us with two other alternatives."

"Yeah," I said, "one, someone pushed him off the bridge and made it look like suicide. Two, he set up a phony suicide to get the heat off for a while and make people think he was dead."

He smiled at me. "Elementary, my dear McKay, elementary."

"But what about Elliott Carson?" I said, shaking my head. "How does he fit into all this?"

"I don't want to know," Gallagher said.

"Why not? You told me you didn't like the guy. Wouldn't you like to expose him if he's up to no good? Don't you want to be the one to bring him down?"

Gallagher sighed. "Look, after a while as a cop you just have an instinct about some things. I've got one about Carson and this whole mess. You say he's involved in it somehow— maybe innocently, maybe not—but involved nevertheless. I think you may be right. But so what? There's no way to come out ahead on something like this. If I cause any kind of a stink and I'm wrong, I can kiss my career good-bye. And if I'm right—well, if I'm right then the shit's really gonna hit the fan and a lot of other people are going to get smeared too. That's not going to make me very popular either. So I'd rather just keep my nose clean. Life's easier that way."

"Does that mean you won't do anything if you find out he *is* involved?"

"No," Gallagher said slowly, "but it means I need more than you've come up with."

After we finished eating, Gallagher gave me a ride back to my place. He parked the car in front and shut off the engine.

"I'll walk you to your door," he said.

"That's okay. I'm fine."

"Maybe I could come up and have some coffee or something. . . ."

I shook my head. "I don't think so."

"Why not?"

"Because we both know what's happening here. If I invite you in for coffee, that's an invitation for something more. We drink coffee, talk a bit, and then you try to get me into the sack. Am I right?"

"Maybe."

"I can read your mind like a book."

"Then again maybe I'm just thirsty for coffee," he said.

"There's a diner on the corner if it's just coffee you're looking for."

He didn't say anything. We sat there silently in the car for a few seconds. Finally I reached for the door handle, opened it, and got out. That was all there was to it. Thank him for the dinner, then go up to my place and call it a night. Let him go back to his sick wife and kids on Long Island. Yep, that was the thing to do, all right.

I leaned back into the open car window.

"So you want to come up and let me make you some coffee?" I asked.

He smiled. "I'd love some coffee."

Actually, I let him make the coffee. While he was doing that, I gave Hobo his evening walk. Then we sat around in my living room for a while drinking coffee, chatting and watching TV.

The end of the eleven o'clock news was on, and then "The Honeymooners." I love "The Honeymooners." Seen them all about a hundred times. This was the one where Ralph tries to convince Alice to give him money to sell a kitchen device called the Vegamatic, then goes on TV to peddle it. I watched until somewhere around the time they started doing the beginning of the ad—"whoa, yes, it can core an apple," Ralph says—and then that's all I remember. Maybe because by that time Rick Gallagher and I were in each other's arms and kissing up a storm on the couch. By the time "Star Trek" came on at midnight and the *Enterprise* was exploring strange new worlds, we were in the bedroom exploring each other, making love.

It was past 2 a.m. when Gallagher finally got out of bed and started to get dressed.

"You can stay the night, if you want," I said.

"I can't," he said as he pulled on his clothes.

"Okay."

"I'm sorry. I'd like to. But I've got to get home. My wife and . . ."

"I understand."

He leaned down and kissed me.

"I'll call you."

"Promise?"

"Promise."

He kissed me again. A longer kiss this time. I felt a tingle go through me.

"I want to see you again, Jenny," he said. "I want to see you a lot. Are we going to be able to do that, Jenny?"

I sighed. "I wouldn't be a bit surprised."

After he was gone, I couldn't fall asleep right away. I wandered into the kitchen and found some chocolate marshmallow ice cream in the freezer. I figured it would go good with the buttered lobster I had earlier. I carried it back into the bedroom and ate it in bed.

Hobo was at the foot of the bed staring at me.

"I know what you're thinking," I said. "I'm not proud of myself either. I know he's a married man, I know he's got responsibilities at home. I probably shouldn't have gone out to dinner with him. I probably shouldn't have invited him up here. And I definitely shouldn't have gone to bed with him."

Hobo just kept staring.

"The trouble with you," I told him, "is you're just a dog. You don't understand life. Sometimes the choices aren't so easy. Sometimes these things just happen. Trust me."

Hobo heaved a big sigh, put his head down on the blanket, and closed his eyes.

I don't think he bought it.

I finished off the last of the ice cream, which was probably a mistake. My stomach didn't feel so good. Neither did my conscience. I made my way toward the bathroom. On the way I passed by a mirror and happened to catch a glimpse of myself in it. I didn't like what I saw.

Forty-one years old, kid, and you're alone again. You're falling in love with a married man. You had sex with him while his sick wife and kids waited for him to come home. And you've got chocolate marshmallow ice cream all over your chin.

Way to go, McKay.

This one's a new low, even for you.

17

From the Same Folks Who Gave You Pearl Harbor

We were supposed to show up at an advertisers' reception the next morning at the Plaza Hotel.

The idea was to let potential advertisers get to meet all the on-air Channel Six personnel. The WTBK news team; Fitz Donnelly, who had a daytime talk show; Gail Benton, our morning exercise lady; and even Zach Gilroy, who dressed up in werewolf makeup and hosted a Saturday night monster movie for kids. It was the first time I ever saw Gilroy without his makeup. He had a flushed, drinker's complexion and big blue veins running through his nose and really bad teeth. Frankly, he looked better with the werewolf makeup on.

Carstairs had explained it to me after the newscast the night before.

"These are very important people, Jenny," he said. "There's a lot of money at stake here. And a lot of our careers too. Don't screw this up."

"Meaning what?"

"Meaning don't do anything stupid or embarrassing. Don't insult anybody. Don't question anyone's political views. And, for God's sakes, don't mention anything about Elliott Carson and this goddamned dead hooker you're so obsessed with. Got that?"

"So what am I supposed to talk about? The weather?"

"Sure. Or, if all else fails, just tell everyone, 'I'm really glad to have the chance to meet you.' "

"B-o-o-o-ring," I said.

"Boring is good. I like boring. Boring will make me a very happy man."

I didn't say anything.

"I'm asking you nice on this, Jenny. Don't screw it up. I mean it."

"Can I get off the Betty Crocker beat?" I asked, gesturing toward the kitchen area on the news set where I'd baked the pie.

"You do this right, and we'll talk about it afterward. Okay?"

"Okay."

After he left, I turned to Sanders, who'd been listening to the whole thing. "What do you think?" I asked.

He shook his head. "My advice to you is to begin drinking very heavily very early tomorrow."

"Great. Why?"

"That way, if you're lucky, you'll be unconscious before this thing is over."

"I don't know," I said, "somehow I think passing out drunk in the middle of a roomful of advertisers falls under the category of doing something stupid or embarrassing."

So here I was now walking through the lobby of the Plaza, heading for the Oak Room where the reception was being held. I knew I was in trouble when I met Linda Fairmont at the door. She handed me a name tag and told me to wear it on my chest. The name tag said: "Hi, I'm Jenny McKay."

After she walked away, I took out a pen and drew a smiling happy face in the corner of the tag. Then I crossed out Jenny McKay and wrote in the name "Squeaky Fromme." I put it back on my chest and went inside. My own little protest.

Walking into a roomful of advertisers is a terrifying experience. A lot of Madison Avenue types dressed in pin-striped suits. All talking about advertising slogans and sales curves and demographic surveys. I kept picking up little snatches of conversation that meant nothing to me—stuff like "Didn't he just lose Proctor and Gamble?" or "I hear they're going two years, two million dollars with J. Walter Thompson."

I know very little about the advertising business. In fact, when I think about Madison Avenue, I always think about the Japanese. That's because a few years back I read a best-seller some advertising guy did about the business in which he tells about struggling to come up with a slogan for a new line of Japanese TV sets. This goes on for hours, so finally the guy gets giddy and announces: "I got it! How about 'From the Same Folks Who Gave You Pearl Harbor.' " No one in the room even smiled. But it always cracked me up.

I walked over and found Carstairs talking to a group of advertisers. He was drinking a Bloody Mary and holding a bagel. He introduced me around to everybody.

"I'm really glad to meet you all," I said. Carstairs looked on approvingly.

"Jenny McKay, huh?" one of the men said. "I've seen you. You're good. Really good."

"Well, thanks. I've broken a few pretty good stories, but I've been lucky. For instance, when I did a political corruption story last year . . ."

"It was last night I saw you, as a matter of fact. You were giving a demonstration of how to bake a pie. I brought the wife into the study and told her to watch it. We were both damned impressed."

"Uh . . . yeah."

"You know, there are so many women running around these days trying to prove they're something they're not. It's good to see a woman on TV who's not ashamed—"

"To know her place is in the kitchen?" I suggested.

"Hey, I know that sounds bad, but there's nothing wrong with the kitchen. My mother spent her life in the kitchen. And it didn't hurt her at all."

Carstairs was eyeing me nervously, waiting for the explosion. But there wasn't any. I just kept a phony smile plastered on my face.

"Did I mention," I said to the guy, "that I'm damned glad to meet you?"

I wandered off to another group of men who were standing around talking. They were discussing what the best shows have been on TV for the advertising dollar. One of them said "L.A. Law" because it had really upscale demographics. Another said "The Cosby Show"' because it reached into the black community.

"How about 'The Brady Bunch?' " I asked.

Everyone turned around to look at me.

" 'The Brady Bunch' is what America is all about," I said. "Family, home, middle-class values. It touches everyone you want to reach. Did you see that Brady Bunch Christmas reunion a few years ago? The ratings went through the roof."

"Miss . . ." one of them of peered at my name tag, "Miss Fromme?"

Dammit, I'd forgotten about that. "No, it's a mistake. I'm Jenny McKay, Channel Six News."

They nodded in recognition now.

" 'The Brady Bunch' was to the seventies what 'The Cosby Show' was to the eighties and what we need for the nineties," I continued.

"In other words," one of them said, "you're saying the best demographic buy for our advertising dollar would be an updated version of the Brady family?"

"Exactly."

"But didn't they try to bring them back and they flopped?"

"That's because they brought back the real Bradys. We don't want the real Bradys anymore, because they're *not* the real Bradys. Am I making myself clear? I mean Florence Henderson isn't Mrs. Brady anymore to most people—she's just some middle-aged woman who does cooking oil commercials."

"Well, then how . . ."

"We create a new family like the Bradys. Only hipper. More nineties. And one that cuts across all demographic lines. We get a black guy like Bill Cosby to play the father. Then he marries an Asian—like Connie Chung or somebody. And they adopt all these kids—black, Chinese, Hispanic—maybe even throw in an Indian. And they've got to have a dog too. And that's the Bradys of the nineties."

There were murmurs of agreement all around. They liked it. They liked it a lot.

Hey, maybe this advertising business wasn't so hard after all.

It was about forty-five minutes of banal conversations later that I saw Carstairs standing next to me again. I quickly told the guy I was talking to, "I'm really glad to meet you." But Carstairs didn't seem to notice. I noticed that the Bloody Mary in his hand before was now straight vodka.

"You're doing good," he said. "I appreciate it."

"Thanks."

I looked around the room. The rest of the news team—Conroy, Liz, Stormy—were still milling around talking to people. Suddenly I thought about something. I turned to Carstairs.

"Where's Hanrahan?"

"Hanrahan?" He pronounced it sloppily. Not exactly drunk, but just with the slight slurring people get when they've had a bit too much to drink. "Hanrahan is . . . history."

"You fired him?"

"I fired him. Last night."

"Amazing." I watched as he gripped his glass tighter. "So what is this now—guilt? Getting yourself drunk because you feel bad about axing ol' Billy?"

"What do you know about firing anyone, McKay?"

"Not much. But I know a lot about guilt."

He stared down at his glass.

"So are you?" I asked.

"Am I what?"

"Feeling a little guilty this morning?"

"Maybe. So what?"

"Well, I don't think it's a very good idea to drown it in that stuff," I told him. "You're not going to do the station or yourself any good. Get drunk on your own time if you want to."

I reached over and took the drink out of his hand. He didn't stop me.

"How about you and I get some coffee and take a walk?" I said.

I poured two cups of coffee from an urn on one of the tables and then led Carstairs out of the Oak Room. We wandered through the hotel down toward the lobby. There was an empty couch there next to a window overlooking Fifth Avenue. We sat down and Carstairs drank the coffee in silence for a few minutes.

"He cried, you know," Carstairs said. "Bill Hanrahan broke down and cried when I told him he was fired. Said I was destroying his life and begged me to let him stay."

"But you didn't."

"No. I wanted to, but I couldn't."

"Why not?"

"Because everyone else said he had to go. The fuckin' ratings people and the fuckin' demographics people and the fuckin' station owner and fuckin' Linda Fairmont and her fuckin' media consultant agency. . . ." He stared down at his coffee cup. It was empty now. I hadn't touched mine, so I handed it to him.

"Did you think Hanrahan had to be fired?" I asked.

He shook his head. "Not really."

"So why didn't you go with your instincts? Do what you thought was right?"

"That's what you'd do, huh?"

"I like to think so."

"Yeah, you probably would."

He took another sip of his coffee and grunted.

"Jenny McKay, the ultimate idealistic newspaperwoman. Truth and justice and morality will always prevail. You must have watched too much Lois Lane when you were a kid. You really believe that crap."

"Maybe you'd understand it if you ever worked for a newspaper instead of in TV. . . ."

"I did."

"Huh?"

"I used to own this little newspaper in northern California," he said.

I was stunned. "I didn't know that."

"Yep. Bought it with my life savings. I wanted to be a small-time editor fighting for good and right and noble causes. And I found one too. I discovered that some of the local restaurant owners were keeping their liquor licenses by paying bribes to state officials. Boy, I was gonna blow the lid off with this one. I could smell Pulitzer prize if I broke the story."

"Did you?"

"Oh, I broke it all right. Only I didn't get a Pulitzer. What I got was an advertisers' boycott. Followed by a reader boycott. The state officials I wrote about were so powerful that they turned everyone in town against me and I lost the paper. I lost my life savings. I lost everything."

"So you got scared, huh?"

"Not scared, McKay. I got smart. I decided to play the game from the inside. So I got me a job in the TV industry, and I've been very successful."

"You really think it's success?"

"Hey, don't give me that holier-than-thou bullshit. I've made a lot of money and I've got a big office and I've got a house in the Hamptons and I drive a BMW."

I nodded. "And those restaurant owners in California are probably still paying bribes to state officials, huh?"

He stared at me for a few seconds. "Probably," he said.

"Maybe sometimes it's not such a good idea to be smart," I told him. "Maybe sometimes—every once in a while—you need to do something dumb. Something you just feel in your gut is the right thing to do. Something that makes you remember why you got into journalism in the first place."

Carstairs smiled. "Like going after a story about a dead hooker even after everybody tells you not to?"

"That's one example."

"Do you really think Elliott Carson's involved in all this?"

"Yes. I'm just not sure exactly how."

"He's a very powerful man in this city," Carstairs said. "Knows a lot of people. Not the least of whom is the owner of our station. If you're wrong about this—or maybe even if you're right—the shit really hits the fan and we all get splattered. I don't like the odds."

"It's not a smart thing to do," I agreed.

He thought about it for a second. "Okay, dig into it a little more. But quietly. Very quietly."

"You mean I'm back on the story again?"

"Yeah."

"You really mean it? I mean, this isn't just the liquor talking? You're going to remember this conversation tomorrow?"

"I told you you're back on the story, that means you're back on the story. You want me to get a goddamned notary public in here and sign an affidavit saying it?" He drank some more coffee. "So what do you know about it?"

I told him about Johnny Camancho's car being found and the possible suicide attempt.

"Great," he said, "that sounds safe enough. We'll just report it straight tonight and it'll keep the story going. You go back to the office, pick up a film crew, and go up and shoot some live footage with the Tappan Zee Bridge in the background."

"I'm on my way."

I stood up.

"Oh, and McKay . . ."

"Yeah?"

He glanced down at the name tag on my chest. "Just make sure that when you do your tag line tonight, you don't sign off by saying: 'This is Squeaky Fromme, reporting live for Channel Six News.' "

On my way out of the Plaza, I saw one of the advertising guys I'd been talking to earlier. He was waiting for a cab with some people. "What we need to find," I heard him say, "is a new Brady Bunch family. 'The Brady Bunch' was to the seventies what 'The Cosby Show' was to the eighties and what we need for the nineties."

This made me very happy. I whistled "The Brady Bunch" theme song all the way back to the office.

18

Sex and the Single Reporter

I had a helluva joke ready for Hobo when I got home that night. A humdinger. A Class-A, guaranteed thigh-slapper. Well, it wasn't actually very funny at all, but it was an animal joke so I figured he'd go for it.

"Here it is," I announced to him. "This duck walks into a restaurant, sits down at a table, and orders dinner.

"WAITER: I can't serve you.
DUCK: Why not?
WAITER: You've got no money. How are you going to pay?
DUCK: That's okay. Just put it on my bill.

"Put it on my bill!" I chuckled. "Don't you get it? He's a duck—put it on his bill." I laughed loudly, and Hobo licked my face excitedly. "I got a million of 'em, kid."

I was just finishing with his walk and supper when the telephone rang. It was Rick Gallagher.

"Hi," he said. "You up for a little romantic liaison tonight?"

"Sure." I paused. "With you?"

"That was the general idea. How about I come by at eleven or so?"

"Eleven?" I looked at the clock. That was a couple of hours away. "What happened to the whole seduction routine? You know—dinner, movie, flowers? I mean we've had one date and now it's 'I'll see you in bed.' "

He laughed. "I've got to work the night shift until ten-thirty. Look, if it's too late . . ."

"No, it's not too late," I sighed.

"Great. I'll see you then."

Since it looked like a long night, I decided to take a little nap while I was waiting for him. I'd just taken my clothes off and crawled under the covers when someone buzzed me from the lobby. I got out of bed and pressed the intercom.

"This better be good," I said.

"It's . . . it's Mike Stoner. Can I come up?"

Damn, I had a dinner date with him for tonight. I'd forgotten all about it.

"Uh . . . sure. No problem."

I managed to pull on some clothes by the time he knocked on the door. Hobo gave him the same greeting I got when I got home. Thumping tail, slobbery kisses. As a matter of fact, Hobo gave that greeting to everybody—jokes or no jokes, whether he knew them or not. If Charles Manson walked in someday, I have no doubt Hobo would welcome him like a long-lost friend.

We sat in the living room and talked for a while. Stoner was wearing a dark blue suit, white shirt, and a striped navy blue and white tie. Very color-coordinated, very conservative. I was neither. I was wearing a pair of faded blue jeans with a hole in the knee, yellow bunny slippers that Hobo had chewed all the fur off of, and a bright orange T-shirt that said "Born to Party." I was starting to feel underdressed in my own house.

"Do you think maybe you could loosen your tie or something so you don't look so much like an IRS agent?" I asked finally.

Stoner smiled, unbuttoned his collar, and undid the knot. "How's that?"

"Like an IRS agent with his tie loosened," I said.

"Sorry. . . ."

"Just kidding. It's fine."

He looked at me and over toward the kitchen, where nothing was happening. "I didn't catch you by surprise or anything, did I? I mean you did say we were going to have dinner here tonight. . . ."

"Oh, sure."

There was a long pause.

"So are we?" he asked finally.

"Are we what?"

"Going to have dinner here?"

"Well, there could be a slight problem. You see, I don't have anything in the house to eat."

"People always say that." He smiled. "But they don't really mean it. Let's go check out the kitchen. I'll bet we can find something."

"It's your funeral." I shrugged.

We went into the kitchen and opened up the refrigerator.

"What we basically have to work with here is some eggs, a half a head of lettuce, one very small tomato, and some lunch meat that looks like it used to be salami," I said.

"What do you recommend?"

"That we stay away from the lunch meat."

"I'll go along with that."

"How about we cook the eggs and judiciously divide the tomato and lettuce for salads? I'd also suggest the eggs be scrambled, since that's the only way I really know how to make them."

"Didn't you say something about being a great cook when I came by your station the other day?"

"I lied."

He laughed. "That's okay. I lied too when I said I had some business in the area."

I cooked the eggs while he sliced up the tomato and lettuce for the salad. Then we carried it into the living room and put it all on the coffee table, sitting side by side on the sofa.

"You know," he said as he ate, "I don't usually make it a point to meet women like this. I mean audit them, then come over their house for dinner."

"Not to mention saving them from the clutches of desperate gunmen." I took a forkful of eggs. "So how do you usually meet women?"

"Actually I don't very often."

"C'mon, a guy like you? Good-looking, good job, decent salary. You probably have to beat them off with a stick. You ever been married?"

"Not yet."

"How old are you?"

"Thirty-six."

"Hey, you're going for my record. I'm at forty-one and counting. Where do you live?"

"Queens."

"Queens?"

"Anything wrong with that?"

"Nope. Nice borough." I tried some salad. "A little far away though. How long have you been there?"

"Thirty-six years."

"Jesus! You mean you—"

"I live where I grew up," he said. He saw the look of amazement on my face. "Oh, I don't mean I still live with my mother or anything like that, if that's what you're thinking. . . ."

"Where does she live?" I asked.

He cleared his throat nervously. "Oh, a good block and a half away."

"Boy, you really cut the ol' apron strings, didn't you?"

"I like living in Queens. I just don't think I'm the Manhattan type. It's okay for work during the day, but not at night."

"You're in Manhattan tonight," I pointed out.

His face reddened noticeably. "That's because . . ."

"Of me?"

"Yes." He seemed to summon up all his courage now. "Because I like you."

I smiled. "That's nice. That's very nice."

There was an awkward silence for a few seconds.

"How about you?" he asked finally. "How'd you manage to avoid marriage for so long?"

"I guess I'm just waiting for the right man to come along," I said.

"The right man? You mean as opposed to the wrong man?"

"Oh, I've met a lot of those. Almost married a few too. But it never worked out, so it's just me and Hobo."

I'd finished my meal. I pushed my empty plate away and leaned back on the couch.

"It's funny, I always sorta thought I'd get married. Even now, I figure it's just a matter of time, that I'm just not ready for it yet. Only time seems to be slipping away more rapidly these days. I think I'm moving into the 'it's now or never' age zone. Forty-one is a serious age."

"You don't look forty-one," he said. "You seem very youthful."

I gave him a funny look. "You want to run that past me again?"

"I said you look very youthful. What's the matter—you don't believe me?"

"Oh, I believe you, all right. I just wanted to hear you say it again."

He laughed and moved close to me on the couch. Very close. He still seemed nervous, but determined too. He put his arm around the back of the couch and touched my hair. "I *really* like you," he said as he leaned over and kissed me.

I kissed him back. Sort of. I mean, I wanted to kiss him the right way, I really liked him. But I knew where this was headed and I also knew Rick Gallagher was coming over soon to spend the night. This worked out, according to my calculations, as one man too many.

He seemed to sense something was wrong after a few minutes. "Look, I guess I'm not very good at this. . . ."

"You're fine," I said.

"Well, then why . . ."

"It's . . . I've got a little problem. Someone else is coming over."

He seemed puzzled. "Who?"

"A friend."

"I see. Can I stay?"

"Well, no, he's not really a friend. He's more of a . . ."

"A lover?"

I sighed. "Yeah."

He moved away from me on the couch now. The moment was over, I could tell that from the body language. "Is this someone you're serious about?" he asked.

"No." I thought about it for a second. "Actually, yes."

"Serious as in getting married to him?"

"He's already married," I said.

Stoner was staring at me as if he'd never seen me before.

"Oh, it's not what you think," I told him. "He's married in name only. You see, his wife is sick and he can't leave her so he just dates on the side and . . ."

I stopped. It still didn't sound any better. Somehow it only worked when Gallagher was telling it.

Stoner stood up. "I better be going then. Thanks for dinner."

"Hey, wait," I yelled after him. He kept walking. "This is really awkward. I'm sorry it worked out this way, but I can't even reach him to tell him not to come so . . ."

"Why did you even invite me over here if you're in love with this guy?" he asked. "I'm curious."

"Because," I said, "I wasn't in love with him then."

"Oh? So when did this great love affair start then?"

"Last night," I managed weakly.

He shook his head and stalked out the door. I called after

him to stop, but he didn't. He just kept walking and disappeared down the steps. I sighed, shut the door, and looked at Hobo.

"Well, all things considered," I said, "I think I handled that rather well, don't you?" Hobo just gave me that same funny look he did when I slept with Rick Gallagher.

Gallagher showed up a little while later. At first I couldn't get Mike Stoner out of my mind, but then we went to bed and I started thinking about other things. I made love with him wildly, passionately—almost angrily. It was almost as if by throwing myself totally into it I could somehow erase the guilt I felt over what I was doing. I wondered if that had ever happened to Rikki Stiles.

When it was over, we fell asleep together with my head on his chest. Later, in the middle of the night, I woke up to find his chest gone and only Hobo sleeping next to me. There was no sign of Rick Gallagher. Only a note on the pillow which said he was sorry to leave so soon, but . . . .

Damn, he did it to me again!

I was too mad to sleep so I switched on the TV. All I could find at that hour of the morning were home shopping networks and Richard Simmons telling me how to lose weight. Finally I watched the tape I'd made the other night of the movie with Alan Ladd and Donna Reed called *Chicago Deadline*. Alan Ladd finds a murdered call girl's little black book with the names of a lot of bigwigs in it and solves the case in two hours flat. Made it look easy. I wondered why I couldn't do the same thing. Why didn't Rikki Stiles leave behind a little black book with her clients' names in it?

Besides, no one ever left Donna Reed in the middle of the night.

I was finally drifting off again when something in the movie dawned on me. I sat up with a start.

"Jesus Christ!" I said aloud.

Hobo looked over across the bed.

"I think I have an idea," I told him.

He yawned and went back to sleep.

19
There's Something Happening Here

I called Gallagher the next morning.

"I guess I must have missed your departure last night," I told him.

"I left you a note."

"Thanks, it was really romantic too. What did it say again? Oh yeah—'Gotta run. See ya. Rick.' "

"Actually it was 'Love, Rick.' "

"Really? Jeez, I guess I was so overcome with emotion I missed that."

"Did you just call to bust my chops?" he sighed.

"Nah. I'm looking for some information. What happened to all the stuff in Rikki Stiles's apartment?"

"You mean her clothes?"

"Clothes. Books. All her personal belongings. Where're they at now?"

"Hold on a second. Let me check."

He came back on the line in a few seconds. I could hear him rustling through some sheets of paper.

"Stiles . . . or Callandro, I guess . . . personal belongings.

Let's see . . . okay, here it is. They were held by us for a couple of days because we didn't know the next of kin. Then, when the next of kin turned up, it was forwarded on. Personal property always goes automatically to the next of kin, once we know who it is."

"The next of kin in this case being . . ."

"Her mother. In Cleveland. You should know, you're the one who found her. She called us that day after you talked to her, made arrangements for the burial, and had her daughter's things shipped on to her."

"Right. The mother in Cleveland." I tried to word my next question carefully. "Was there anything in that stuff you sent to Cleveland that seemed . . . well, seemed pertinent to the case?"

"Pertinent to the case? My, my, don't we talk fancy? You been watching 'Murder, She Wrote' a lot?"

"Okay, were there any clues there?"

"Clues?"

"Yeah. Something that might help solve her murder."

"Sure, lots of them. But we didn't do anything. We were waiting for you to come along and brilliantly solve the whole thing for us."

"There were no clues," I said.

"Of course there were no clues. Do you really think we would have released her stuff to the mother if there were?"

"No, I guess not." I thought for a second. "Do you have the mother's address in Cleveland?"

"You talked to her."

"Yeah, but only on the phone. I can get the address through the phone company, but this would make it easier."

He looked through the papers again. "Okay, here it is. 5155 East Sixty-first Street in Cleveland. I don't know where the hell that is."

"Terrific." I wrote it down. "I'll keep in touch."

"Hey, wait a minute. When are we going to get together again? I thought maybe tonight we could—"

"Gotta run," I said. "See ya."

I hung up and went into Carstairs's office to tell him what I had in mind. He seemed pretty much back to normal today. He didn't say anything about our conversation the day before and neither did I. He gave me the approval I needed to make reservations for myself, Sanders, and Jacobson on a flight to Cleveland. Then I went back to my desk where my phone was ringing.

"Miss McKay?" the voice at the other end said.

"Yes, it is. Who is this?"

"My name is Hurewitz, Mark Hurewitz. I'm with the Medical Examiner's office." He hesitated for a second. "I wonder if you might spare a few minutes to come to our offices this morning to help us out with a matter."

"Help you? How can I do that?"

"Well, we think you may be able to identify a body. It was brought in here overnight."

"Why do you think I know who it is?"

"Because," he said, "your business card was found with the young woman's personal belongings."

I sat there staring at the phone and didn't say anything.

"Miss McKay? Miss McKay, are you still there?"

"Yeah, I'm here," I said. I knew which young woman I'd given my business card to recently.

"Can you come over to the morgue to identify the body?"

"I'll be right over," I told him.

The Medical Examiner's office is located at Bellevue Hospital, on First Avenue at East 27th Street. It's a big, white brick building. Inside when you enter is a receptionist sitting behind a desk with a row of filing cabinets behind her. All very neat. Bureaucratic. Just like any other office. Except this office deals in bodies. Dead bodies. And they're all in drawers in the back.

Mark Hurewitz reached down and pulled out one of the drawers now. The body on it was covered with a white sheet. He pulled back the sheet to show me what was underneath. The eyes were closed, the skin beginning to get a deathly pallor. Attached to one of the feet was a tag with a number on it to identify her from the rest of the bodies in the morgue.

"Do you know her?" Hurewitz asked me.

I nodded. "Yeah, I know her." I took a deep breath and stepped back a pace. I felt like I was going to be sick. "Her name is Donna Willis."

He pulled the sheet back up and pushed the drawer back into the wall. Then he picked up a clipboard and a pen.

"Do you have any knowledge of where she lived?" he asked. "Or next of kin?"

"No," I said. "She was a hooker. She worked out of a fleabag on Fourteenth Street called Helena's Hideaway. They might tell you something, but I doubt it."

"I see," Hurewitz said. He was writing everything I said down. Precise. Attentive to every detail. A professional at work. "How about friends? Did she have any?"

"Yes, she had a friend," I said.

"Really? Do you know her name?"

"Rikki Stiles," I told him. "But it won't do you any good. She's dead too."

He arched an eyebrow in surprise. "Rikki Stiles? The hooker killed on the Upper East Side? I saw that on TV. That was your story, huh?"

"Right. Listen, how did she die? Donna Willis, I mean."

Hurewitz cleared his throat. "Well, the results of our investigation indicate she succumbed to an overdose of heroin. There was a large quantity of it in the body. In addition, the track marks on her arms show she'd used heroin in the past quite frequently. So the cause of death seems rather obvious. An overdose."

"Obvious," I said. A heroin overdose. Nice, neat, and clean. Good-bye, Donna Willis.

He put the clipboard down and looked at me.

"Are you suggesting maybe it wasn't an accident?"

"I don't know. It does seem to be a helluva coincidence—two hookers who were best friends dying within a matter of days of each other. Couldn't somebody have given her the overdose? Deliberately injected her with a huge dose of heroin that would kill her? Wouldn't that look the same as an accidental overdose?"

"It could, I suppose, only . . ."

"Did the police investigate that possibility at all?"

"Miss McKay," Hurewitz said, "the police were called, found the body, and had it brought here. Let's be frank. I don't think they did very much else. A hooker who's found dead of an overdose is not exactly a top priority. No one really cares that much."

I thought about Donna Willis's body lying on that metal slab.

"Maybe I can convince them to care now," I said.

"You mean you think it's a homicide?"

"That's what I think."

I found a pay phone in the hall and called Carstairs at the station. I told him what had happened and said I wanted to do a piece for tonight on the latest in the series of mysterious deaths in the Rikki Stiles case. Then I phoned Gallagher back and filled him in too. When I was finished, I walked back through the morgue area where Hurewitz worked. He was talking to a sad-faced man and woman who seemed to be on the verge of tears. The woman was wringing her hands nervously. The man was staring down at the floor and trying hard not to look at the surroundings.

"Mr. Hurewitz," the woman was saying, "we're the Jensens. Our son was in an auto accident and they said we needed to see you to . . ."

Her eyes started to well up with tears now.

"To identify the body," Hurewitz said.

She nodded.

He turned and led the Jensens to another wall drawer and started to pull it out. Both the woman and her husband began to cry when they saw the body. I looked at Hurewitz and wondered what it must be like having a job like that. Maybe you got used to it after a while. Maybe it didn't get to you anymore. But I didn't think so.

Hurewitz saw me walking toward the door. "Thanks again, Miss McKay," he called out. "You've been a big help."

"Yeah," I muttered under my breath. "Have a nice day, Hurewitz."

I walked out the door onto First Avenue. It was cold outside, with a bitter wind blowing into my face, but anything felt good after being in that room with the drawers filled with dead bodies. I started walking down First, thinking about a lot of things. Donna Willis lying there in that white brick building. Rikki Stiles shot to death on Sutton Place. Nicky Camancho in a car trunk. Johnny Camancho's empty car on the Tappan Zee Bridge. Leo Kluge, the hit man from Chicago, sitting in my apartment. An old lyric from a Buffalo Springfield song kept running through my head: "There's something happening here—what it is ain't exactly clear." Finally I looked around and saw I was standing in front of Helena's Hideaway on 14th Street. I walked past it and went into the bar where I'd sat with Donna Willis a few days earlier.

Mickey, her pimp, was inside again. There were about a half dozen other people in the place, and all of them looked like the kind of faces you'd expect to find in a police mug-shot book. They were all watching the TV. A show called "Glamorous Ladies of Professional Wrestling" was on. Someone named Amazon Audrey had Helga, the Red Menace, in a headlock and was smashing her head into one of the posts alongside the ring. The men cheered loudly each time she did this. I slipped onto one of the stools.

"How you doin', Mickey?" I said.

"Huh?" He looked around at me. His eyes were glazed, like he was stoned or drunk. Probably both. "Who are you?"

"Jenny McKay," I said. I took out a card and showed it to him. "Channel Six News."

"I don't talk to press," he said, turning back to his drink.

"Yeah, you and Madonna," I said. "Listen, greaseball, this may come as a shock to you, but we in the media don't care all that much about you either. I mean you're not going to be on the cover of *People* or anything."

The bartender walked over and gave me a tough look.

"What's up, lady?" he asked. "You don't belong here. What are you doing—looking for trouble?"

I leaned over the bar toward him.

"I'll tell you about trouble," I said. "Trouble is what you're going to have if you start hassling me. Because I'll talk to my friends downtown on the vice squad and have them pay you a little visit. This isn't exactly the roster of the Society Register you have here for customers. I figure it would take them about three seconds to get this place closed down as a blight to civilization."

The bartender stared at me for a few seconds. Finally Mickey laughed, gestured that it was okay, and waved him away. The bartender grunted and walked down to the other end of the bar to watch the end of the wrestling match. Audrey had Helga's head in a scissors hold between her legs now. Boy, talk about your Excedrin headaches.

"Okay, so what do you want, TV lady?" Mickey asked.

"I hear you lost one of your girls."

He shrugged. "It happens. It's part of the business. There's a lot of drugs on the street. Drugs can do bad things to you."

"Especially if someone makes sure you get too much," I said.

Mickey took a sip of his drink and looked at me strangely. "You think someone did Donna in?"

"That's the way it seems to be going down," I told him.

"Who? Some nut case?"

"Maybe not. Maybe the same person who killed her friend, Rikki Stiles. Who was with Donna right before she died?"

"A trick."

"Anybody you knew?"

"No, this dude was a first-timer. He paid for her, spent about thirty minutes upstairs, and then left. Later, I found her dead. Hey, I just assumed she shot up afterward. She'd done it before. She was a goddamned junkie."

"You didn't tell the cops any of this, did you?"

"C'mon, give me a break. I don't talk to cops about anything. Know what I mean?"

"Got you." That seemed to be a code of honor among
pimps I talked to. "Tell me more about the trick she saw
before her death. What'd he look like?"

"I don't know. A big guy. No one I'd want to mess with.
Blond hair. Cut very short, kind of a crew cut. Does he sound
familiar?"

He sounded familiar, all right.

"Oh, one more thing," Mickey said. "I know the name he
used. It was Leo."

"Leo," I said.

"Yeah, as they were going up to the room, I heard Donna
say to him, 'What do I call you?' And he answered, 'Leo.'
He had a funny look in his eyes when he said it. Well, not
really funny. Kinda scary. Know what I mean?"

I knew what he meant. I'd seen that look before. The night
Leo was in my apartment.

"What do you think?" Mickey asked. "That this dude did
Donna in because she was a friend of the Stiles chick? Like
maybe he tried to find something out from her, then killed
her? Made it seem like an accidental overdose?"

"That's what I think, Mickey, my friend," I said. "That's
what I think."

I could have told him some other things too. That I felt
responsible for her death. That Kluge probably zeroed in on
her because he saw her on TV with me saying how she and
Rikki were such close friends. That if I'd never tracked her
down that day, she might not be lying on a cold slab in the
morgue right now. But I didn't. Instead I ordered a scotch
from the bartender and drank it down with the sounds of
"Glamorous Ladies of Professional Wrestling" in my ears.
Then I polished off a second in the same way. It didn't
help though. The image of Donna Willis in that drawer was
still there.

I found a pay phone and dialed the number for Victor Galena. He answered on the second ring.

"Jenny McKay," he said happily when he recognized my voice. "I knew you'd call. Reconsidering my suggestion for us to maybe meet and—"

"Keep it in your pants, Victor," I said. "I'm calling to try to save your life. Although I can't figure out why."

"Huh?"

I told him about Donna Willis and how I thought it was connected to Leo and all the other dead bodies.

"This guy's a professional killer," I said. "I think he killed Rikki and now he's killing everyone who came into contact with her. I don't know the reason, but I figure you're in real danger. Belinda too. You're about the only people close to Rikki who're still alive. If I were you, I'd lay real low. Maybe get out of town."

Galena chuckled. "I'm afraid that's impossible."

"Why's that?"

"I have many business interests which require my presence here."

"Business interests, my ass. You're a goddamned pimp. Give the girls a rest for a few days. I'm telling you, this guy's gonna come after you too."

"Well, I do appreciate your concern for my well-being, but—"

"Let me tell you something, Galena. I don't care if you live or die. As far as I'm concerned, you're scum. In fact, I think anyone who killed you probably ought to get a good citizenship medal or something from the government. I'm giving you a break you don't deserve with this warning. You ought to listen to my advice."

"Maybe you should listen to it too."

"What?"

"Well, if this madman is killing anyone who came into contact with Rikki Stiles, then you're in danger too. Isn't that right?"

He was right, of course.

"Maybe *you* should get out of town," Galena suggested with a laugh.

"Victor," I said, "that's a hell of an idea."

20

Mrs. Callandro

My plane touched down at Cleveland's John Hopkins Airport a little after 9 a.m.

Sanders, Jacobson, and I rented a car from a woman at the National counter who gave us a road map that showed us how to get to 61st Street. It was about an hour trip because the airport is ten miles outside of town, and we had to go through downtown Cleveland to get there.

Comedians love to make jokes about Cleveland. The Mistake By the Lake. The place where the Cuyahoga River once caught fire. Quips like, "I spent a week in Cleveland one day." But the downtown area really didn't seem so bad. Like a lot of big cities, it was undergoing a revitalization project and new buildings, cafés, and shopping malls were springing up all over. And the view of Lake Erie to the north was damned pretty. A sign we passed proudly proclaimed it as "The Best Location in the Nation."

The revitalization project hadn't gotten to Susan Callandro aka Rikki Stiles's mother's house yet. It was nearly noon by the time we finally pulled up in front of it, and my first reaction was to turn around and go back the way I had come. The house was in what is sometimes referred to as the inner city. The area had probably once been nice, a long time ago, but now everyone who could afford it had fled to the suburbs. At the same time, slums had expanded outward, enveloping all the once middle-class neighborhoods like this one that stood in their path.

Actually 61st Street wasn't exactly a slum. It was more like a forgotten land. Boarded-up storefronts and buildings dotted the block, the owners obviously having pulled up stakes and gotten out while they could. Many of the homes seemed closed up too. Only a few seemed to have people still living in them. The result was a kind of ghost-town effect—no people, no businesses, just a memory of what a neighborhood had once been.

The Callandro house stood defiantly in the midst of all this devastation. It was tiny, badly needed repairs, and wasn't exactly ever going to be a cover shot in *Better Homes and Gardens*. But the grass on the front lawn was neatly trimmed, there were flowers in the window, and a welcome mat sat in front of the door. It was as if the occupant was delivering her own message of determination and grit to a world gone to pot around her.

We parked the car and I started to open the door.

"What are you doing?" Sanders said. "We're not getting out of the car here, are we?"

"That was the general idea. Why?"

"I'm too young to die."

"Are you saying you're afraid of this neighborhood?"

"In a word—damned straight."

"That's two words. Besides, aren't you Mr. Ghetto? Didn't you tell me once you were the only guy on the staff who could walk down a street in Harlem and feel no fear?"

"Yeah, that was Harlem. Here I'm scared shitless. What are we doing in Cleveland anyway, Jenny?"

"Trying to find out some information."

"What kind of information?"

"I don't know."

"Well, then how—"

"I'll know when I see it."

Sanders shook his head. "This is crazy. It's crazy for us to be here." He turned to Jacobson in the back seat. "Isn't this crazy, Artie?"

Jacobson was working on an ever-present crossword puzzle. This one was from the Cleveland *Plain Dealer*. He told me he liked to pick up the local paper every time he went to a new city and try out its crossword puzzle. Maybe there was a book idea in that somewhere for me. You know, *The Travelers' Guide to Crossword Puzzles*.

He looked up from the paper now and said in a bored tone: "Hey, as long as they keep paying me, they can send me to the South Pole if they want. I don't give a fuck."

We got out of the car, walked up the steps, and rang the bell. A minute later the door was opened by a middle-aged woman wearing a blue housedress and slippers. Her hair was grey, her face beginning to line with age, and she had a weary look to her. But you could still tell from her features that she had once been beautiful. Just like her daughter.

"Mrs. Callandro," I said, "my name is Jenny McKay. From Channel Six News in New York. These gentlemen are my film crew. I talked to you on the phone a few days ago. About your daughter's death."

She looked at all of us strangely. "What are you doing here?"

I'd thought about calling her in advance, but decided against it. If you give people too much time to think, sometimes they won't talk to you. The spontaneous approach seems to work better.

"I want to talk to you about your daughter. May we come in?"

She hesitated for a second, then nodded and led us through a hallway to a neatly furnished living room. There was a couch in the center, a coffee table in front of it with a picture of her daughter in a gold frame, a plastic easy chair across from the couch. In one corner stood a battered old desk, in another a baby crib. Clean, white curtains hung on the windows and blocked out the grime from outside. Mrs. Callandro motioned for us to sit down and asked if we wanted coffee or anything to drink. We said coffee was fine. She went into the kitchen, came back a few minutes later carrying a plastic tray with four cups which she set down on the coffee table in front of us. Then she sat in the easy chair and looked at me.

"So tell me, Miss McKay," she asked cautiously, "what's so important that you traveled five hundred miles to see me?"

"I'm trying to track down your daughter's killer," I told her.

She arched an eyebrow. "Really? And are you having any success?"

"I think so. I think that whoever killed her killed some other people too. And may kill more."

"Why?" she asked. "Why would he do that?"

"That's something I don't know the answer to yet," I said. "In fact, it's one of the reasons I came today. I'm hoping you can help me to find out."

"Me? How?"

"Tell me more about your daughter. Everything you can think of."

"Well," she began slowly, "Susan was a very nice daughter. Loving. Responsible. She never really gave me any trouble. And she was quite a good artist. Her drawings . . ."

"Did you know she was a prostitute, Mrs. Callandro?" I asked.

I could feel Sanders flinch next to me when I said it. I glanced over at him, and he gave me a funny look. "I know what I'm doing," I whispered to him under my breath. That wasn't strictly true, but no sense in letting him know that.

Mrs. Callandro picked up her cup of coffee, took a sip, and gazed at me evenly.

"Yes. . . . I suppose I did."

"Did she ever talk to you about it?"

"No. Not in so many words. But I'm not stupid, Miss McKay. I knew she really didn't have a job in New York. And when I saw her clothes, heard her talk about her apartment . . . well, it doesn't exactly take a genius to figure it out."

"Were you surprised at how she was living her life?"

Mrs. Callandro sighed. She fiddled with the coffee nervously. Somewhere I heard a baby crying. "Surprised? Let me put it this way, Miss McKay. Susan was a good girl. Deep down she always meant to do the right thing. But she was impatient. Always had been, ever since she was a little girl. Always looking for shortcuts to get what she wanted. She wanted to get out of here, didn't want to live like me for the rest of her life. So she went to New York thinking she was going to find fame and fortune in the art world there. Her father died when she was very young, and I've always had to struggle to make ends meet. We managed, but just barely. That was never good enough for Susan, she wanted more. So when she went to New York and discovered in the beginning that she wasn't living any better there than I was back in Cleveland, she took a shortcut to get what she wanted. That shortcut was becoming a prostitute."

I nodded. "I talked to a friend of hers in New York," I said. "Her name was Donna Willis. She's dead now too. This Willis woman said that your daughter had left the city for a while about a year ago. She said she came home here to Ohio. Did she stay with you then?"

Mrs. Callandro's face got a funny expression on it. I wasn't quite sure what to make of it. "Yes," she said finally, "she was here."

"For how long?"

"Oh, a few months, I guess."

"Uh-huh. But then she went back to New York City. And the same life-style she was living before."

That look came across her face again. "Yes, that's right. She went back."

"Do you know why?"

She smiled sadly. "Look around you, Miss McKay. This isn't exactly Sutton Place here. Do you think someone like my daughter could have been happy staying here for very long?"

"Maybe. At least it could have been the start of something."

"No, Miss McKay, being in Cleveland was wrong for her. Do you know that I didn't even have her body shipped back here after she died? I had her buried instead in a little cemetery out on Long Island. She didn't belong here. I knew that. And so did she."

I thought about Rikki Stiles telling me how badly she needed money for a new start.

"So she went back to New York," I said.

"Yes, to try to make enough money for a stake on a new life. Not here. And not as a New York prostitute either. Something totally fresh. But she needed money first, and she said she was going to do whatever she could to get it."

Even sell information about her customers to the police, I thought.

"Except someone killed her first."

"Yes," she said. "Someone killed her."

It was time now to ask one of the questions I'd really come for.

"When your daughter died," I said, "the police kept her possessions from the Sutton Place apartment until they found the next of kin. You. They said they later sent it all on here to Cleveland. Do you have the stuff in the house?"

She nodded. "Yes, of course."

"I'd like to look through it. Would that be possible?"

"I suppose so. But why? What are you hoping to find?"

"Ask me that when I find it."

She shrugged. "All right. I'll get it for you."

She disappeared for a few minutes, then came back carrying two big cardboard cartons. She laid them down on the living room rug in front of me.

"I haven't brought her clothes," she said. "They're all in a closet in the bedroom if you'd care to look at them."

"That probably won't be necessary," I said.

I didn't think there were any clues in Rikki Stiles's clothing. I wasn't even sure there were any clues in these boxes of personal possessions. But I was hoping.

The first box contained a lot of bills, financial records, and canceled checks. Might be some leads there if I wanted to wade through it all. But I didn't. Not now anyway. I rifled through the stuff a few times, then put it aside. The second box was more personal. Inside was a lot of jewelry. A few pictures—one of her and her mother, another of her with Donna Willis standing in front of the Empire State Building. An artist's sketchbook with her drawings inside. That was about it. The rest of the stuff was just odds and ends. A few theater programs. A dozen record albums. Some matchbooks. Actually there were maybe thirty matchbooks, all from the St. Regis Hotel. Probably stayed there with some of her dates. Although when I thought about it for a second or two, I wondered why she went to a hotel with a customer when she had that beautiful apartment on Sutton Place. I didn't know the answer to that one either.

"There's nothing else?" I asked Mrs. Callandro.

"No. Like what?"

"I don't know. Maybe a book of phone numbers or addresses she kept."

"You mean a little black book?" Mrs. Callandro smiled. "Like prostitutes are supposed to keep. I guess that would make it easy, wouldn't it? But no, I haven't seen anything like that. And even if there was, wouldn't the police have gone through it already before sending this stuff on? They would be looking for the same thing as you are."

"Yeah, I guess you're right," I said. There was no little black book. And I wasn't Alan Ladd. I wasn't going to solve this case the way he did in *Chicago Deadline*.

My coffee cup was empty now. "I'll get some more," Mrs. Callandro said.

She left and went into the kitchen. I could hear her working out there. Outside a car horn honked. Somewhere a baby was still crying.

"Can we get out of here now?" Sanders was saying impatiently.

"Soon," I told him. "Very soon."

Damn, I was so sure that something would be here in Rikki's things. A name. A clue. Something. Alan Ladd had a little black book to work with, I didn't have anything. There were no books here for me. The only book she left behind was her sketchbook.

Just like that, it hit me. Jesus Christ, that was an idea. I actually had an idea. Maybe.

I reached back into one of the cardboard boxes and took out Rikki Stiles's sketchbook. This time I went through all the drawings carefully. There was a knight in shining armor. A football player scoring a touchdown. A cowboy holding a six-gun. But there was something the same about all of the drawings. *They were all men!* Rikki Stiles's sketches—that was her little black book! Of course, she was an artist. She kept her little black book in drawings.

I paged through the sketches until I came to the one I knew would be there. It was a picture of a man on horseback. A strapping, handsome man with locks of hair flying behind him as he rode a white horse. I'd seen something like it once before. In a picture. In the lower right-hand corner of the drawing, near one of the horse's hooves, were some numbers. Maybe a phone number. I'd check it later. Behind the rider in the background was a smaller horse with a smaller person in the saddle. Like a midget. Or a little boy. A son.

I heard the sound of the baby crying again. It was all coming together now.

"Aha!" I said out loud.

Sanders and Jacobson looked at me strangely. "What did you find?" Sanders asked.

"I think I have solved the case," I proclaimed proudly.

Just like Angela Lansbury.

Mrs. Callandro returned carrying the coffee. She put it down on the table in front of us and sat down again. The baby cried one more time. I nodded toward the baby crib I'd seen in the corner when I came in.

"Mrs. Callandro," I asked, "whose baby is it?"

She looked startled. "Baby?"

"I heard the baby crying before. The first time I called you up and told you about your daughter's death. It didn't dawn on me then, but later I started thinking about why you would have a baby crying in your house. You're about fifty, aren't you, Mrs. Callandro? A little past normal childbearing age. So that's really one of the reasons I came to see you. To ask you about the baby."

"Well, I'm just taking care of it for someone until they—"

"It's your daughter's baby, isn't it?" I asked softly.

She hesitated for a second, then nodded. "Yes, it's Susan's son," she said quietly.

"That's why she came home for those few months, wasn't it? She was having a baby. And she didn't want anyone in New York to know. Not her clients. Not Victor Galena. Not even her friend, Donna Willis. It was going to be her secret."

"That's right," Mrs. Callandro said. "At first, I hoped she'd put New York and that life behind her for good. I wanted her to have the baby, stay here, and raise it. I offered to help. And she did stay for a while. But then . . ."

"She went back to New York."

"Yes. She said she had to make some money. I knew she was right. She could never live with me here . . . like this. She wanted to take the baby and start a new life somewhere. Not New York and not here either. But she needed money to break away. She said she knew how to get it in New York. That's all she was going back for, she said. It would only take a matter of months, she promised, and then she'd be free of it all."

I thought about Rikki Stiles sitting across from my desk that day, after Victor Galena had confiscated her secret cash savings, and telling me how desperate she was for money. Why she was willing to turn in Johnny Camancho for the Lancaster Hotel heist. Now I understood why.

"And then someone killed her," I said.

"Yes, they murdered my daughter. But why? What happened?"

I took a sip of the coffee and looked across at her. "Mrs. Callandro, did your daughter ever tell you who the baby's father was?"

"No. I asked, but she wouldn't say. She said that he didn't know about the baby and never would. She said he was someone very important. That it would ruin his career if people ever found out. So she never told me. I never found out his name."

I thought about the drawing in Rikki Stiles's sketchbook.

"That's all right," I said. "I know who he is."

21

My Lunch With the Godfather

Someone once said, "The ends justify the means." Barry Goldwater said, "Extremism in the pursuit of liberty is no vice." Vince Lombardi said, "Winning isn't everything—it's the only thing." And Leo Durocher said, "Nice guys finish last."

I was running all these thoughts through my head to justify why I was sitting at the bar of Enrico's, downstairs from my apartment, waiting for Anthony (Big Tony) Mosconi to show up for lunch.

My motive for asking to meet with him was logical, I thought. Desperate, but logical. My thinking went something like this: Tony Mosconi was one of the city's top mob bosses, the main rival of Jerry Rossiello. I knew Rossiello was at the center of this whole mess somehow, but I didn't know how or why. Mosconi might. After all, the two of them were the number one and number two underworld leaders in New York. So maybe it was like Macy's and Gimbel's used to be. I mean Macy probably never talked to Gimbel, but they damn well knew everything the other guy was doing.

I looked at my watch. It was almost twelve-thirty. Mosconi had said he'd be here a little after twelve. I'd been here for forty-five minutes already. God, I hated hanging around bars and restaurants like this. I thought about how many times I'd done it over the years—hunting for tips or waiting for news sources. It never bothered me as much as it did lately. Maybe I was getting too old for this line of work. Maybe I should do something new with my life—move out of New York to Miami or out West somewhere and start fresh. I thought about what it would be like living in some small town out West. Growing vegetables in my garden. Walking to the general store. Sitting out on my porch. On the other hand, maybe I'd just be hanging around some little bar in Arizona or Nevada waiting for a news source to show up. Some things you can't change about yourself.

Mosconi finally got there a little before 12:45. He was about sixty, probably no more than five feet eight inches tall, and he must have weighed close to two hundred and fifty pounds. You might say his presence filled the room. I figured the only exercise he got was walking up to the buffet table.

There were two bodyguards with him. Tall, muscular, swarthy-looking. Mosconi sat down at a table in the corner, then one of the bodyguards motioned me over. I sat down across from Mosconi. The two bodyguards stood alongside us—arms folded, not moving, staring straight ahead at the door. I sat down.

"Miss McKay," he said.

"How are you, Mr. Mosconi?"

I reached across the table and shook his hand, then looked up at the two bodyguards. They still hadn't sat down. They were just standing there like statues. Impassive. Stoic.

"What's with them?" I asked.

"These are just two of my associates," he said. "A necessary security precaution, I'm afraid."

"Oh, I thought maybe they were just practicing their act in case Francis Ford Coppola decides to hold a casting call for *Godfather IV*."

No reaction from either of the bodyguards. This was a tough room to work. Mosconi stared at me from across the table.

"You said you needed to talk to me," he said. "What do you want?"

"I need a favor."

"What kind of a favor?"

"Some information."

He shrugged. "So why not call 411? Or go to the public library. They've got lots of information there."

"Not the kind I need."

"Which is?"

"It's about the Rikki Stiles murder."

The waiter brought us some wine and a plate of antipasto and another filled with some sort of veal cutlets. There was also a big bowl filled with bread and two large salads.

"This is wonderful antipasto," Mosconi said, scooping half of it onto his plate in one motion. "I eat it here often."

I'll bet you do, I thought. I helped myself to one of the veal cutlets and nibbled at some salad.

"You owe me, Mr. Mosconi," I told him.

"Listen," he said as he worked his way though the food on the table and at the same time signaled for the waiter to start getting ready a big plate of eggplant parmigiana, "I'm very grateful for what you did in helping to get my granddaughter back. But I did repay you. I've given you a very lovely apartment."

"It's not *that* lovely," I said.

He looked surprised. "You don't like the apartment?"

"Hey, it's got some problems. The paint's peeling, the pipes are rusty, the freezer won't defrost, and the heat thermostat is broken."

"Those are all things that can be taken care of."

"Besides," I said, "there are roaches."

"So you've seen a few roaches in the apartment? Is that such a big deal?"

"A few roaches! There's roaches that hold conventions there. It's like the Atlantic City of roachdom. I've got roaches in my bread box, in my cupboard, in my bedroom, in my closet. Do you know I even found one in my makeup the other day? I'm thinking of making them pay half the rent."

"Miss McKay, what exactly is your point here?"

"My point is I got a lot of fuckin' roaches in my place!"

Mosconi smiled and shook his head. "My father had a word to describe someone like you. An Italian term he used."

"What's that?"

"He would have called you a '*vucca granni*' ."

"*Vucca granni*, huh? What's that mean? Pretty as a flower or something like that?"

"No." He paused. "Actually the closest translation I could give you in English would be . . . smart mouth."

"Oh," I said.

Mosconi picked up a piece of the veal and devoured it in a matter of seconds. He ate quickly. Effortlessly. I love a man who's good at what he does.

"The Rikki Stiles murder has nothing to do with me," he said.

"I know," I told him.

"So why come to me for information?"

"Because I think you make it your business to know what Jerry Rossiello is up to. And I think Rossiello's involved in this somehow."

Mosconi nodded and took a sip of the wine. "Tell me what you know," he said.

"I know there's a hit man in town," I said. "His name is Leo Kluge. He's from Chicago."

"Mr. Kluge is a bad man," Mosconi sighed. "A very bad man. Even in my business. Almost uncontrollable, I hear. You give him a job, but then he ignores your guidelines and takes it to . . . well, extremes."

"He killed Nicky Camancho?"

There was a nod from Mosconi.

"And Donna Willis, Rikki's friend?"

Another nod.

"And Rikki Stiles and Johnny Camancho too?"

Mosconi laughed this time. "Johnny Camancho. That was quite melodramatic, wasn't it—a car on the bridge, wallet left behind, someone making a mysterious report of a body going into the water."

"Meaning you think it was a stunt?"

"If I were a betting man, I'd say so."

"So where's Camancho then? What's he doing?"

Mosconi shrugged. "How would I know?"

"Oh, you know, all right. I think you know about everything that goes on in this town."

He seemed pleased with that. There was a big grin on his face. McKay, you old flatterer, you.

"Why?" I asked. "Why all the killing?"

The waiter came with the eggplant parmigiana and also refilled our wine glasses. Mosconi took a big bite of the parmigiana, swallowed, and said softly: "In my business, the worst thing a man can do is break a promise. It is a matter of honor. The price for violating that code can be very high— sometimes one's life."

"Who broke their word? Rikki? Johnny Camancho?"

Mosconi dismissed them contemptuously with a wave of his hand. "They're bit players in all this. Nobodies. No, the real target of Mr. Rossiello's wrath is someone very important. A man of high public profile. A man who has made things very difficult for Rossiello."

"You mean Elliott Carson?"

He nodded his head almost imperceptibly.

"The word on the street is that there is a contract out on Mr. Carson's life. A very big contract, paid for by Mr. Rossiello. The person trying to carry out this contract appears to be the man you referred to. Leo Kluge."

"And what about the others?" I asked. "Why did Kluge kill them?"

"I suppose they were just in the way. Like I said, Mr. Kluge tends to carry things to extremes."

Most of the parmigiana was gone by now. There was one piece of veal left on the plate. Mosconi paused for a second, apparently as a polite gesture to see if I wanted it. But not too long. When I didn't immediately grab for the plate, he did. He popped the veal into his mouth and then looked down at the empty plate. I wouldn't have been surprised if he'd picked it up in his hands and started licking the grease off. He didn't. But I bet he thought about it.

"Now I understand," I said. "Carson indicted Rossiello. So Rossiello got mad and hired Kluge to . . ."

Mosconi shook his head. "You don't understand. You're not listening to everything I'm saying."

"But the indictment . . ."

"Indictments and troubles with the law are a part of our business. Rossiello understands that. These things happen from time to time. An ambitious young District Attorney takes office, decides to go after us to further his career, gets some front-page stories . . . well, you know how it goes. But time and the courts have a way of diluting these things. No, I don't think Jerry Rossiello would take out a contract on a law enforcement official simply because he indicted him. There has to be more to it than that."

"Like what?"

"Like I said before, someone broke their word. The story I hear is it was Carson who reneged on a promise."

"A promise? You mean to Rossiello?"

"Yes. That's really all I know. But I assume it had something to do with the indictment. My assumption is that for some reason Rossiello got a promise from Carson that he wouldn't be indicted. When Carson went back on his word, Rossiello took it as a personal affront to his honor. That's when he called in Leo Kluge."

"Why would Carson make such a deal in the first place?" I asked.

"I don't know. I can only assume that Rossiello—"

"Had something on Carson," I said.

"Exactly. But I have no idea what that was."

I do, I thought. Son of a gun! Rossiello found out about Elliott Carson sleeping with Rikki Stiles and was blackmailing him. Figured Carson would never go after him because he could ruin him politically. They made a secret deal with each other. Then Carson blew everything sky-high with the indictment. But why? I thought of one person who might know the answer.

"Where's Johnny Camancho?" I asked.

He started to tell me again how he didn't know, but I interrupted him.

"I need your help, Mr. Mosconi," I said. "When you got your granddaughter back, you told me she was the most important thing in your life."

"I know, but . . ."

"You said if I ever needed a favor, just come to you. Well, now the bill has come due. I don't give a damn about the apartment, you can take it back if you want. But people's lives are at stake here. Maybe mine. Tell me what you know about Camancho."

The waiter brought an entire cheesecake, two forks and two coffees to the table. Mosconi stared down at the cheesecake, started to stick his fork into it, and then stopped. He pushed the plate away. Boy, I must really be getting to him. He was so confused about what to do he'd lost his appetite.

"Do you get to New Jersey much?" he asked.

"Sometimes. Why?"

"There's a place just over the George Washington Bridge, not far from Hackensack," he said. "A motel called the Sunset Motor Lodge."

"The Sunset Motor Lodge?"

"Yes, you should visit it sometime."

"Okay."

He picked up the fork again and this time took a big piece of the cheesecake. He chewed it slowly. Thoughtfully. Almost lovingly.

"Exquisite," he pronounced. "You must try some."

"I don't think so. . . ."

"I insist."

"Look, if I eat that on top of this lunch, I'm going to bear a startling resemblance to Delta Burke. Not the actual Delta Burke, but an amazing re-creation. So, like Nancy Reagan used to suggest, I'm going to 'just say no.' "

He picked up a second fork and handed it to me. "Eat," he said.

"Well, maybe just a little bitty piece. . . ."

When the Godfather talks, I listen.

Twenty minutes later the two of us had finished off the whole thing. I was stuffed, nauseous, and starting to feel sleepy. But Mosconi seemed fresh as a daisy. Probably was going to stop off at a Carvel for dessert on his way home.

Somehow I managed to stand up and push myself away from the table.

"This Sunset Motor Lodge," I asked him. "By any chance, does Leo Kluge have the directions to it?"

"Not yet."

"How can you be so sure?"

Mosconi smiled. "If he did, do you think Mr. Camancho would still be alive?"

22
Johnny Camancho

The Sunset Motor Lodge was located on Route 46 in Little Ferry, about fifteen miles northwest of Manhattan. It was a shabby-looking, white, two-story building with peeling paint and a roof that badly needed repairing. Across the street was a diner and a gas station, next door a discount drugstore.

I'd brought Sanders and Jacobson along with me, figuring there was safety in numbers. We parked in the lot next to a sign which said: VACANCIES—INQUIRE WITHIN.

"Okay, here's the plan," I said. "Sanders and I go inside and nose around for a while. See what we can find out. Artie, you wait in the van. If we don't come out again in twenty minutes, you go get help."

"I like that plan," Jacobson said.

"Well, I don't," Sanders yelped. "How come he gets to sit in the van? Why can't I sit in the van?"

"Because, you're young, you're black, and there's a chance you might just be a little intimidating to someone." I looked over at Jacobson, who was already starting on his ever-present crossword puzzle. "Artie sure as hell isn't going to scare anybody."

We went inside. There was a kid sitting behind the desk chewing on a toothpick and watching the "Price Is Right" on TV. Whenever Bob Barker would ask a contestant to guess the price of some item, the audience would scream out a number. The kid quietly mouthed a number too as he watched. Audience participation.

"Hi," I said. "Can I get some help?"

The kid turned the sound down on the TV, took the tooth-pick out of his mouth, and stood up. He looked me over carefully. Then he checked out Sanders, who was examining a rack of postcards next to the front desk.

"You with the pickaninny?" the kid asked.

I looked over at Sanders. He was glaring in our direction, but didn't say anything. "You mean the gentleman of African-American extraction?" I asked.

"Yeah, the pickaninny. Are you together?"

I nodded.

"Well, keep him out of the lobby. I mean I don't care what you two do in the privacy of your room. But our clientele gets nervous when they see his kind hanging around the place. Know what I mean?"

"Sure, I understand," I said. "I can see you run a really classy operation here."

He didn't say anything.

"The truth is," I said, "I'm not looking for a room. I'm looking for a friend." I'd decided not to identify myself as a reporter right away because it might scare somebody off. "I think he may be staying here. I wonder if you've seen him."

I reached into my purse and took out a picture of Johnny Camancho I'd copied from a newspaper clip. I handed it to the kid. He barely glanced at it, shook his head, and handed it back.

"Nope, never seen him."

"You're sure? Maybe if you took a longer look . . ."

"I said I never saw him. That's it."

He went back to his chair and turned up the volume on
the game show again. He was finished with me. I was of no
use to him.

"Hey, one more thing," I yelled, "do me a favor. Change
a fifty-dollar bill for me, okay?"

The kid groaned but got up, walked over, and took the
fifty from me.

"How do you want the change?" he asked.

"That depends."

"Depends on what?"

"On how you answer that question about the picture the
next time I ask it. Get my point?"

He looked at me with a surprised expression on his face
for a second, then smiled. "Yeah, I get your point. Let me
take another look at it."

I handed the photo back to him. This time he looked at it
longer.

"You know, my memory's coming back to me on this
guy now. He is here. Checked in . . . oh, maybe a week ago
or so."

"You see him around much?"

"No, he stays in his room most of the time. Has his meals
sent up and left outside. The only time we see him is when
the help goes in to clean the room. He even gives us a hard
time about that."

"No question about it, your memory has definitely
improved," I said.

"Yeah, funny how that happens, isn't it?" He slipped the
fifty-dollar bill into his pocket. "So what is this guy—your
husband or something?"

"No, just somebody I'm looking up for a friend. How
about his room number? How's your memory on that?"

"I might know it."

"Might? Do you or don't you?"

"Not for the same fifty dollars I don't."

I took two twenties and a ten out of my purse this time
and slid them across the counter to him.

"Room 216. Second floor, back entrance."

Sanders and I started off in that direction.

"Hey," the kid called out after us, "I don't want no trouble."

"My sentiments exactly," I told him.

We took the stairs up to the second floor. Room 216 was at the end of the hall, next to a door which said HOUSE KEEPER. There was a window next to the door overlooking the discount drugstore and an industrial park in the distance. New Jersey was definitely not as romantic as it sounded in Bruce Springsteen's songs.

"Did that guy back there really call me a pickaninny?" Sanders asked.

"I think it was a term of endearment." I looked at the open door. "Listen, I've got an idea."

"Oh, jeez!"

"What does that mean?"

"Look, why don't we just call the cops? Tell them we think we know where Johnny Camancho is. Let them handle the whole thing, huh? Isn't that a good idea?"

"We will call them."

"When?"

"Soon. Very soon." I looked inside the closet. There was a cart of cleaning stuff in there. I brought it out. "Take off your jacket and sports shirt, try to dress down as much as possible, and then take this cart."

"You're not going to tell me to—"

"Sure. It's the best way to get in there. Tell him you've got to clean the room."

"Why me? Why not you? Or Artie?"

"Well, I hate to sound like the guy in the lobby," I said, "but of the three of us, you've got the best chance of passing for one of the hired help."

He grumbled some more, but a few minutes later he was standing in front of Room 216 with the cleaning cart. I watched from a hiding spot around the corner. Sanders knocked on the door.

"What do you want?" a voice called from inside.

"I clean room now," Sanders said. He used a heavy Jamaican accent as he talked.

"Don't worry about it," the voice said. "I don't need any cleaning."

"I clean room now," Sanders repeated mechanically, as if he didn't understand English.

"Later! Come back later."

"I clean room . . ."

The door opened. An angry-looking man stood there. He had dark hair, a swarthy-looking complexion, and was wearing a white T-shirt with slacks. Johnny Camancho.

"Look, I told you," he said, "not now."

"Boss man downstairs said I clean room for you. . . ."

He threw up his hands in disgust. "All right, all right. Come on in and get it over with. I don't have the energy to explain it to you."

Sanders smiled at him and rolled the cart into the room. Camancho followed him, then walked into the bathroom where he'd been shaving. Once he was out of sight, I slipped into the room too and looked around. The television set was on, the bed unmade. On the table next to the bed was a stack of newspapers. There was a chair next to them with a shirt hanging on the back. I lifted up the shirt. There was a holster with a gun underneath it.

"We call the cops now," Sanders whispered frantically, "right?"

"Right. In a minute."

I rolled the cleaning cart over to the chair, took the gun out of the holster, and dropped it into the bin with all the cleaning equipment. Then I walked into the bathroom.

"You're Johnny Camancho, aren't you?"

He whirled around and made a start for the other room to get the gun.

"Don't bother," I told him. "It's not there anymore. I was afraid you might use it on me before I got a chance to explain why I'm here."

He sat down on the closed toilet seat and looked at me closely. "Who the hell are you?"

"Jenny McKay," I said. "From Channel Six News. I'm a reporter. The guy out there is my cameraman."

"A reporter." His mood relaxed a bit. I think he was beginning to realize I really wasn't a threat to him. "How did you find me?"

"You've got something more important than that to worry about, Johnny."

"What do you mean?"

"I mean if I was able to find you, so will Jerry Rossiello. And when that happens, you're dead. You know that as well as I do."

Camancho stood up and walked into the other room. He took out a pack of cigarettes from his shirt pocket, lit one, and sat down on the bed. I followed him in there. Sanders was standing by the open door, looking like he was ready to bolt if there was trouble. I went over and whispered to him that everything was fine.

"Yeah, I know," Camancho was saying. He looked around the motel room. "That's why I've been living like this."

"What about the empty car bit on the Tappan Zee Bridge?"

"I was hoping to throw everybody off my trail."

"All you did was maybe buy a little extra time," I said. "You're not really solving the problem. They're going to find you unless you do something."

"Like what?"

"Turn yourself in."

"Huh? You mean to the police?"

"Sure. You tell them what they want to know about Rossiello, maybe they let you cop a plea on the Lancaster Hotel job. Plus they give you protective security."

"I don't know. . . ."

"It's the only way out, Johnny," I said quietly. "The only way to save your neck."

He stood up and began pacing alongside the bed. "Christ, how in the hell did things go so bad? It was such a sweet deal. But now everything's screwed up. Rikki's dead, Nicky too, and they're after me." He shook his head disgustedly.

"Why don't you tell me about it?" I said.

He sat down again and didn't answer me. I looked over at Sanders, who just shrugged. We waited.

"Look," I told Camancho, "I think I already know part of it. The Lancaster Hotel heist is involved. And Elliott Carson. Rikki Stiles was having an affair with Elliott Carson, the District Attorney, wasn't she?"

He nodded. "Yeah, they were making it. For more than a year."

"And you and Rikki too?"

Camancho smiled. "Rikki had a lot of men, all right. But then that was her business, wasn't it?"

"Okay, so what's the connection?" I asked. "Between you and Elliott Carson and the Lancaster Hotel job? Why does Jerry Rossiello have a hit man out looking for you? And why are Rikki and the others dead?"

Camancho looked down at the floor and shook his head. "It seemed so easy at the beginning. Like a goddamned gold mine. And I just lucked into it . . . the break of a lifetime."

"What are you talking about?"

He sighed. "Look, I found out by accident one day about Carson and Rikki. She kept it a big secret, no one knew. They used to meet in hotels and everything so no one would ever spot him going in and out of her apartment. But I got a feeling something funny was going on so I followed her. Watched her go into this hotel and take an elevator up to the twelfth floor. A few minutes later, I see Carson in the lobby and recognize him from his picture in the papers. This was a couple of months before he got elected. Anyway, he goes up to the twelfth floor too. Bingo! An hour or so later, they come down separately and leave, a few minutes apart."

I remembered Rikki talking about working as an informant. "You don't think she was helping him on a case," I suggested sarcastically.

"No way." He laughed. "He wasn't even the DA yet. And believe me—I saw the look on this guy's face in the lobby. He wasn't there to play crime-buster. He was there to ride the bumpy love train with her."

"So what did you do?" I asked. "Confront Rikki with it?"

Camancho laughed. "Nah, nothing like that. Hey, I wasn't jealous or anything. Like I said, men were her business. I mean, she fooled around with a lot of them. I wasn't upset at all. In fact, I was delighted. This was my big chance. I knew this, and no one else did. Even Rikki didn't know I knew. Yeah, I liked the situation a lot."

He took out another cigarette and lit it. The smoke filled the room. I wanted to open a window a crack and let some air in, but the curtains were drawn and I didn't want to suggest opening them. It would make us too visible. I wasn't kidding about Rossiello's men being able to find him if I could. It was on my mind every minute we spent in that motel room.

"Anyway," he said, blowing some smoke in the air, "I figured out pretty soon that they met twice a week, on Tuesdays and Thursdays. Same hotel, same room."

"The St. Regis?" I said, thinking about the matchbook covers she'd saved.

"Yeah, how'd you know that?"

I just shrugged.

"Anyway," he said, "once I knew that, the rest came easy. I let myself into the room one day before they got there and set up some video equipment, cameras and stuff, so that they couldn't see them. Then I waited until they showed up and bingo—candid camera."

"Blackmail," I said. "You were blackmailing Elliott Carson. How much?"

"Oh, nothing so crude as that. I simply took the pictures to Mr. Rossiello. Told him I could work out a deal to keep this new guy running for DA off his back once he got elected. It was apparent even then that Carson had the goods to make it to the job. And having a guy as DA who was under his thumb really appealed to Rossiello. So he told me to set it up."

Camancho took a deep breath. "And that's what I did. It was a breeze too. I got in touch with Carson's people, told them what I had, and said Rossiello would even contribute a bit of money to his campaign to help him get elected. We wanted to make sure he won. All Carson had to do was look the other way as far as the Rossiello family was concerned once he was in office. In return, we wouldn't send the pictures on to the newspapers or TV stations or his wife and family."

"Did Carson see the pictures?"

"Oh sure, I sent a couple of them along as proof." Camancho smiled. "Real nice. The two of them in a really interesting position, his face turned toward the hidden camera. You could make him out clear as day. Once he saw that, I knew he'd agree to anything to make sure these never became public."

"And he went for it all?"

"Yeah. A couple of days later the word came back. We had a deal. So I told Rossiello. The campaign money he had to contribute didn't matter a thing to him; it was small potatoes considering what he was getting. Carte blanche from the District Attorney's office to do what he wanted. Rossiello was ecstatic. So ecstatic, in fact, that he gave me a reward. A big reward."

"How much?" I asked.

"He let me and Nicky in on the Lancaster Hotel job that he was planning then. Can you imagine it? Me in on a high-class job like that? Hell, I couldn't believe it. Rikki didn't believe it at first either. But I proved it to her, showed her some of the jewelry from the robbery. Even gave her a few pieces. That knocked her eyes out. Of course, she didn't have any idea how I pulled the thing off."

I thought about the jewelry from the heist Gallagher said they'd found in Rikki's apartment. Of course, that's why a nobody like Johnny Camancho was involved in a top operation like the Lancaster job. No one could understand that in the beginning. But now it made sense. It was a payoff for setting up the blackmail operation against Carson.

"So Carson got elected," I said. "But what went wrong? Why did it all blow up?"

"I don't know," Camancho said, shaking his head. "Everything just went sour overnight. Carson broke the deal, went after Rossiello with this indictment—don't ask me why. All of a sudden Rossiello's before a grand jury, his guys are being picked up off the streets, and I'm in hot water with him."

"Rossiello blamed you?"

"Sure. I'm the guy who set up the deal. Told him he'd be safe from the DA's office. He believed it. So when it all fell apart, he went crazy. They told me he was furious at everybody. Carson. Me. Anyone connected with the whole thing. It was like this blind rage, he just had to strike out at someone."

"And that's where Leo Kluge comes in, huh?" I said.

Camancho nodded. "Leo Kluge, hit man extraordinaire. Do you know what they say about him? He's never missed a contract. Never once, not in his entire career. You tell him you want a guy knocked off, that guy's dead meat. And now he's after me. Shit!"

"And Elliott Carson too."

He smiled. "Yeah. Elliott Carson's number one on his hit parade."

"So you decided to hide out here in Jersey?"

"Yeah, I grabbed whatever money I could and got the hell out of town."

"Where did you get the money from? The Lancaster heist?"

He shook his head sheepishly. "No, I lost most of that gambling. I was kinda flat broke. But Rikki had some she gave to me before she died. . . ."

I remembered what Donna Willis said Rikki had told her. Someone took her secret stash. I'd assumed all along it was Galena, but it was really Camancho. There was no shortage of lousy men in Rikki's life.

"Rikki didn't give it to you," I said. "You beat her up and took it, didn't you? The whole ten thousand. Everything except a few hundred she'd hidden at the bottom of one of her drawers."

"Hey, I never touched Rikki. . . ."

"Sure you did," I said quietly. "You gave her that bruise on her cheek she was walking around with."

He shrugged. "Okay, I had to slap her around a bit to get the money. It was no big deal."

"Did you tell her why you needed the money?"

Camancho nodded. "Yeah, I did. She was stunned, she had no idea what I'd been doing."

So Camancho's visit to Rikki was what set everything in motion. He took her money and told her enough about the blackmail scheme to make her realize she might be in danger from an angry Rossiello too—she had to move quickly. So she came to me that day in hopes of getting some reward money by giving up Camancho for the Lancaster job. Why not? She certainly didn't owe him any loyalty anymore after what he'd done.

But there was still a piece of the puzzle missing. I've got a couple plans to make some money, she'd told Donna Willis before she died. One of them was the reward on the Lancaster robbery. What was the other one?

"Hey, I didn't kill her," Camancho said. "I just hit her a couple of times, that's all. She was alive when I left. Honest, it's the truth."

I didn't figure Camancho told the truth all that often, but I had a hunch he was this time. "Yeah, I know," I said.

I stood up and walked over to where Sanders was sitting. He looked up at me anxiously. "Now we call the cops?" he whispered.

"Now we call the cops," I told him. I reached for the telephone. "It's your only chance, Johnny."

Camancho didn't stop me.

23
Man of the Year

Elliott Carson didn't throw me out of his office this time.

I sat opposite him in front of the big walnut desk. The picture of him riding the horse was still there next to the Man of the Year trophy. The man on the horse still looked dashing, swashbuckling. Except it had a different meaning for me this time. I thought about the St. Regis Hotel and Rikki Stiles's sketchbook and the baby boy crying in the little house back in Cleveland.

Sitting next to me was Capt. Dave Hanson of the Police Dept. Intelligence Division. I'd gone to the cops with Camancho and told them everything I knew. Everything except the baby. That was Rikki's secret, and I wasn't going to be the one to reveal it. Hanson ran through it all for Carson now.

"Mr. Carson," he was saying, "we're here today because information has been uncovered in the course of this investigation that leads us to believe your life may be in danger."

Carson raised one eyebrow in surprise. "As I told McKay

here before, someone in my position hears a lot of wild threats and—"

"This is much more serious than that," Hanson said. "We believe that Jerry Rossiello has employed the services of a mob hit man named Leo Kluge to assassinate you. Kluge is very, very dangerous. We believe he means to carry out the assignment."

He took out a police mug-shot photo of Kluge and handed it to Carson.

"Have you seen this man around anywhere in the last few days?" Hanson asked.

Carson shook his head. "No, never."

He slid the picture back across the desk.

"Where does this intelligence information about the danger to me come from anyway?"

Hanson cleared his throat. "It was given to us by a former Rossiello associate who is also currently a target of his wrath."

"You mean this Camancho joker?" Carson asked.

"Yes. He's confessed to the Lancaster Hotel robbery and is giving us other information about Rossiello and his mob activities. In return, we've agreed to keep him in protective custody." Hanson looked over at the DA. "He appears to be telling the truth."

Carson nodded. "So Rossiello is really going after me because of the indictment I brought against him. Well, I suppose I should have expected something like this. No one's gone after the mob this hard in years, so it makes sense that they want to stop me. But they won't. Threats and intimidation can't prevent me from doing my duty in ridding the city of this kind of despicable element. We will not waver—even for a second—in our appointed duty to . . ."

I turned to Hanson. "Can I borrow your gun?"

He looked stunned. "Why?"

"Because if this guy doesn't shut up, I'm gonna want to shoot myself in about five seconds."

Carson glared at me. "What is *she* doing here anyway?"

"Uh, Miss McKay is actually the person who tracked down

Johnny Camancho and uncovered this whole plot."

"Yeah. I could give you some crime-fighting pointers afterward, if you want."

"She's been a key contributor to our information on this matter," Hanson was saying.

"She's a nut case!" Carson said.

"Oh yeah? Sticks and stones may break my bones, but names will never hurt me."

"A fuckin' fruitcake. A looney tunes. A basket case."

"Now wait a minute," Hanson said, "we're all adults here and I think we can find a mature way—"

"I'm rubber, you're glue!" I screamed at Carson. "Whatever you say bounces off me and sticks to you!"

Hanson just stared at me. He looked like he wished he was a million miles away. "The fact of the matter is," he said slowly, "Miss McKay thinks she knows the reason why Rossiello wants to kill you."

"I already know why," Carson snapped. "Because of the indictment."

"There may be more to it than that."

"Says who? Her?" Carson said.

"Her information has been awfully good so far," Hanson told him. "Maybe we should listen to what she has to say."

Carson turned toward me.

"All right, Miss Know-It-All. What else is there? Why do you think Jerry Rossiello wants me dead?"

"Because you broke your deal with him."

"My deal? What deal? What in the hell are you talking about?"

"Rossiello was blackmailing you," I told him. "I know all about the pictures. About the afternoon meetings between you and Rikki Stiles at the St. Regis. You reneged on the deal with Rossiello not to go after him, you broke your word. So now he wants you dead. It's as simple as that."

Carson's face was flushed a beet red. He looked like he was going to have a stroke. "I don't know what the hell she's talking about," he finally said to Hanson.

"Did you know the Stiles woman, Mr. Carson?" Hanson asked.

Carson licked his lips nervously. "Okay, I was having a thing with her, I'll admit that. It wasn't the smartest thing in the world to do, I know. That's why I never admitted I knew her before. But nobody's blackmailing me. I don't have the slightest idea where you're coming from on that. If Rossiello was blackmailing me, I'd damn well know about it, wouldn't I? And I don't. The only thing I did was have an affair with this Stiles woman, who wound up getting herself killed. That's stupid on my part, but that's all there is."

Hanson looked over at me with a questioning look. Carson seemed to be telling the truth.

"But Camancho told me . . ." I started to say.

"I don't give a damn what anyone told you!" Carson snapped. "I don't know anything about any blackmail. You want me to prove it to you, I will. I'll take a lie detector test, anything you want. Okay, Captain?"

Hanson nodded. "Let's put that aside for a minute. The most important thing right now is keeping you out of danger. Do you accept that?"

Carson shrugged. "What can I do?"

"We can protect you," Hanson said. "Twenty-four hours a day, maybe hole you up in a secure place somewhere, until we have this guy Kluge in custody."

"I don't know . . ."

"Kluge's a very bad man," Hanson told him. "He's already killed a number of people. He means business."

"Do you have any idea how he might try to get at me?"

"I don't know—probably some sort of public appearance. Can you tell me what you have coming up?"

"Christ, I don't know all that stuff off the top of my head. Carrie handles all that for me, tells me where to go and when." He reached over and pushed a buzzer on his intercom. A few seconds later Carrie Macklin came in from the outer office.

"What is it, Mr. Carson?" she asked. She looked around

at both Hanson and me with bewilderment, but didn't say anything else. I think she was dying though to know why we were there.

"Miss Macklin, run through my schedule for the next few days. All my appointments, appearances, speeches—things like that."

Carrie Macklin still didn't look like she understood, but she cleared her throat and said: "Of course. Tonight you're having dinner with Senator Endicott at Four Seasons. Tomorrow it's lunch at '21' with Judge Jamieson, a talk to a law class at NYU, and a cocktail party at the Israeli Mission. The day after that you're speaking at the Republican fund-raising dinner at the Sheraton Centre. . . ."

"Hold it," Hanson said, "that's enough." He shook his head. "Jesus, we can't have you running around town like that. You'll be like a clay pigeon in a shooting gallery."

Carrie Macklin stared at him.

"That's all right, Carrie," Carson said, dismissing her with a wave of his hand. "You can go now. That will be all."

"Certainly," she said, and that tight little smile I'd seen before came across her face.

"Can you cancel all this stuff?" Hanson asked after she'd left the room.

"Cancel? I don't see how. It's all been arranged and—"

"Then you could die," Hanson told him.

"Yes, I see what you're saying," Carson said slowly. He appeared a bit shaken.

"Here's the plan. We relocate you somewhere for a while where we can guard you easier. Maybe a hotel room or something. With twenty-four-hour protection, men on the door at all times—that sort of thing."

"But how can I do that?" Carson asked. "I've got a job here. I can't let people know I'm cowering in a hotel room somewhere. I mean my whole image as a fearless crime fighter . . ."

"We're not talking about image here, sir," Hanson said. "We're talking about your life."

Carson nodded. He was sweating profusely.

"It would only be for a short time, until we can shake this guy Kluge loose," Hanson said. "Like I said before, he's a very professional killer. If you're walking around in public, having lunch and keeping appointments, I can't promise to protect you. It would be easier if we had your cooperation."

"I just . . . I just don't know. . . ."

"I'd like you to at least think about it," Hanson said. "Will you do that?"

Carson sighed. "All right, Captain, I'll think about it."

24

A Channel Six Exclusive

Barry Kaiser, the producer, was cueing us up now for the show.

KAISER: Ten seconds, everybody ready?

McKAY: I think I have to go to the bathroom.

KAISER: What?

McKAY: Just kidding, Barry.

KAISER: Okay, here we go. Five seconds . . . four . . . three . . . two . . . one. . . .

The theme music came on, followed by the announcer's voice. . . .

ANNOUNCER: It's the News at Six on Six—with the WTBK team of newsbreakers:
Conroy Jackson and Liz St. John at the anchor desk,

Stormy Phillips with the weather, and special guest sports commentator Monty Montez.

And now here's Conroy and Liz. . . .

ST. JOHN: Good evening, ladies and gentlemen. There is a major story developing in our town. Channel Six News has learned that Manhattan District Attorney Elliott Carson is currently under twenty-four-hour guard after authorities uncovered a mob plan to assassinate him. We go for a live report to our Jenny McKay. Jenny?

She turned and smiled at me on the screen. I smiled back. Jeez, I wish the viewers knew what we were really thinking. Maybe we should run little subtitles across the bottom of the TV, like at a foreign movie. *Up yours, McKay. Blow it out your ass, St. John.* Then again maybe that wasn't such a good idea after all.

McKAY: Thank you, Liz.

The camera was on me now. I was standing in front of the District Attorney's office on Centre Street. Superimposed on the screen was a logo that said CHANNEL SIX EXCLUSIVE.

McKAY: Manhattan District Attorney Elliott Carson has been taken to an undisclosed location after Channel Six helped uncover evidence that a mob hit man was in town stalking him.

The underworld plot is believed to be linked to Carson's recent indictment of mob boss Jerry Rossiello and also—in a startling turn of events—to the slaying of Sutton Place call girl Rikki Stiles.

The hit man has been identified as Leo Kluge, a hired killer from Chicago with a long arrest record. Authorities say he is responsible for several other murders in the metropolitan area during the past few weeks. These include Rikki Stiles, another call girl named Donna Willis, and small-time underworld figure Nicholas Camancho.

But his real target is DA Carson, who works out of a command center in the building behind me. . . .

The picture cut to a shot of the offices inside.

Carson marshals a force of one hundred and fifty investigators from here in the battle against underworld figures like Jerry Rossiello.

But sources say this story really begins at the posh St. Regis Hotel. . . .

The picture now went to a shot of the St. Regis, first the outside, then the lobby, and finally the inside of Room 1214. . . .

Channel Six News has learned that Elliott Carson and call girl Rikki Stiles met for sex in this room numerous times. Rossiello, after discovering this from an underworld informant, tried to use it to blackmail the DA who . . .

The piece went on for nearly ten minutes, a healthy chunk in TV news. Finally I wrapped it up by saying:

For his part, Elliott Carson admits having a sexual relationship with Rikki Stiles, but denies ever being approached with any sort of blackmail deal by Rossiello.

Carson remains in hiding and under guard somewhere in the metropolitan area.

Rossiello has dropped out of sight, and authorities are conducting a massive search for him and for hit man Leo Kluge—who is described as armed and extremely dangerous.

From the District Attorney's office on Foley Square, this is Jenny McKay, Channel Six News, reporting live from New York.

There was silence in my earpiece for a few seconds. Then I heard Kaiser's voice. "Jesus!" he said.

"What? Something wrong?"

"No. That was super. A helluva story."

"Barry," I said, "I'm a helluva reporter."

There were more congratulations all around when I got back to the office. The only person who didn't seem to like it was Liz St. John. She just sat there sullenly and glared at me across the room. The highest praise indeed.

My telephone rang. I figured it was either Barbara Walters looking for an interview or Rick Gallagher.

"Hi, Barbara," I said.

"Huh?"

It was Gallagher.

"Oh, hi. You were my second choice. Did you see it?"

"Terrific. Hey, I thought I could come over tonight and . . ."

"Gee, I'm exhausted. How about tomorrow?"

"I'm busy tomorrow night."

"Tonight is fine," I said quickly. I paused. "Where do you have to go tomorrow?"

"Oh, this big annual affair at the Sheraton—the Patrolmen's Benevolent Association Ball. A formal dinner, dance, all that crap."

"Perfect. I've got a formal gown I've never worn yet and . . ."

"Uh, Jenny—I have to take my wife."

"Oh."

There was a long silence.

"It's something she's looked forward to for a long time, a chance to get out of the house for once and meet some people. Even if she has to do it in a wheelchair. The doctor thinks it would be good for her to—"

"I understand."

"Really?"

"Sure. No problem."

No problem at all. A guy should take his wife to an event like this. That's what marriage is all about. Love, honor, and obey. Till death do you part. Of course, there's nothing in those vows about having a squeeze like me on the side. . . .

"So what's the plan for tonight? Another quick toss under the sheets with the TV babe and then home to Long Island again?"

"Jenny . . ."

"Sorry. I'm just being bitchy."

"We'll talk about it tonight."

"Boy, that ought to be fun."

"What does that mean?"

"It means I don't think it's a good idea to see you tonight, after all."

"Aw, c'mon, Jenny, what am I supposed to do?"

"Go home to your wife," I said and hung up the phone.

I sat there for a while being mad. Mad at Gallagher. Mad at his wife. Most of all, mad at myself. What the hell did I expect anyway? Rick Gallagher wasn't some Prince Charming who was going to sweep me up in his arms and take me off into the sunset where we'd live happily ever after. The guy was married—with a capital M. Christ, I seemed to specialize in screwed-up relationships.

The phone rang again. Probably Gallagher calling back.

I picked it up. "I've been thinking about it and I'd love to see you tonight. . . ."

"Gee, that's great, McKay, but I'm all booked up."

It was Carstairs.

"Sorry, Bob. I thought you were someone else."

"Can you come to my office for a minute?"

"Sure."

"That is, unless you're too busy setting up your social schedule. I mean if Mr. Right is going to be calling . . ."

"I'm on my way."

When I got there, he complimented me on the piece and then asked what I was going to do next.

"Well, I was thinking about a nice Caribbean vacation for a week or two. . . ."

"I meant on the story."

"Oh."

"Can we find out where they've got Carson hidden?"

"I don't know. . . ."

"I mean I'm not going to reveal it or anything. But it would be great to say we know where it is. Even greater if we could get an interview with him in hiding. I mean you've got this sort of special relationship with the guy. . . ."

"Bob, he hates me."

"Well, see what you can do."

I started to leave, then turned around. "By the way, where did you get that new sports reporter?"

"Monty Montez? What did you think?"

"I thought," I said slowly, "that he made Bill Hanrahan sound like Red Barber."

"Yeah," Carstairs agreed, "he might be a bit too intense."

Montez's shtick was sound effects. All kinds. He made a cracking sound for a Yankee or Met hitting a home run. A whooshing sound for a basket. A crunching sound for a tackle on the football field. Sort of like the guy from the *Police Academy* movies who makes all the motorboat and machine-gun sounds. Saliva's flying all over, and you practically need an umbrella to sit next to him.

"Where'd you find him anyway?" I asked Carstairs.

"He was working at this comedy club downtown, doing routines about sports and stuff. I thought it might work."

"Here's a radical thought," I said. "Why don't we find an actual sports journalist who talks like a normal human being and simply put him on the air?"

Carstairs smiled and shook his head. "Boy, you are a dreamer, aren't you?"

Back at my desk a few minutes later, I continued to muse on the Rick Gallagher situation. I really didn't know what to do. My unhappiness must have shown, because Stormy Phillips came by and gave me a funny look.

"You look like a woman with a problem," she said.

"Very perceptive," I told her.

"Professional?"

"Personal."

"You want to be more specific?"

"Men."

"Uh-huh. Can you narrow it down a little more?"

"Married men."

"Now we're getting somewhere—a subject I have extensive expertise in." She sat down. "Let's hear all the disgusting details."

I told her about Gallagher and his wheelchair-bound wife and the sick kid and how guilty I felt when he talked about them and yet how excited I was when we made love.

"The first thing you have to understand," she said when I was finished, "is there is no way you can win in a relationship with a married man. You're always going to wind up with the short end of the stick. Lonely nights. Holidays by yourself. Jealousy every time a crisis comes along and he has to go home to deal with it. . . ."

"So I shouldn't do it, huh?"

"I didn't say that. I just think you should understand the rules before you do."

"I've never done anything like this before," I said. "I wouldn't have gotten involved this time except he's really unhappy with his wife and he's looking to get out anyway. . . ."

"They always are."

"What are you saying? That he's lying to me about that?"

"I'm saying you don't know exactly what's going on in the marriage. He says he's miserable with her. Fine. So it would be better if you could get a firsthand look at them together to see for yourself."

"You mean spy on him?"

"Spy is a strong word. Let's just say you discreetly appear

at someplace where he and his wife are going to be and see what happens. Scout out the opposition, you might say."

"You're talking about this police ball tomorrow night?"

"Why not? You can get an invitation, can't you?"

"Probably. I'd feel stupid going all by myself though. I'd need a date."

"So get one. Isn't there someone who's dying to go out with you? Even to do something like this?"

I thought about that for a while after she left. Mike Stoner was out. I couldn't start that up again after what I had done. Most of the other men I knew were either married or gay or not speaking to me. Some of them a combination of all three. The telephone rang.

"Jenny McKay," the voice at the other end said, "I just saw you on TV."

It was Victor Galena.

"That was some story." He laughed. "Boy, you really got the ol' DA by the balls on this one."

"An apt description," I said. "You sound in a good mood."

"Why not? I figure you've also insured my own safety. Probably yours too. I mean you've got the whole town looking for this guy Kluge so he's not going to try anything against us now."

"Probably not. Victor, is there some reason you called?"

"Like I said, I saw you on TV and you were great. It got me to thinking about . . . well, I feel a lot safer now that the cops are out looking for Kluge. You know?"

It was a nice gesture. Galena, huh? I thought about the Patrolmen's Benevolent Association dinner. Why not? I needed a man. Galena was a man. Well, sort of.

"Victor, what are you doing tomorrow night?" I said.

25
True Love and Other Myths

I laid out the ground rules for Galena before we walked into the Sheraton.

No touching. No flirting with me. No suggestive remarks. No come-ons of any kind. He was there simply because I needed a man to get into this thing, and Victor Galena—God help me—was the best I could do on such short notice.

"Let me explain it this way, Victor," I told him. "If you put any moves on me, I will kick you as hard as I can and as many times as I can in an extremely sensitive part of your body. When I am finished doing this, you will no longer be able to father children. You will not be able to engage in your favorite coed recreational activity. You may not even be able to stand up straight again. Do you hear what I'm saying?"

"Yes, ma'am."

It was a formal affair so I'd told him to wear a tuxedo. I was afraid he'd show up in a pink one with tails or something, but he was dressed in a conservative black tux just like everyone else there. I guess he did have a certain amount of class. Sleazy class, but class nevertheless.

I had on a robin's-egg-blue, off-the-shoulder taffeta eve-
ing gown that I took out of my closet about once a year for
vents like this. Wearing it always made me think of going to
my high school prom. I tried to remember if my date for that
was better or worse than Victor Galena. I finally decided it
was a toss-up.

The dinner was being held in the ballroom on the second
oor of the hotel. There was a bar alongside the wall there,
nd we immediately repaired there so I could devise my plan
f action. Galena ordered a whiskey sour for himself and a
cotch and soda for me.

"You got any peanuts or chips or anything?" I asked the
artender. "I'm starving to death."

He pointed to a tray alongside the bar. "There's compli-
nentary hors d'oeuvres for the guests," he said. "A choice
f shrimp or salmon and caviar on crackers."

"I don't like shrimp, salmon, or caviar," I told him. "I like
eanuts and potato chips."

He gave me a "what-do-you-want-from-my-life?" look and
noved down the bar to wait on someone else. Galena picked
p a shrimp on a toothpick and tasted it. "Excellent cuisine,"
e announced. "Definitely excellent."

I sipped on my drink while I studied the layout of the room
nd tried to spot Gallagher and his wife. Shouldn't be too
ard to find 'em. I mean how many women in wheelchairs
ould there be here?

"Jenny! Jenny McKay!"

I turned around. It was Pat Shockley, a uniformed cop I
new from doing stories on the street during my years as a
ewspaperwoman.

"What's the matter?" he asked. "You don't remember your
ld friends from the force now that you're a big star on TV?"

"It's not that," I told him. "I just didn't recognize you in
 tuxedo. Boy, you look great. I thought for a second you
ere Donald Trump."

Actually he didn't look great. His tux seemed like a bad
ental. The coat was worn, the pants shiny, and the shirt

wrinkled. Plus it was all about a size too small for him—giving him that two pounds of bologna in a one-pound ba[g] look. Frankly, he looked sort of like a maître d' at Beefstea[k] Charlie's.

"What are you doing here anyway?" he asked.

"You know me—support your local police. I thought i[t] would be fun."

"Fun," he grunted, shoving his empty glass toward th[e] bartender and getting a refill. "The free drinks are fun. Al[l] the rest is crap."

He was staring at Victor Galena now. "Pat, this is m[y] friend, Victor," I said as casually as I could.

Shockley shook hands with Galena. He was looking at hi[m] funny.

"Have we ever met before, Victor?"

"I don't believe so," Galena said in perfect measured tones. There was no trace of the street lingo he used most of th[e] time. I liked that. He was a real piece of work, all right.

"What do you do?" Shockley asked. "Besides hang ou[t] with McKay here."

"I'm a trader," he said evenly.

"You mean on Wall Street?"

"Yes, he does some business on Wall Street," I said.

"Well, I better get back to the wife," Shockley sighed. "She's probably getting drunk as we talk. Nice meeting you[,] Victor. Take care of yourself, McKay."

"You too. Hey, you know a lieutenant named Ric[h] Gallagher? I'm looking for him."

"Sure, he's here tonight. Sitting a couple of tables awa[y] from me." He pointed toward his seat. "Well, he's not ther[e] now. But I can tell him you asked and—"

"No, don't do that," I said. "I want to surprise him."

After Shockley left, Galena let out a huge sigh of relief. "Boy, that was close," he said.

"What do you mean?"

"That guy busted me last year."

"Oh, Christ. . . ."

"I was sure he was going to make me there."

"I know I'm going to regret asking this, but what did he arrest you for?"

"Nothing. All I was doing was standing at the corner of Broadway and Forty-eighth at four o'clock one morning talking to this woman and . . ."

"I'll bet you were waiting for a bus, huh?"

"That's just what my defense lawyer said."

He looked around the room. "So where *is* this guy you're looking for anyway?"

"I don't know. You see a woman in a wheelchair?"

"A wheelchair?"

"Yeah, she's really sickly. Hardly ever gets out of the house. That's why he had to bring her here tonight. You see, they've got this problem with one of their kids too and—wait a minute, there he is."

Gallagher was back now at the table near Shockley's. A woman was sitting next to him. She was blond, maybe ten years younger than me, very pretty, and very buxom. She was wearing a clinging red formal dress with a plunging neckline that left very little to the imagination.

"She doesn't look all that sickly to me," Galena observed.

"That can't be his wife," I said.

"Probably not."

The two of them stood up now, Gallagher and the blonde. There was not a wheelchair in sight. They walked over to an open area where people were dancing and began moving to the music. I mean *moving*. The blonde looked like she was trying out for a dance show on MTV.

"Professionally speaking," Galena said, "that's one fine piece of woman out there."

"Victor," I said, "shut up."

The music was over now. Gallagher went back to his seat. The blond woman headed for the ladies' room. I told Galena to wait for me at the bar and followed her inside.

She was standing in front of the mirror fixing her makeup. Up close she looked even better than on the dance floor. Nice figure, tanned face and body, not a trace of fat anywhere. I stood next to her and looked at my own reflection. I didn't like the comparison.

"Boy, I hate going to these things," I said, turning to her and trying to sound as casual as I could. "I mean you work all day on your hair and you get all dressed up just to watch your husband drink himself into a coma."

She smiled and kept working on her makeup.

"Well, I guess you've got to expect that when you're married to a cop," I sighed. "Are you married to one? I mean you must be because you're here, right? Who else would come to a boring event like this?"

She nodded.

"Say, you're not Tony Abalone's wife, are you?" I asked. "The street vice guy from the Fifteenth Precinct?"

"No, my husband's a lieutenant, Rick Gallagher. . . ."

"You're married to Rick Gallagher? Oh, I know him."

She was combing her hair now. I looked back at the mirror.

"Damn, I think I'm putting on a few pounds," I said. "You look pretty good. You must starve yourself, huh?"

"Not really." She laughed. "I just exercise a lot—tennis, swimming, I like to jog a couple of miles a day too."

"Sounds very healthy."

"Yeah, well, I'm kind of a fanatic about my health."

"You know what really ruins your figure," I said. "Kids. I was a perfect size six until I had mine."

"I wouldn't know about that." She smiled. "I've never had any children."

She was still fixing herself up when I left. Back out in the ballroom, I walked over to where Gallagher was sitting and plopped down in the empty chair next to him. "Amazing what medical science can do, isn't it?" I said.

"Jesus, Jenny! What are you—"

"I mean yesterday your wife was in a wheelchair, and tonight she's out on the dance floor. It kind of makes you believe in miracles."

"Listen, I can explain this."

"Really?"

"That woman I was dancing with wasn't my wife. She's a friend of my captain. I just brought her here as a favor to—"

"I talked to her in the ladies' room," I said. "Women in a bathroom have no secrets."

He didn't have an answer for that.

"The whole thing about her being sick and the family and the problem with the imaginary kid—you just made it all up, didn't you?"

Gallagher spread his hands. "What do you want me to say, Jenny?"

I shrugged. "The truth?"

"Okay, you want the truth—here it is. I wanted to go to bed with you, you wanted to go to bed with me. But I knew you wouldn't because I was married. So I just made up a little white lie so we could—"

"You son of a bitch!"

"Hey, we had some good times. You enjoyed it too."

"Good times? Is that all it was?"

"What exactly did you think was going to happen between us, Jenny?"

"I don't know—love, maybe. But I sure as hell thought it was going to turn out better than this."

His wife came back to the table. "Oh, you two found each other." She smiled at her husband. "We ran into each other in the ladies' room, and she said she knew you."

I stood up.

"I was mistaken," I said. "I didn't know him after all."

It's funny how getting older doesn't make the pain of rejection any easier to take. Walking back to Galena at the bar, I flashed back to all the times my heart had been broken before. From the time Bobby Giles down the block took my best friend to the eighth grade graduation dance to when I caught a politician I was living with in flagrante delicto with a young lady not even old enough to vote. You always think

it could never get any worse, but it always does. My eyes
were burning now, and I started to cry. I asked the bartender
for a double scotch on the rocks.

"I guess it didn't go well," Galena said.

"I've had better evenings," I said.

He put his arm on my shoulder. At first it was just a
friendly hug. A sympathetic gesture. Then it became something more.

"That man Gallagher must be crazy," he said. "I would
never treat you that way."

"Don't . . ."

"You're very beautiful. You know that, don't you?"

"Victor, I'm a ticking time bomb. Get your goddamned
hands off of me."

He squeezed me tighter. Then he went into what must have
been Pimp Speech 1A. The one he used on all the runaways
from Kansas and Minnesota he picked up off the buses at the
Port Authority. "You just don't know what you need," he was
saying. "Victor knows what you need. Let me make you feel
good again. . . ."

When I hit him, I wasn't just hitting him for mauling me.
I was hitting him for Rikki Stiles and Donna Willis and all the
other women who'd fallen for his line of crap over the years.
I guess I was also hitting Rick Gallagher and the politician
and about a dozen other guys too. In any case, my aim was
perfect. He grabbed his crotch and dropped to the floor in
agony.

A crowd quickly gathered. His screams could be heard
throughout much of the ballroom. He appeared to be in a
great deal of pain.

"Jesus," the bartender said, looking down at him on the
floor, "what happened to him?"

I finished off my scotch in one big gulp.

"Beats me," I said. "Maybe he got hold of a bad piece of
shrimp."

26

Enquiring Minds Want to Know

The cops were stashing Elliott Carson at the Gramercy Park Hotel on Lexington and 21st Street.

I found this out over my fifth cup of black coffee as I tried to shake the cobwebs out of my head from the night before. Sanders came over and sat down on the side of my desk. He shook his head.

"Jesus, McKay, you look terrible."

"Beauty is in the eye of the beholder," I groaned. I took a sip of the coffee.

"Bad night?"

"The worst."

After I finished decking Victor Galena at the Sheraton, I decided I needed a nightcap before going home. So I wound up at The Lion's Head in Greenwich Village. The Lion's Head has a reputation in New York for being a literary hangout. When I first came here out of college, I expected to find J. D. Salinger and Joyce Carol Oates hanging around the bar, discussing theories of writing. Mostly though all you ever found were a lot of drunks who told you about the novel they were going to start writing as soon as they quit their jobs or left their wives or whatever. I usually found it depressing.

Last night though, everyone seemed brilliant and funny. They felt the same way about me. Everyone's always brilliant and funny when you're drinking a lot. The only problem is the next morning you can't figure out who any of them were or what you talked about or why you were there.

I'd promised myself I'd only have one drink there, no more. But then someone bought me a round and I had to buy them a round and things started getting fuzzy after that. My only vague recollection of the rest of the evening was standing on a table at one point and delivering a stirring rendition of "Danny Boy."

The next thing I remember was Hobo licking my face in the morning. I still had my formal gown on. "Wake me up in about thirty-six hours," I said. He started barking. It was 7:30 a.m.—time for his first walk. Some things wait for no man or woman.

Later, as I was feeding him after the walk, I gave him a lesson on some of the pitfalls of life:

"Never let demon rum pass through your lips," I intoned solemnly. "Or demon scotch or bourbon, for that matter."

He gobbled down his food, oblivious to what I was saying.

"Don't burn the candle at both ends. Early to bed, early to rise."

Still no response.

"And most of all," I said, "never fall in love. If love makes the world go round, then I want to get off the ride. You're better off without it. I'm telling you, Hobo—you don't know how good your life is."

He'd finished his meal now. He came over and licked my face some more. His tail was wagging furiously. It made a thump-thump sound on the kitchen floor as he drooled all over me.

Then again, maybe he did.

I'd tried to find out where they were hiding Carson from Capt. Hanson, but he wouldn't tell me. "I don't want another scene like the one we had in his office," he said. "Carson wants to see you about as much as he wants to see Leo Kluge."

I'd finally gotten the Gramercy Park location from a cop I knew at the 13th Precinct. This guy owed me a favor. About six months ago, I was supposed to do a story on how he'd been wounded while heroically trying to stop a robber. Only I found out after a little digging that he'd actually shot himself with his own gun. I decided not to tell anyone. Life's full of little compromises.

"Okay, so we know where Elliott Carson is," Sanders was saying. "Now what?"

"We go up there."

"To the Gramercy Hotel?"

"Right. You, me, and Artie."

"You really think he's going to give you an exclusive interview about his life in hiding?"

"I don't know. Let's ask him."

Sanders shook his head. "The story's over, Jenny. You exposed the guy's relationship with a hooker and the blackmail scheme and the mob hit plot against him. So why are you doing this?"

"Enquiring minds want to know," I said. That was the *National Enquirer*'s slogan. But we weren't that different from the *National Enquirer* some days, so what the hell.

"Know what?"

"I'm not sure yet."

He sighed. "Sorry, I just don't get it."

I didn't get it either. There was still something wrong with the story. Something horribly wrong. Why didn't Carson admit to the blackmail scheme? He admitted to the affair with Rikki, so why continue to deny that unless . . .

Unless he had more to hide!

Unless . . .

"Look, I've got a hunch," I told Sanders, "something I hadn't thought about before. I've got a call in to a friend of mine who's a reporter at the *Chicago Sun-Times*. She's trying to check some stuff out for me. It might answer the questions I still have about this case."

"Then what?"

"Then we ask Carson about it."

He stood up and sighed again. "I suppose you know what you're doing, Jenny."

"Gee," I said, "I don't know what I could have said to have given you that idea."

First I made another call to the cops. A guy I knew in ballistics.

My friend from Chicago called back twenty minutes later. What she told me was very startling. I hung up the phone and sat there for a few minutes trying to sort it all out in my mind.

"Incredible!" I finally said out loud. "In-fuckin'-credible!"

Then I headed uptown to confront Carson again.

The Gramercy Park is a middle-class hotel, not in the same league as the posh spots uptown like the Plaza or the Pierre, but still very comfortable. The rooms are spacious, there's a grand old bar and restaurant in the lobby, and a beautiful private park running along the south side of the hotel.

Sanders, Artie, and I walked into the lobby. There was somebody checking out at the front desk. A couple of people were sitting around in chairs. One of them was reading a newspaper. Or rather he was pretending to read a newspaper. Pretending very badly.

"Cop over there," I whispered.

"You know him?" Sanders asked.

"No, but he might as well be wearing a sign that says, 'I'm on stakeout duty.'"

"So how do all of us—plus this equipment—make it past him and up to Carson's room?"

"We don't. Not right now. I'll go up myself first and check things out. A lone woman will have an easier time of it. You guys go someplace and wait for me."

"Hey, that's a great idea," Artie said, brightening up for the first time. "There's a place down the street where I smelled them making fresh, hot popcorn when we walked by."

I stared at him. "Artie, try to understand something. This could be the biggest story of my career."

He shrugged. "So what do you want me to do? Stop eating?"

After they went back outside, I pretended that I was looking in my purse for a key and made my way to the elevator. The cop in the chair never gave me a second look. New York's finest. Ever vigilant.

Carson was being kept in a suite on the fifth floor. I knocked on the door and waited. A few seconds later, a voice asked: "Who's there?"

I decided honesty was the best policy. I didn't want anyone mistaking me for a killer, shooting first and asking questions later. "Jenny McKay. Channel Six News."

The door opened. Hanson was standing there. He shook his head disgustedly. "How'd you ever find us?"

"I need to talk to Carson," I said.

There was a noise from the room and then I saw Carson. "Not you again."

"You know I had a feeling you were going to say that."

"What do you want?"

"Let me in. I need to talk to you."

Hanson looked over at Carson. The District Attorney just shrugged and motioned me inside. "Why not?" he said. "You're the reason I'm stuck here anyway. How can it get any worse?"

"By the way," I said to Hanson as I passed by him, "can you call down to the lobby and ask them to find two guys with me—Sanders and Jacobson? Just tell them it's okay to come up too."

"Sure," Hanson said, "anything else you want done while I'm at it? Maybe I can park your car or something."

I ignored him and walked into the living room. Another cop was there who introduced himself as Ron Bilecki. A TV set was on in the corner, with the sound turned way down. On the screen you could see images of daytime TV, Vanna White turning over letters on "Wheel of Fortune." Several newspapers were spread out on a couch nearby, all open to stories about the case. Elliott Carson had apparently been reading about himself.

Carrie Macklin sat in a chair in the corner, her hands folded neatly in her lap, her legs pressed stiffly together. The tight look was on her face again and she seemed scared. She didn't look like the calm, efficient person I'd met those times in Carson's office. It was as if she'd glimpsed what the future was going to be like for her and Elliott Carson, and she didn't like it.

"What do you want?" Carson asked me.

I sat down on the couch. "We need to talk."

"About what?"

"About who really killed Rikki Stiles."

Carson stared at me with an incredulous look. "Why this guy Kluge, of course. . . ."

"No, he didn't kill Rikki," I said evenly. "You did."

"What? I don't know what the hell you're talking about!"

"Sure, you do. Oh, I assumed it was Kluge too for a long time, and Kluge did kill Donna Willis and Nicky Camancho. But Rikki came first."

I leaned forward and stared directly at him.

"The bullet that killed Rikki doesn't match with the slugs in Camancho. It took a while for the cops to determine that for sure. But I just had the ballistics report read to me."

Carson seemed flustered. "So? Kluge's a hit man. He probably has more than one gun. . . ."

"There's more. I checked with the cops in Chicago. It seems that they had Kluge under surveillance as a dangerous felon. They reported he left town on a flight for New York on the morning *after* Rikki Stiles was killed."

"What are you saying?"

"He's got an airtight alibi for the murder, Elliott."

Carson looked like he was going to faint. "I—I don't understand. . . ."

"Rikki Stiles said she had a couple of ideas on how to get some money fast. One was to give up Camancho for the Lancaster reward money. I think the other was you. She was desperate. So I think she met you at her apartment and told you everything had blown sky-high and demanded money to keep her mouth shut. That's when you killed her."

"No! No! No!" he screamed.

"It has to be you," I said. "Who else had a motive?"

"I don't know anything about Rikki's murder," he sobbed now. "Just like I don't know anything about this blackmail deal that Rossiello's trying to kill me over. I don't know why any of this is happening to me. . . ."

There was a knock on the door. Bilecki moved toward it and asked: "Who's there?"

"Lunch."

He looked around. "Anybody here order lunch?"

"It's for Mr. Carson," the voice said. "He called down for it before."

Bilecki nodded and reached down for the doorknob.

"I didn't—" Carson started to say.

"Hold it!" Hanson screamed.

But it was too late. The door blew open, and a figure rushed in with a gun in his hand. He pushed Bilecki into the living room and got the drop on Hanson before he could draw his own weapon. He ordered them to throw their guns over into a corner of the room.

"Jesus, who the hell are you?" Carson screamed in anguish.

I knew who it was. The close-cropped blond hair. The tiny smile. And the eyes. Most of all I remembered the eyes.

I'd seen them that night in my apartment. Donna Willis and Nicky Camancho probably saw them too, just before they died.

"It's Leo Kluge," I said softly.

27
Leo Kluge

Carson was in shock. His face turned white, and his whole body trembled. The more scared he looked, the bigger the smile on Kluge's face. I could tell he was enjoying this. He gestured to Carson, Carrie, Bilecki, Hanson, and me to all come together in the center of the room where he could see us.

"How could this happen?" Carson mumbled. "I mean the police promised me protection. They said I'd be safe here."

"How did you find us anyway?" I said.

"Simple, McKay. You seemed to be at the center of everything that was happening, so I just followed you. You led me right here."

"Shit!"

Kluge deftly slipped something out of a pocket with his free hand and screwed it onto the barrel of the gun. A silencer.

"Oh, my God!" Carson cried out. "He's going to kill us all!" He began to weep. "Please don't kill us, please let us live!"

He fell to his knees and began pleading with Kluge. The guy was really going to pieces.

"Please, please . . . let me talk to Mr. Rossiello," he sobbed. "I'll have the indictment against him thrown out. Whatever he wants. But please don't kill me. I have a wife and kids. . . ."

Kluge's lip curled in disgust as he looked down at the crying District Attorney. "You should have thought of all that before you welched on your deal with Mr. Rossiello. Mr. Rossiello doesn't like welchers."

"Deal? What deal? I don't know what you're talking about. I swear to God I don't know anything about it."

Now I finally believed Carson. He was too scared to lie. And, I suddenly realized, too dumb to pull off a double cross like this.

But if it wasn't him, then who was it?

It had to be someone smart. Someone well-connected to his office. Someone very close to him. . . .

"That's not the way I heard it," Kluge was taunting him. "I heard you were a bad boy, Mr. DA. Not keeping your promises. Unfortunately for you, Mr. Rossiello is a very bad person to break your word to. . . ."

I thought back to that first day in Carson's office and how he could hardly make a move without Carrie Macklin's help.

"No, no, no," he pleaded. "I didn't . . . I wouldn't . . ."

That little lady takes good care of me! That's the way Carson had put it to me.

"He's telling the truth," I blurted out. "He doesn't know anything about a deal with Rossiello."

"Huh?" Kluge looked at me. He seemed momentarily nonplussed.

I wondered if he'd just kill Carson or do everyone in the room. Probably all of us. I looked over at Hanson and Bilecki, who never took their eyes off Kluge. I figured sooner or later they'd make a try to get the gun out of his hand.

Maybe we should all try for it. He couldn't shoot all five of us at once. Or could he?

"What are you saying?" Kluge asked me now. "That the scumbag Johnny Camancho lied when he told Rossiello that Carson agreed to the deal?"

"No," I said, "I don't think Camancho would lie about something like that to a man like Rossiello."

"Well, then . . ."

"What exactly did Camancho say he'd done?" I asked Kluge.

"He said he'd worked out an agreement with Carson. In exchange for not going public with pictures of him and the hooker, Carson would lay off Rossiello."

"Did he say he'd talked to Carson personally about this?"

"Well, he said he'd contacted Carson's top people and . . ."

"Which top people?"

"How the hell do I know?"

I pointed toward Carrie Macklin. "That's Elliott Carson's top person over there," I said. "Nothing gets done without going through her."

Carson's head jerked around in surprise. "Carrie, you mean you . . ."

Carrie Macklin stood very still, with her face pale and her eyes riveted on the gun Kluge had aimed at Carson.

"Hey, wait a minute!" Kluge said. "Are you telling me she agreed to the whole deal on the pictures herself and never told him anything about it?"

"Is that true, Carrie?" Carson asked.

She didn't say anything. Just kept staring down at the gun.

"Why?" Carson wailed in anguish. "Why would you do something like that?"

Now she turned to him with a fury in her eyes like I'd never seen before. There was something else there too. Jealousy. She was a woman scorned.

"I did it for you, goddammit! To protect you. All because you slept with that woman. That cheap little whore!"

She almost spat the words out.

"We'd worked so hard to get where we were. Our future was so bright. The governor's mansion in a few years. Maybe even the White House down the road. And then you blow it all with your sordid little affair. Well, I wasn't going to let that happen. Those pictures . . . the things you were doing with that woman . . . they were so disgusting."

Her voice broke.

"I ripped the pictures up. I never showed them to you, not to anyone. I didn't want anyone to ever see you like that. So I told them we'd agree to whatever they wanted."

Carson buried his face in his hands and groaned. "Carrie, Carrie, how could you?"

"How could *I*?" she yelled at him. "How could *you*? And with that woman? I did everything for you, I was always there when you needed me. There was never anyone better for you than me. And how do you repay me? By sleeping with that whore!"

She was sobbing now.

"She called the office. That harlot actually had the gall to try to talk to you there. I couldn't believe it when I took the call. I knew what she wanted—money. And I knew that, sooner or later, she was going to ruin everything we'd built up together."

She looked at Carson pleadingly.

"So I told her that you weren't in, but that you wanted to meet with her at her apartment. Then I went over there to try to talk to her. That's all I wanted to do—talk. I just wanted to convince her to leave us alone. . . ."

The words were pouring out in a rush now.

"I told her about your future . . . about our future. How I'd planned out everything we could have together. I tried to reason with her, I really did. But then . . . then she just started laughing. . . ."

Carrie's voice trailed off.

"So you killed her," I said softly.

She nodded slightly, almost imperceptibly.

"I had a gun in my purse. I always carry a gun. You can't

be too careful in this city, with all the rapists and sex maniacs running around." She looked pleadingly at Carson. "Don't you see, Elliott? I did it for us."

I turned to Kluge. He seemed bemused by the whole scene.

"This is all very touching," he said. "But now it's time . . ."

"Wait a minute!" Carson shouted. His face looked hopeful. "This proves it wasn't my fault. She did it. She did everything. You can tell Mr. Rossiello that. I didn't know anything about the deal. She's the one you should kill, not me. . . ."

Kluge just shook his head. "My, my. Is chivalry dead or what?"

He pointed the gun at Carson's chest.

"No! No! Kill her!"

There was a noise from the door. I looked over and saw Sanders and Jacobson walking in carrying a couple of trays of food.

"You know, they've got a lot of good stuff at that place," Artie was saying. "I got me some soup, some macaroni, even a tub of hot buttered popcorn. I take back what I said about this assignment. It's okay with me if—"

He saw Kluge standing there in front of him with the gun. "Jesus!"

"Put the food down and your hands up," he told them.

Artie nodded. "Sure. No problem."

Then he hurled the entire tray of hot food into Kluge's face. He screamed in pain; but somehow managed to hold onto the gun. Bilecki lunged at him from behind and tried to grab him, but Kluge threw him off. Hanson raced toward the corner to try to retrieve his gun.

"You're still gonna die," Kluge shouted at Carson. He pointed the gun at him again.

Leo Kluge, the man who never failed on an assignment. A perfect record. He wasn't going to fail on this one either. Even if he died doing it.

"No, no, don't kill him!" Carrie Macklin screamed. She lunged toward the gun, blocking his aim.

"Goddammit! Get out of the way!"

Kluge pulled the trigger and Carrie Macklin screamed in agony. A bright red splotch of blood exploded on her chest. But she didn't fall down. She kept holding onto him, grabbing his gun arm. She seemed like a woman possessed.

I had to do something. I looked around and saw a lamp on the table next to me. I ripped it out of its socket, lifted it in the air, and took aim at Kluge's head. Maybe it would stun him enough to . . .

But I didn't have to.

Hanson had gotten to his gun now and came up firing.

He shot Leo Kluge twice in the head, and it was over.

28

This Is Jenny McKay
Reporting . . .

ANNOUNCER: We break into our regularly scheduled programming to bring you this bulletin from the WTBK newsroom.

The picture cut from John Ritter in a "Three's Company" rerun to the newsroom where Conroy Jackson was sitting.

JACKSON: There's been a shoot-out at the Gramercy Park Hotel where an underworld hit man just tried to assassinate Manhattan District Attorney Elliott Carson. Two people are reported dead, one of them an aide to Carson. The District Attorney is believed to be unhurt. For more on this breaking story, we take you live to our Jenny McKay at the hotel.

McKAY: I'm standing in a fifth floor room of the Gramercy Park Hotel. Less than an hour ago, Carrie Macklin, special assistant to District Attorney Elliott Carson, died trying to save the DA from a gunman's bullet. I was in the room and witnessed it all. Here's what happened. . . .

It took a while to get everything straightened out.

Leo Kluge lay dead in front of me. Part of his face was blown away, and there was blood all over the floor. Carrie Macklin's body was a few feet away. Her eyes were still open and staring up at nothing. Bilecki reached down and pushed them shut. Then someone found a blanket and covered her with it.

Elliott Carson was alternating between hysteria over his brush with death and happiness that he was still alive. He never looked at Carrie's body. Probably didn't want to think about how close it came to being him.

"Let me get this straight," Hanson said, glancing down at her, "*she* killed Rikki Stiles."

"That's right."

He still looked confused.

"I really don't think it was premeditated," I said. "I really think she just went over there to talk, maybe scare her a little with the gun. But when Rikki said she had to see Carson and needed money—well, her sense of preservation for her boss took over."

"And the rest of it was all a big mix-up?"

"Yep. Rossiello thought Carson had double-crossed him on their deal, and so he sent Leo Kluge after him and everyone he thought was connected with it. Only there was no deal with Carson. It was Carrie Macklin all along. All she wanted to do was protect him, instead she almost got him killed."

"And Carson had no idea about any of it?"

"No."

I thought about the baby back in Cleveland I still hadn't told him or anyone else about.

"All he knew was a hooker he'd been having an affair with got herself murdered, and she'd told me some secret before she died. That's why he called me in that day. He wanted to find out if the secret was about him and Rikki.

Rossiello's people must have been watching him, and that's why they came to me. After that, well . . . things just started happening very quickly."

Hanson shook his head sadly. "Rikki Stiles. Carrie Macklin. Donna Willis. Nicky Camancho. Even Leo Kluge. All dead— for nothing. It doesn't make any sense."

"Murder never does, does it?" I said.

There was a sound coming out of the bathroom. Hanson heard it at the same time I did. It was someone whistling. Cheerful whistling. We walked over to the bathroom door and looked in. Elliott Carson was splashing water on his face and combing his hair in front of the mirror. He looked on top of the world.

Suddenly he realized we were watching him and turned around. "Yes?"

"What are you doing?" Hanson asked.

"There's going to be a lot of people here in a few minutes," he said. "More media, TV cameras, I'm probably going to have to give a press conference."

"I don't believe you," Hanson told him.

"Huh?"

"There's a woman lying dead out there. She's dead because she saved your life. You might at least try to act a little sad for her instead of looking like you just won the lottery."

"I can't do anything to change what happened," Carson said defensively.

"That's a shame. Because I think this world would be a damn better place if she were in here whistling and you were lying dead out there."

"Now wait a minute . . ."

"No, you wait a minute. If I hear you whistling a happy tune again before we get her body out of here, I'll personally make sure you're not able to whistle again for a long, long time."

Carson pulled himself up to his full height and tried to look dignified. "I am the District Attorney of New York and I—"

"You're scum," Hanson spat out at him. "You're shit. You're something I wish I could just scrape off the bottom of my shoe."

"I'll have your badge taken away. I have plenty of clout in this city. . . ."

"You're not going to be able to get elected dogcatcher in this city when all this comes out," Hanson told him.

Carson licked his lips nervously. "What are you talking about? I didn't do anything wrong. That woman confessed to the hooker's murder and the deal with Rossiello. You heard her say it, everyone heard it. I'm in the clear."

"Legally, yes."

"What do you mean?"

Hanson started talking in a whining, cowardly tone and pretended to cry. "Oh, please, please don't kill me! Kill her instead. I'll do anything for Mr. Rossiello but don't shoot me. . . ."

Carson's face turned a bright red. "You wouldn't?"

"Oh yes." Hanson smiled. "The whole city's gonna know about your little performance here. The way you fell apart under pressure. McKay here's gonna tell 'em. And if she doesn't, I will. I'll take out a billboard in Times Square to spread the word if I have to. I wonder how the voters will feel about their courageous, crime-busting District Attorney then."

He whirled around and stalked back into the living room. I started to follow him, then turned around and looked at Carson. He was staring at himself in the mirror again, running the comb through his hair.

"Hey, Elliott," I said, "there's one more thing."

He looked at me with a confused expression. "What?"

"I think you're starting to get a bald spot in the back," I told him.

Hanson was staring down at Carrie Macklin's body under the blanket.

"I still don't get it," he said to me when I walked over to him.

"I told you, it was all a mistake."

"No, I mean I don't get why she did what she did at the end. She was a smart woman, knowledgeable about the law. She had to know that they'd go easy on her for killing the Stiles woman. I mean she'd never been in trouble with the law before, it didn't seem premeditated—I'll bet she could have cut a deal for manslaughter and walked after a couple of years at some country club jail."

The blanket had gotten pushed and we could see her face now. She looked serene—like she was just sleeping. Looking at her that way, I realized she actually could have been very pretty. Maybe if she'd worked at her looks a bit, wore some decent clothes, used a little makeup . . . but now it was too late for all that.

"Why'd she do it?" Hanson asked. "Kluge was going after Carson, not her. We'd have gotten to him after he got the first couple of shots off. She didn't have to die. Why'd she throw her life away to save him?"

"She's always done everything for him, Captain. Even killed for him. And now she's done this one last thing."

"I know, but why?"

I smiled sadly. "She loved him. Carrie Macklin loved the son of a bitch."

McKAY: We now return you to the studio and rejoin our regularly scheduled programming. But stay tuned. There'll be much more on this major, breaking story on the News at Six on Six. From the Gramercy Park Hotel, this is Jenny McKay reporting. Live from New York.

News Update

The cemetery was on Long Island, about an hour outside the city. Sanders, Jacobson, and I drove out there the next morning. It was a nice fall day to go for a ride—crisp and cool, but with the sun shining brightly. It made you feel good to be alive.

We drove down a quiet country road, parked the van, and turned off the engine. Then I reached over and picked up a large bouquet of flowers from the backseat. $150 worth of roses. The same $150 I'd been carrying around in my purse since that day I showed up to give it to Rikki Stiles and found her dead.

"You want us to come with you?" Sanders asked.

"No," I said. "You wait here."

"Okay. You're sure?"

I nodded. "This is something I want to do myself."

You had to go down a slight incline to get to where she was buried. I looked around as I walked. It was actually quite beautiful here. Green grass, trees swaying gently in the breeze, falling leaves all over. There was even a pond with a few birds flying over it who hadn't gone south for the winter yet. Finally, about two hundred yards down the road, I stopped in front of Rikki Stiles's grave and laid the flowers down on the marble slab.

The whole thing was probably ridiculous, I knew that. But I needed to do it. I wasn't sure why. Maybe it was just my way of tying up the final loose ends in the case. Anyway, I felt the $150 was Rikki's. I owed it to her. And this was the only way I knew to pay her.

I thought of all the things that had happened since the day when Rikki came to my office looking for help. Some of it good, some bad. The murders. Elliott Carson's political career ruined. My affair with Rick Gallagher. She'd set a lot of things in motion that day, even if she never realized it.

Now it was time to say good-bye.

She hadn't been an angel, of course. A lot of the trouble was her own doing. But she knew things were screwed up and had wanted to make it better. And in the end she'd tried to do the right thing. Break away to start a new life with her baby.

I looked down at the flowers lying on the grave.

"Rest in peace, Rikki," I said. "Rest in peace."

Then I turned around and walked back to the van.

They buried Carrie Macklin the next day. I went to the service and listened to the eulogy about how she was a good person whose passions led her astray at the end. I wasn't sure how I felt about her. I mean, I know she murdered Rikki Stiles, but she did it for love. People do a lot of strange things for love, take my word for it. It's almost like a form of insanity.

Whoever said "love makes the world go round" sure knew what they were talking about. Just look at what happened here.

Rikki Stiles had a love affair with Elliott Carson and it wound up costing her her life.

Carrie Macklin loved him, and she died too and ruined his political career.

Me, I fell in love with a married man and learned what I should have known before I started—it's a no-win situation. I got my heart broken, and along the way I managed to break the heart of a very nice guy—Mike Stoner—who seemed genuinely interested in me.

So there were no happy endings. Of the three of us though, I guess I made out the best. I'm still alive.

A while back I read a survey in the paper in which some single women were asked their feelings about men. They described them as mean, manipulative, oversexed, self-centered, and lazy. Nine out of ten of the women polled then said they hoped to get married someday.

The message here, I believe, is something along the lines of: "Men—you can't live with 'em, you can't live without 'em."

Speaking of men, I ran into Rick Gallagher a few months later while I was covering a murder in Bensonhurst. He was real friendly and so was I—what happened between us seemed like a long time ago by then. We even had a friendly drink together. And then a second. By the third drink, he was telling me how his wife didn't really understand him and he was thinking about leaving her. I thanked him for the drinks and said good-bye. I may be dumb, but I'm not that dumb.

Mike Stoner, I never saw again. I think about him every now and then, mostly when I'm struggling with my tax returns. Once I even dialed his number, but I hung up before it started to ring. Some things you just can't go back and do over.

Elliott Carson isn't the District Attorney anymore.

For a while he tried to carry on as if nothing had happened, but there was too much scandal swirling around him. The affair with Rikki. Carrie Macklin's secret deal with Rossiello. His cowardly behavior that day in the hotel room. Pretty soon he became a running joke for call-in radio shows and disc jockeys. One of them even did a whole parody of *The Wizard of Oz* with Elliott Carson as the cowardly lion.

Finally the city's political bosses pressured him into stepping down. He hooked up with a big Park Avenue law firm that specialized in defending big businesses like Exxon in environmental cases and the like, but that didn't last long either. The story I heard was that he got caught in bed one afternoon with the mistress of the firm's senior partner. Anyway, he wound up in Atlanta where he opened up some sort of corporate law practice. Not a bad life, but not exactly the fast track to the White House or the governor's mansion either. I take some small satisfaction out of that.

Victor Galena sells real estate these days.

Damnedest thing I ever saw. It seems Rikki's building on Sutton Place went co-op and he made about seventy-five thousand dollars by turning over her apartment. So he bought another apartment and sold that one for a profit too. Now he thinks he's Donald Trump.

The guy owns apartment complexes in the Bronx and Brooklyn, some tenements up in Harlem, and he even bought some run-down hotel on the Upper West Side recently that he's converting into high-priced condos. He doesn't drive the Mercedes anymore, he's got his own limo driver who takes him everywhere. And he works out of this big suite of offices on Madison Avenue with a lot of cute secretaries running around and waiting on him just like his girls used to in the old days.

"If I'd known it was this easy to go straight, I'd have done it a long time ago," he said. "I was wasting my time before. I'm a changed man now."

I'm not so sure about that. I mean he still makes a living out of screwing people.

Big Tony Mosconi became the undisputed boss of bosses in New York City after Jerry Rossiello was caught, convicted, and sent to prison on racketeering and conspiracy to commit murder charges. So things worked out fine for

Tony. Which is why, I realized, he had that lunch with me and helped me in the first place. Once I broke the case and exposed Rossiello, his main competition for mob supremacy was out of the way. Did I really think Big Tony was doing it because he liked me? Well, yes—but then I'm very naive about these things sometimes.

I don't live in his building anymore either. Somehow it just didn't feel right. I found a sublet on West 77th Street with two bedrooms and a terrace which gives me a terrific view of the drug dealers and hookers on Broadway, but I have to leave when the owner comes back from Europe next month.

Galena wants to sell me an apartment in one of the buildings he bought in Harlem. He says it's a changing area, the hot new up-and-coming neighborhood in New York and he can get me in on it for the ridiculously low, bargain-basement price of two hundred thousand dollars. I asked him if he threw in the Brooklyn Bridge on that deal too.

I never told anyone about Rikki Stiles's baby.

I'm not sure why. Well, actually I am. Rikki never said anything about it to anyone except her mother and made it clear she didn't want Elliott Carson to know. Would she have revealed it to him at the end when she was desperate for money to flee from Rossiello? Who knows? But she didn't get the chance, so I figured she deserved to take the secret to the grave with her.

Besides, no kid should have to grow up knowing Elliott Carson is his father.

The fifty-thousand-dollar-reward money in the Lancaster heist has never been paid out. Most of the loot is still unrecovered, and the government has filed a civil suit against the jailed Rossiello to seek repayment from his other business interests. This will probably take years to go through the courts.

I submitted Rikki's name for the money, which means it would go to her mother and eventually to her son. Who knows—it might work out. Maybe the kid will even get some of it by the time he's ready to go to college.

Here at Channel Six News, not much has changed.

Liz St. John got a screen test out in Hollywood after some hotshot director saw her on TV or in a singles bar or something, and she figured she was on her way to stardom. But she found out when she got there that the town was crawling with hundreds of drop-dead beautiful blondes willing to go to bed with directors. She doesn't talk about it much anymore, so I guess we're stuck with her.

Conroy Jackson got a big journalism award—some local group called the Silurians named him their Man of the Year for "outstanding achievement during a broadcasting career." Now he's got to give a speech next month at the annual Silurian dinner. I'm taking a pool in the office to pick how many minutes into his talk it'll take him to mispronounce the word "Silurian."

Stormy Phillips is finishing up her last year of law school at Columbia during the day, and still dressing up in bikinis for the newscast at night. Linda Fairmont is now a political consultant. And Bill Hanrahan quit broadcasting and opened up a baseball school for girls in Connecticut. Boy, talk about falling into the perfect niche.

As for Bob Carstairs, the way I see it is our relationship has gradually evolved into one of mutual respect. I mean he finally seems to understand that I'm not a Liz St. John or Maria Shriver or Deborah Norville and he can't turn me into one. I'm Jenny McKay, reporter. And a pretty damn good one sometimes too. Maybe I'm not the world's greatest broadcaster, but I bring something to a TV news show that the Liz St. Johns of this business can't. Carstairs knows this. And he may not come right out and say it, but he's glad to have me around.

I think.

Well, there was this one little incident the other day. . . .

I was doing a live interview with a priest at St. Patrick's Cathedral about the church's stand on the use of condoms during sex. Surprise, surprise—they were against it. Midway through the interview my mike went dead. Suddenly there was no sound, no picture. Just dead air.

"What the hell's going on?" I screamed to the control room.

"There's a bunch of protesters outside," I was told. "They attacked our remote van and knocked us off the air."

"Fuck 'em if they can't take a joke," I said.

Suddenly the voices in my earpiece went crazy.

"Jenny!"

"McKay, we're back on the air!"

"Shut up, you idiot. . . ."

There was chaos for a few seconds, until they hurriedly cut to a commercial. Then I heard Carstairs's voice.

"McKay, I want to see you back here in my office. Now."

Damn!

I did it again.

Hey, nobody's perfect.